QUEEN TAKES ROOK

THEIR VAMPIRE QUEEN - BOOK 4

JOELY SUE BURKHART

QUEEN TAKES ROOK

THEIR VAMPIRE QUEEN, book 4
Published by
Joely Sue Burkhart

A Reverse Harem Vampire Romance

The epic showdown between the last Isador queen and House Skye begins.

Strengthened by her new queen sib, Shara Isador plans to return to her mansion-in-progress for some much needed rest. She especially wants to get to know her new twin Blood and fears she may have made a mistake in taking them. She does not love them. Yet.

However, the sun god and the queen of New York City have other plans.

The snares are set to capture the young but extremely

powerful vampire queen. Someone inside Zaniyah's nest has betrayed them, and Shara's trusted butler calls to inform her that a large package has arrived–from Marne Ceresa, the queen of Rome. A trap, surely. Or could the unknown gift be an olive branch from the feared Triune queen?

Copyright © 2018 Joely Sue Burkhart
Cover Art by Cover Me Darling
Formatted by Tattered Quill Designs

All rights reserved. No part of this book may be reproduced, scanned, or distributed in print or electronic form without the express, written permission of the author.

This is a work of fiction. Names, characters, places and incidents are the product of the author's imagination and any resemblance to any organization, event, or person, living or dead, is purely coincidental.

Adult Reading Material

For my Beloved Sis.

Thank you to my comma warriors and beta readers:
Mads Schofield, Shelbi Gehring, Alyssa Muller, Meagan Cannon West, Sherri Meyer, Laura Walker, Briana Walker, Stephanie Cunningham, Kiersten Wukitsch, and Kaila Duff

1

RIK

I would never have thought it possible to fit four full-sized Blood in a double-sized bed, but for our queen, we made it so.

The only way to make it work at all was for her to sleep on top of us. It was a testament to the depths of her exhaustion that she managed to sleep so deeply on such rock-hard "mattresses." Though surely Daire's constant purr helped.

He was curled up tight against my side, his head on my shoulder. His fucking ridiculous hair in my face. Though she liked his longer hair, and Nevarre's, so the rest of the Blood were already joking about starting a hair-growing contest. And yeah, my hair was longer too. The first asshole who thought to try and give me a trim would find himself short a few choice body parts.

Ezra crowded close to Daire, though if he moved an inch, he'd end up on the floor, and likely drag Daire off with him. Guillaume lay on his side facing me, his thigh locked over mine and Shara's so he didn't fall off. His position put her ass tight into his groin, so I don't think he minded in the slightest. She had her face buried in Ezra's chest, though I had no idea how she could sleep with that bear rug tickling her nose.

The six-hour mark approached, when I normally changed who was in bed with her. With her sleeping so deeply, though, I didn't plan to jostle her with new Blood sliding in. The two newest Blood, the Zaniyah twins, were chomping at the bit for their chance to join her. Not that I gave a fuck. They could wait. She had plenty of Blood ahead of them.

Maybe it was petty of me, but I'd do nothing to make it easier for them to come to my queen's bed. I still had a bitter taste in my mouth from how House Zaniyah had "welcomed" my queen to their nest by not revealing the geas laid on their blood circle. Shara had broken that geas, but it'd cost her greatly, and I'd certainly never trust a single person from Zaniyah again.

:Mayte's here,: Mehen said from the guest-quarters door. :She's asking to enter.:

I especially didn't trust their queen.

I would have asked why, but it was only four o'clock in the morning. It could only be for one reason.

Shara had enjoyed her first foray with a queen in the grotto, but I wasn't sure that she'd want to indulge again. She'd been very clear in what she wanted. She didn't want us to touch the other queen. She didn't want to touch Mayte's Blood, which would make taking this queen into her bed more complicated, unlike the light and easy lovemaking we'd shared in the grotto.

:*She comes alone,*: Mehen added. :*No alpha. No Blood.*:

I huffed out a breath. Fucking hell. If my queen tried to go somewhere without me...

Every muscle in my body objected. Strenuously. Though I had allowed her out of my sight already, like when she'd taken Mehen. I'd hated every moment, even though she certainly hadn't gone to him for sex, but to free him from his prison.

What if one day she ordered me to stay behind while she went to another queen's bed? If she ordered us all to stay behind?

The thought made the rock troll heave beneath my skin, begging to be freed so he could smash down the entire house around us. Though the truth sliced through me, shredding my heart into ribbons. If she ordered it... I would do it. We all would. No Blood ordered his queen. Not one. Even her alpha.

Although it was petty of me, I gave the order to Mehen to allow Mayte inside simply to torment her alpha, who'd been forced to stay behind. :*Cover yourselves if you can,*: I told the rest of the Blood. :*You know our queen's opinion of pants around other women.*:

Ezra tugged the sheet up over him and Daire, cursing under his breath when he almost fell off the bed. Guillaume grabbed the corner of the blanket and at least managed to cover his pertinent parts.

Dressed in a thin, long robe that dragged on the floor behind her, Mayte stepped into the bedroom, and inhaled deeply when she saw all of us in the bed. She tiptoed closer and met my gaze.

I felt a tickle in the back of my mind. Fucking hell. She wanted to talk to me through her bond with Shara. I debated for a moment, not relishing the touch of a queen in my head who wasn't mine. But she was trying to be polite, I assumed, by not waking Shara, so I allowed her access to my mind. :Yes?:

:Thank you for allowing me to see her. I can't sleep.: She laughed wryly in the bond, her gaze locked on my queen. :I wanted to be near her, even if...:

She didn't finish the thought, but I understood completely. I wanted to be near her every moment, day or night, whether she wanted me involved in whatever lovemaking she wished to indulge in or not.

:She sleeps like this every night? With so many?:

:She would sleep with us all not on guard duty if we had a big enough bed.:

:Oh.: Her eyes widened and she nodded. :If she graces us with a visit again, I will see to it. May I lie with her? I don't mind being on top, or squished. Whatever's necessary.:

:It's not that simple.:

Her gaze dropped to the floor, her shoulders drooping. I didn't want to send her away if Shara would like waking up to see the other queen's eyes shining back at her. But she wouldn't be pleased if Mayte touched any of us, even to get close to her. Getting everybody out of bed, naked, while not letting the other queen get an eyeful...

:*We could shift, one by one,*: Guillaume suggested.

Ezra growled out a curse—softly, because Shara stirred and nuzzled his chest. :*I don't want to leave. Not for her.*:

:*Yeah, I get that,*: Guillaume replied. :*Me, neither. But which would Shara prefer? After one more night, we'll go home to her nest and have her to ourselves again. Mayte only has two nights, and this night is nearly over.*:

:*The stud has a point.*: Ezra grumped, but acquiesced, letting his bear flow up to the surface as he carefully slipped out of the bed.

Guillaume's hell horse was trickier, without the same flexibility as the grizzly. He chose instead to drop backwards off the bed and shift from the floor. Watching a hell horse try to tiptoe so his gigantic hooves didn't ring loudly on the tiled floor and wake our queen made me choke back a laugh.

:*You're next,*: I told Daire.

He'd flattened out enough beside me to cradle Shara's head on his chest, taking up more room without Ezra at his back. He inched closer, his purring shaking the bed. :*She'll wake if she doesn't hear me.*:

Probably true, but maybe she would want to wake up, now that her queen had come to her. :*Go. If she wakes and wants you back, then she'll call you.*:

Daire shifted to his warcat and Shara rubbed her face in his fur. Even in her sleep, she tangled her fingers in his fur and held on. Daire let out a pleased little huff as if to say, *"I told you so,"* and continued purring without leaving.

I looked at Mayte, standing silently as the Blood left the room. Her eyes searched my face. :*She doesn't want them to touch me, does she?*:

:*Not at all. But she doesn't want to touch your Blood, either.*:

:*I'm grateful that she allowed me to keep my Blood at all.*: She sidled closer, coming around the foot of the bed to the opposite side. :*I'll be careful. I won't touch anyone but her.*:

Without Guillaume against her side, Shara's lower body sagged down to the mattress, though she still draped across my chest. Mayte slid in close to her, and pressed her face into the hollow of Shara's lower back.

Even though Mayte's bond was not mine, I felt an intense surge of pleasure and longing in the bond. She breathed deeply and lightly stroked her fingers along the curve of Shara's hip. She kept her touch soft and gentle, but I still felt the stirring in Shara's bond. She didn't lift her head or move to indicate awareness, but she touched my bond. :*She's here?*:

:*She asked to be near you while you slept. She came alone, and agreed to touch no one but you.*:

She lifted her head, and I felt the leap in Mayte's bond. Hope, longing, agony that she might be sent away. Shara rubbed her face against the warcat's neck, but released him. :*Go, my furball purring machine.*:

He rumbled deeper into a lower register that made my bones throb, but agreeably hopped down lightly and padded to the door. She watched him go, and laughed softly when he flipped his tail from side to side and looked back over his massive shoulder.

:Even when I'm a warcat, you can't stop staring at my ass.:

:You know it. Thank you for shifting so she didn't see how gorgeous you are.:

She rolled over a little to look into my face. I lifted my head, pressing my lips to hers. *:Would you like me to leave too, my queen?:*

Slipping her hand around my nape, she held my head, as if she feared the strain on my neck. When I would crack every vertebrae in my spine to be close to her. *:No. I want my alpha to stay, unless you wish to leave.:*

:Never.:

Mayte sat up on the edge of the bed and slid the silken robe off her shoulders. "I'm at your disposal, my queen. How may I pleasure you?"

SHARA

Waking up with the assurance that I'd never be alone again was wonderful, though I had never woken up to the smell of flowers before.

Mayte's dark hair fell loose about her shoulders, trailing over her full breasts. Her nipples were hard, peeking out from behind her hair, and I suddenly wondered what they would feel like on my tongue. What mine would feel like on hers.

"What do you like?" Eagerness tightened her voice. "You allow Blood to take Blood, so perhaps you like to watch. I can call Etzli or Tepeoyollotl to fuck me for you. Any way you like. Maybe you want them to hurt me. Or we can deny our Blood and make them watch us together. Torment them with what they cannot have."

I tried not to frown, but none of that sounded... sexy to me. I did like to watch, at least when it came to my Blood, but I didn't get off on watching someone being hurt, humiliated, or denied. Mehen had hurt Daire, yes, but it hadn't been punishment or denial. Mehen had only given Daire what he wanted, and I'd been privileged to see how carefully the more dominant Blood had handled him. Rough, but not brutally so. Even the mighty king of the depths could be tender, and he'd controlled himself to make sure Daire was safe. That kind of rough lovemaking I'd watch anytime, day or night, and want more, more, more.

But I didn't like the idea of making our men stand at the bed, watching their queens touch. Denying them. Making them hurt with need simply because I could. It was a fine line. I didn't mind pain, or watching someone deal pain to their lover, as long as they were all getting off on it. Rik would never get off on that kind of play. If I made him stand beside the bed and watch while I touched someone else, even another woman, it'd be torture for him.

Not pleasure.

"I don't like such games," I finally said. "I don't want to encourage any kind of jealousy, resentment, or denial among my Blood."

Mayte relaxed, a soft look coming into her eyes that made my throat tighten. "And that is only one of the many reasons they love you so much. What would you like, my queen?"

"Just call me Shara, please. As for what I would like, I don't really know. I've never been with a woman before you. Have you?"

"No. I still want my Blood, but I want to touch you too. I've never felt like this before. Knowing that you were here, under my roof, I couldn't stay away. I had to be with you, close to you, even if you were sleeping."

Staring at her, I felt my hunger stir. Need swelled inside me like a wave deep in the ocean. The wave lifted me higher, building strength. Pushing me closer to the beautiful woman in my bed.

I tasted her lips again, reveling in her softness. I loved a man's rock-hard body, but she was lusciously soft. Her skin was like satin. Her hair, heavy silk sliding over her shoulder. Her lips were lush and full, opening for me, asking me to slide deeper. I took my time exploring her mouth, imprinting the taste of her in my head. I didn't know when I'd ever come back to Mexico City, or if I'd ever feel like this for another woman.

I was so hungry, and she was a rare delicacy. I had to concentrate so I didn't devour her.

My fangs ached, but I only pressed my lips to her throat below her ear.

She moaned. "Yes, Shara. Let me feed you again. Please, take what you need from me."

I looked over at Rik to gauge his reaction. He watched me, his eyes heavy and dark.

Only for me.

You might think that such a healthy, virile alpha in his prime would be looking at both women. Mayte was naked, after all, and certainly beautiful. Most men had probably fantasized about watching two women make love.

But Rik was *mine*. Wholly, irrevocably mine. My rock. My always. Forever.

He looked at me like I was the moon and stars, and he'd die if he took his eyes off me for a single moment.

"Have your queen, Shara," he rumbled, reaching out to rub his thumb over my bottom lip. "And have me too, as you want, when you want, how you want."

My throat tightened, and my heart thumped hard against my ribcage like it wanted to escape. :*I love you more than life itself.*:

:*And I love you, my queen.*:

I pushed Mayte down onto her back. I tried to be gentle, but her breath rushed out on a soft gasp that made something perk up inside me. While I knew my Blood were predators, I'd never considered myself one, unless I was the cobra queen. But looking down at her shining eyes, her parted lips, her hair spread out on my pillow, I felt like a prowling jungle cat.

Mayte called jaguars. That was her gift. Was she calling something out of me? Something new?

I shivered a little, too turned on to worry very much about it. At least yet.

I leaned down and closed my lips over her nipple. The unique delicate hardness of a female nipple in my mouth made goosebumps race down my arms. There wasn't any part of my Blood's body that was so small, yet so hard, pillowed in softness.

Her desire became my desire. My hunger, hers. Lightly, I trailed my fingertips up her arms, across her shoulders and throat, down her flanks, while I sucked on her nipple. Softly, at first, but she pushed up against me, urging me on. Her bond glowed in my head. The more I touched her, the more she glowed like soft, pearly moonlight. Her scent warmed, growing sweeter and spicier the more I touched her.

Fuck, she was so soft. Her breasts filled my hands, her skin like fragile flower petals in my mouth. I quivered with the need to sink my fangs into the plumpness of her breast. To mark her as mine. To taste that sweet, hot blood simmering beneath the surface of her skin.

Was this how Rik felt when he touched me?

"Like a ravenous beast?" He moved closer, mindful of my wishes that he not touch the other woman. He leaned down and pressed soft kisses along my hip. "Yes. Every fucking time."

I shifted forward and flattened out on my stomach, giving Rik access to my legs and ass. He kneaded the muscles of my thighs and licked the hollow behind my knees.

Mayte tangled her fingers in my hair, pulling my head up a moment so I looked into her eyes. "I'm supposed to be pleasuring you, Shara."

"You are."

"But—"

"Is it alright if I touch you? If I taste you?"

She quivered beneath me, her eyes darkening. "Are you aware of what tasting a queen's desire does to a Blood?"

"Yes. What does it do to us?"

One shoulder lifted slightly, a wry, yet deliciously wicked, smile curving her lips. "I don't know. Would you like to find out?"

"Yes. Very much. And I'd like to feed from your thigh too. But I should warn you that I often feed so deeply that my Blood pass out. I'll try to hold back—"

"No," she broke in, her eyes flashing with emotion. "Don't hold back. Not for me. I want you all, Shara. I want to feed you as much as I can. I've given you so little in this arrangement. Surely you realize that you could have taken everything I have. Everything that I love. You could have even taken my daughter or killed her outright as a threat to Isador."

Her words thickened, as if tears clogged her throat, which made my eyes fill with tears too. "I would never hurt anyone like that, let alone you and your daughter."

"You could have, but you didn't. You wouldn't. Please, take me, any way you want. And if I pass out, or, goddess forbid, I die, so be it. Drain me as you wish. I make myself a willing sacrifice to Shara of House Isador."

Power swelled inside me, turning my desire even darker. Her words triggered something in me. Maybe it was the location, or the lineage of her house, but my predator side liked the idea of this sweet-smelling, beautiful woman stretched out on an altar for me to devour at will. :*Don't let me hurt her,*: I told Rik in the bond.

He rubbed his cheek against my calf, a deliberate rasp to help settle me. :*As you wish, my queen, so it shall be.*:

His words twisted inside me, his bond leaking a darker meaning. He would support me wholeheartedly if I decided to decimate her entire house after the mess with the geas. He didn't care about her in the slightest. But he did care about me, and he knew how badly I'd feel later if I actually hurt her.

I slid lower on her body, rubbing my mouth against her skin as I went. I scratched her with my fangs, fighting down the urge to feed. I'd wait. I'd wait until her cries hurt my ears, and her blood simmered with so much pleasure that her body couldn't contain it. Then I'd feast. But the silken heat of her skin against my mouth was a torment. I could smell her blood, rich and sweet like warm caramel, just below the delicate surface of her skin. Sweat beaded on my forehead, and my fangs throbbed in beat with my heart.

I kissed her stomach from one pelvic bone to the other. The skin in the crook of her thigh was paper thin, making me tremble with hunger. But I only licked the crease and breathed in her musk. She wanted me. She wanted this.

This was what Rik felt when he leaned over my pussy.

:*Not even close.*: His whisper was like distant thunder in my head, reverberating through my skull. He stroked his big palm up the back of my thighs and squeezed my ass. :*You smell like the finest, rarest perfume in all the world. I'd do anything to breathe your musk. To taste your desire. There's nothing better in this world, except your blood. Even better if I can mix the two into a heady concoction that makes me doubt my ability to retain control.:*

Yes, that was exactly what I was feeling now. That razor-wire dance of control. One misstep and I'd sink my fangs in her thigh and be done. Or I'd come myself. I could, easily, I realized. Desire hummed in me. If Rik slid his fingers between my thighs, he'd find me wet and swollen, aching for his cock.

Exactly like Mayte. Only she wasn't aching for him. She was aching for my mouth. My fingers. My tongue. My teeth.

She ached for me.

2

SHARA

I pressed a soft kiss to her pussy, letting the sensations pour over me. The crinkle of pubic hair. The scent of her desire, earthy, musky, and intoxicating. It made me connect to my own desire in a new way. My scent rose when I was turned on. My pussy swelled like this, pumped with blood, aching for touch. I tasted like this when Daire nuzzled deep between my thighs. A bit salty, but sweet, too. Very much like a peach, soft and luscious and perfect. Her desire coated my lips and tongue and sent a buzzing spark through my head.

The fine hairs on my arms tingled as my power rose. When I'd tasted Mehen's semen, my desire had fired to lust in a heartbeat, the kind of desire that needed to be filled, stroked, pounded, as hard and long as possible. I didn't feel that way with Mayte's cream hitting my system.

No. Instead, I wanted to seize a big mouthful of her tender thigh in my jaws and let out a rumbling growl.

Her hips undulated in a slow roll that made my blood simmer in my veins. I slid my index finger inside her, feeling the hot clench of her inner muscles. She moaned and pushed harder against me. Her fingers tangled in my hair. Her mind opened to me. In the bond, we floated in the secret grotto with a huge, full moon shining down on us.

I licked every crevice, and twisted my fingers deeper into her, stroking inside her. Seeking her pleasure. I wanted to hear her cries, taste the fresh flood of her desire on my tongue.

:*Let him taste you as you taste me,*: she whispered in my head.

Rik heard her words, whether she intended him to or not. He kept up the steady, slow stroking on my calves and knees, his mouth still on my thigh, but I felt his eagerness in the bond. I shifted up on my knees and that was all the invitation he needed.

He pressed nibbling bites to the sensitive line where my thigh met my buttock, following that curve to my hot, aching core. He flattened his tongue against me in a long, delicious swipe that made me groan against Mayte. He feasted on me, as I feasted on her. I stroked her, sliding deeper into her through our bond. A dark shadow that wound inside her, my power sparking against hers like a lightning storm.

She came against my mouth, and I could feel her pleasure thudding against my tongue, her muscles tight on my fingers. Her power flooded me with a lush, dark jungle, the scent of rich loam bursting with life. In the vision, she walked toward me with sprouts breaking free of the soil in her footsteps, vines winding up her body, and flowers blooming in the night.

Rik pushed his tongue deep inside me as I came, drinking me down on a low rumble of hunger. I threw my head back, letting the climax roll through me, his big hands on my hips holding me steady. Then I struck, hard, sinking my fangs into her inner thigh. Her blood exploded on my tongue, rich and hot, mixing with the sweet, honeyed taste of her desire. My spine bowed, and I quivered in Rik's grasp.

Moving closer, he pushed deep inside me in one smooth thrust. Filled by my alpha while my pretty queen fed me—it was almost more than I could bear. I came again, a sudden, hard climax that winched my muscles so tightly that Rik let out a soft grunt of pleasure. He didn't even have to move in me. He just filled me. Hard. Steady.

And then I came again. I couldn't stop coming.

Gasping, I raised my head, hoping that if I stopped tasting her blood that the pleasure would crest and ebb a bit. Her head lolled on the pillow, her eyes heavy and dazed, but I hadn't taken enough to make her pass out. Rik flexed against me, nudging a little deeper, and my back bowed, my head falling back helplessly like Mayte's.

Something surged inside me. Something large.

Bones cracked inside me.

Rik paused, his hands tensing on my hips. "Shara…"

But I didn't want him to stop. I pushed back onto my knees, leaning into him, and he automatically wrapped his arms around me.

Giving me something to bite.

I sank my fangs into his forearm, and he heaved up into me, lifting my knees off the mattress. Climax shook his big body as he emptied into me. I could feel the hot flood of his semen filling me, dripping down my thighs. A growl trickled through my lips.

I don't think I'd ever made that sound before. It almost sounded…

Mayte stretched out her hand toward me, calling something inside of me.

Two eyes glowed like lamps in the darkness of my mind.

She cupped my head in both her hands and pulled me down toward her, her thighs slipping around me. "Yes, my beast. Come to my call. Let me give our queen this gift."

Power surged upward like a geyser, pulling the dark, massive shape through me, shifting bones out of its way. My skin slipped away to something else with fur. And feathers. And claws.

Afraid I'd accidentally hurt her, I tried to move away, but she held my head in her hands. Her power sang to mine, and the goddess's gifts inside me reveled in that call.

I stared down at her and saw through new eyes. Eyes that could trace the smallest capillary beneath her skin. My heart pounded frantically. I didn't want to kill her like I'd killed Rik, when I'd shifted into the cobra queen.

But I didn't feel that same detachment this time. Even though I'd been dreaming when I hurt Rik, I still remembered the horrible realization that I was hurting him... and I hadn't cared. This form didn't have that same emotionless detachment. I still felt very much like myself, aware and wholly present in whatever creature I'd shifted into. Something large. The bed frame creaked beneath our combined weight. I was afraid to move, for fear I'd turn it into kindling. Another bed destroyed, like the one when Rik had made love to me in that very first time.

I laughed, but it wasn't a human sound. It came out of my throat more like a coughing growl.

"Oh," Mayte whispered, her eyes shining with excitement and pleasure. "You're beautiful, Shara. Look what our goddesses have given you."

Something fluttered in my peripheral vision. I turned my head and couldn't comprehend what I saw. Wings? But I didn't feel like a bird or even the wyvern.

She called jaguars.

Jaguars didn't have wings.

:*What am I?*: I asked them both.

"I don't think you have a specific name," Rik said, his voice soft with reverence. "You're a winged cat. More specifically, a black jaguar with blue-black wings." He stroked his hand down my rear haunch, his fingers pushing deep into my fur.

Fucking *fur*. Every single hair quivered with the sensation of his fingers gliding through them.

Mayte stroked her fingers over my jaws, despite the

sharp teeth I felt against my tongue. "Your head looks more lion to me, almost like the sphinx."

I loved that they both touched me without fear or hesitation. I didn't think she'd be looking at me with that soft light in her eyes if I'd shifted into the cobra again. Though Rik hadn't scrambled out of the bed when I'd unknowingly shifted into a massive snake.

"I think you're a hybrid," she continued. "Lion and jaguar. Jaglioness, maybe? You have the jaguar rosettes, but the shape of your head is definitely lioness. And these wings… Some kind of eagle, maybe?"

I couldn't even find the words. Why now? Why this shape?

"Do you remember the shapes on the jars in the legacy?" Rik asked. "Wasn't one of them a cat head?"

Yeah, I was pretty sure one had been some kind of cat, and another a cobra. If I'd had human skin, goosebumps would have raced down my arms. I'd needed the cobra to save Mehen. What would I need this shape to accomplish? More, what if I'd sent Mayte back to her own bed? Would I have still been able to shift to this winged cat form? Or was it a gift that only fully materialized when I took advantage of the chance to make love to her?

My head ached, even if I had fuzzy ears.

Laughing softly, Mayte leaned up enough to loop an arm around my neck and pulled me down to lie beside her. Still unafraid, stroking my fur like it was the most natural thing in the world to lie naked with a giant cat. The wings flopped awkwardly, until Rik helped me fold them up close to my sides.

:*How do I shift back?:*

"My power is yours now, Shara. Call your cat back inside to sleep. She'll obey without question."

I hesitated, wondering if I could purr like Daire. How did he do it? I huffed out my breath, and it came out a growl again.

In the bond, Daire rumbled that low, deep purr, sliding through me until he found the spot low in my throat. He touched those muscles, making them twitch crazy fast. And yeah, a purr vibrated through me.

Oooooooh. I loved Daire's purr without question, but it was a whole new crazy level of vibration to have my own organs humming from the inside.

He laughed softly in our bond. :*Now you know the truth about why I purr so much. It feels fucking fantastic, and I get to make you feel good too.:*

Rik fell down beside me as if I'd sucked the last drop of blood out of him, even though I'd only bitten him to make him come. He rubbed his hand up my side and caressed where my right wing sprouted from my back.

My eyes rolled back in my head, and my purr rumbled lower.

:*Rest, my queen. Enjoy your new shape as long as you like. Transforming back will probably require a great deal of energy, at least this first time, and this trip has already taxed your reserves.:*

I rubbed my face up beneath his chin and lightly touched

my tongue to his throat. Thousands of tiny details flooded my brain. His body temperature. The number of blood vessels that were so close to the surface. How many ounces of blood would spurt on my tongue if I bit him. The cat wanted to grip his throat in her jaws and purr directly against his flesh, knowing how easy it would be to kill him. He'd let me do it. Without question. The thought made me queasy, because I knew how easy it'd be to accidentally tear open that paper-thin skin.

But my alpha didn't even flinch. In fact, he dropped into a heavy sleep, with his vulnerable throat pressed against my wicked sharp teeth.

3

SHARA

When I woke again, sunlight streamed in through the windows and Mayte was gone. Rik sat beside me on the bed, already dressed. I looked down at myself, relieved to see that I'd shifted back to my normal human shape at some point. Though I couldn't help but feel vaguely cheated. I'd slept the rest of the early morning hours away instead of enjoying another Blood or touching Mayte in another delightful three-way session. I couldn't believe I'd slept so long and heavily. My stomach rumbled like I hadn't eaten for days.

Rik handed me a cup of coffee with a grin. "You needed it. There will be plenty of three-way sessions anytime you wish, my queen." He waggled his eyebrows at me, deliberately making me snicker. "Or more, of course. We're eager to serve in as many ways as you'd like."

I took a sip and sighed with bliss. I might live after all. "But not with Mayte."

He grunted softly. "Very true. I didn't send her away. She woke an hour ago and scurried out of here like the house was on fire."

Triggered by his words, the tapestry in my mind flared to life without conscious effort, sending me a mental picture of the entire home and beyond to the land and people living nearby. *Her* nest, now mine. I felt her with her child, laughing on her knees beside the bathtub. Her Blood were grumpy and silent, giving me a glare as I touched them briefly. Every living soul inside the perimeter, their health, needs, fears... available to me at a moment's notice. It was staggeringly easy to immediately assess one hundred and twenty-three people.

Drawing back to my immediate vicinity, I couldn't help but linger on each of my Blood. Mostly, I felt fierce determination mixed with some wicked glee and a healthy dose of possessiveness. But from the two newest Blood, Mayte's twin brothers, I felt impatience and hunger bordering on desperation.

I focused solely on Rik's bond. :*I think I may have made a mistake.*:

His eyes narrowed. :*What concerns you, my queen?*:

Despite my misgivings, I didn't want to hurt the twins' feelings, or give my other Blood cause to act out even more in some twisted desire to protect me. I sighed softly and slid to the edge of the bed while Daire and Nevarre brought me some clothes. Another pretty dress, this one made from a white gauzy material. White made me nervous—I had the annoying habit of dribbling blood all over me if I wasn't careful. :*I said I wouldn't take a Blood I didn't love. I don't love them.*:

:*You felt the rightness of it, though, so my guess is that you will love them eventually. The foundation is there. You wouldn't have even considered them if you hadn't felt the possibility.*:

:*But?*:

Rik made no noise, but I could hear the sigh in our bond. :*I don't trust them yet. I can't forget that they did nothing to protect you from the geas, yet wanted to serve as your Blood.*:

:*They made it sound as though they didn't know Mayte hadn't told me.*:

:*It doesn't matter.*: His bond hardened, molten steel in my mind. :*They wanted to be your Blood before we came here. They knew of the danger. They should have been present at your arrival to voice that concern, rather than trusting someone else, even their sister and queen, to take care of the warning. If they're careless with your safety and assume another Blood will take care of a risk, no matter how small, then I'll kill them.*:

He said it calmly, though every single word reverberated with intent in our bond. He didn't exaggerate. He'd snap their necks without hesitation if they didn't live up to his expectations.

:*Make them wait until they've earned the right to touch you. Remember that most Blood rarely ever touch or feed from their queen.*

It will do them no harm to wait until you're fully assured of their love and dedication.:

Dressed and caffeinated, I headed downstairs, driven by my grumbling stomach. I wasn't sure what time it was, although it was certainly too late for any meal to be called breakfast. Luckily, Mayte's people must have been used to late risers, because the breakfast room was well stocked with both traditional breakfast foods as well as soup and sandwiches.

Gina smiled at me, already at the table with a cup of coffee nearly gone. "Good morning, my queen. When you're ready, I have some things to go over with you."

"Me too." I sat down and trusted Rik to get me a plate. "When we get home, I'd like to take a look at the legacy again."

She immediately picked up her phone and typed rapidly. "Of course. I'll make sure it's there and waiting for you."

I loved that she did as I asked without question. "What else is happening at home?"

"Our general contractor was eager to get some work done despite the holiday. Evidently, we had some unseasonably nice weather, so your bedroom and bathroom should be ready for you when we return to Eureka Springs."

Rik set my plate in front of me and I dove into scrambled eggs with peppers and onions. I normally wanted something light, like fruit, but I'd slept so long that my body was eager for protein. Of course, he'd somehow known that, more in tune with my body than I was. "Oh wow, really? That was fast."

She smiled. "He had a small army of workers who were eager for bonuses in an otherwise slow time of year. Next up will be the kitchen. Even with that small army, Winston estimates a full week of work, but he's arranged for all the meals to be delivered indefinitely until he's satisfied with the renovations."

Mayte came in with her daughter in her arms, both of them dressed in bright, colorful dresses. "Good morning, Your Majesty."

I started to rise, but she quickly dropped her hand on my shoulder. "Please, don't trouble yourself. Not for me."

"Then you shouldn't call me Your Majesty, either. Especially under your own roof."

Smiling, she sat down beside me with Xochitl on her lap. "I have to set a good example for her, and this is still my roof only by your good graces." The little girl giggled and reached for me. "Oh, no, sweetie. Wait until our queen has finished eating."

"Nonsense." I put the fork down and opened my arms for her. The little girl crawled over into my lap, her eyes bright. "Good morning, Xochitl."

She giggled. "It's afternoon, silly."

"So it is. I was up way too late last night, and I sleep a lot."

"Mama slept in late today too."

I didn't look at Mayte for fear I'd blush. "What have you been doing today?"

"Papa took me riding this morning. I have my own pony."

"You do? What's her name?"

"Esperanza."

"That's a pretty name. What color is she?"

"White. How did you know she was a girl?"

I smiled and leaned down to whisper, "Because girls are the best."

"Could you ride with me today after you eat? Please?" She drew the plea out for several long seconds, her eyes glistening with excitement.

"I'm afraid I don't know how to ride."

"I can show you. It's easy. Papa has lots of horses that you can pick from."

I quirked my lips and tipped my head in Guillaume's direction near the door. "I have a horse to ride. I just don't know how to use the reins, or how to keep from getting bucked off."

Guillaume let out a huff in our bond that sounded very much like a disgusted nicker. :*As if I would ever allow you to fall off me, even if I'm bucking beneath you.*:

I couldn't help but look at him, then, my hunger stirring. I'd like to have him bucking beneath me. Very much indeed.

"He shifts into a horse?" Xochitl wiggled around to look at her mother. "Mama only has jaguars. Can I call horses, Mama?"

"It's too early to know what you'll call, sweetie."

I sensed hesitation in Mayte's bond, a reluctance to disappoint her daughter. Mayte's mother and grandmother before her had only ever called jaguars, so it was very likely that Xochitl's goddess would give her the same gifts.

Xochitl looked back at me. "What else do you have in your Blood?"

"A rock troll, warcat, hell horse, wolf, dragon, raven, and a bear. Plus, your uncles can shift into a giant black dog and a feathered serpent."

Xochitl tipped her chin up, her eyes gleaming with sudden determination. "Then I'm going to call unicorns."

My power stirred, my hair fluttering softly about my face. Staring into her brown eyes, I asked her solemnly, "Are you sure that's what you want? Unicorns?"

"Yes. That's all I want. Forever and ever."

My power shimmered inside me, shifting with her intention. Isis could give her this gift through me. I touched Mayte's bond. :*My goddess is willing to make this gift, if you aren't opposed.*:

I felt a surge of tearful emotion from her. :*Blessed be, thank you, Great One. Yes, please, I would give her anything in my power, but I cannot give her any Blood but jaguars.*:

:*Has she had blood before? I don't think I can give this power to her otherwise.*:

:*Yes, she's had mine and her father's. She knows what it means, though she has no need to feed yet. She doesn't have fangs yet.*:

I looked back into the child's eyes, shining with such promise. I didn't want to call down my massive fangs and scare her, so I held my hand up for Rik. He carefully punctured the tip of my index finger and I offered my blood to the child. "Take your gift of unicorns, Xochitl. Make them yours."

Her rosebud mouth closed over my finger and she

sucked hard, like I was a piece of candy and she was determined to get every drop. Her eyes spun rainbows for a moment, glittering like crystals and diamonds. Then she pulled back and smiled brightly. "I can't wait to grow up now, so I can have my unicorns!"

Mayte smiled, her eyes glittering just as brightly as her daughter's, but with tears. "What do you say, dearest?"

"Thank you, my queen."

"You're very welcome, Xochitl, Princess of Unicorns."

"I'm going to go tell Papa!" She jumped off my lap and raced for the door, but paused, looking back at me over her shoulder. "You will go for a ride though? Please?"

I laughed and nodded. "Of course. If Guillaume doesn't mind."

"Yay!" She skipped out the door.

I turned my attention back to my food. After a few moments, Mayte said, "You're very good with her. You will make a wonderful mother."

"Maybe someday."

Mayte gave me a questioning look, her brow furrowed. "You don't want children? I assumed… Well, I mean, if you can have a child, and children are so rare to our kind, I thought you'd be eager to have as many children as possible. The power you'll gain will be immense."

"How old were you when you had Xochitl?"

"Nearly two-hundred-and-thirty years old, but only because I couldn't have children. I tried everything we could think of for decades. Every queen does."

"I'm only twenty-two. I've been alone for the last five

years, on the run and scared to death. I've only had my Blood and known what I even am for a few weeks. There are a million things I must do before I can even think about settling down into my nest and having a child. Not the least of which is making sure we're all safe."

"Certainly, take care of Keisha Skye and Marne Ceresa first, but—"

"They're not my only enemies," I whispered softly. "In fact, they're not even the worst of my enemies."

Mayte's eyes widened and she dropped her voice to a whisper. "Who's worse than Marne?"

"Ra."

"The god of light? What does he have to do with you?"

My knee gave a phantom twinge as I remembered the skeleton trying to drag me through the portal in my bedroom. "Everything."

4

GUILLAUME

I tried not to twitch my tail with impatience, although I would have loved to snap at the man droning on and on about the different pieces of tack as he saddled me.

Picking up on my irritation, Shara asked in the bond, :*Are you sure you don't mind?*:

:*Not at all, my queen. You need to learn how the saddle and bridle work so you can ride a regular horse. I simply wish he wasn't quite so dedicated in telling you everything you could possibly ever wish to know about a piece of leather.*:

The new Blood, Itztli, gave a hard tug to tighten the girth one last time. Unnecessarily, because I was no standard horse that would employ such tricks to loosen the girth and risk giving my queen a tumble off to the ground. I picked my rear hoof up and deliberately planted it on the fool's foot.

I was a hell horse. The smell of brimstone burned my nose, along with the scent of scorched leather.

To his credit, the man didn't make a sound, even when his boot started to smoke.

"G," Shara chided.

:*Oops.*: I picked up my hoof and the idiot moved his foot out of my way. Even better, he received the message loud and clear that I was finished with this lesson.

"May I assist you in mounting, Your Majesty?"

"Of course."

"On a smaller mount, I'd suggest putting your left foot in the stirrup and swinging up onto his back, but he's rather too tall." He bent down and laced his fingers together. "Give me your left foot, and I'll toss you up. Carefully," he added that last word hurriedly, sensing our alpha's unspoken warning.

She picked up her foot, encased in borrowed boots, since we hadn't thought to shop for riding gear in Dallas, and Itztli gave her a gentle toss up onto my back. Even with the leather separating my sensitive skin from direct contact, her weight brought the nerves in my back to life. I had a warhorse's instincts. I could feel the tightening of her muscles, the slight press of her thighs and heels as she shifted her weight in the saddle. I would have dearly loved a thinner English-style saddle rather than the heavy Western-style roping saddle they'd used. Bareback would be even better.

I'd had her bareback and bare-ass naked. Once. Having

my queen's bare pussy on my back had been a life-altering experience, to say the least.

"The stirrups are a bit too short," Itztli said. "Let's drop them down a notch."

His brother stepped closer on my other side, their eagerness to touch our queen, even for something so minor as fixing her stirrups, painfully obvious. I watched Rik, his gaze merciless. He didn't care one whit how desperate they were to be taken by our queen. He'd make them wait as long as possible.

"Stand on the balls of your feet," Tlacel said, smoothing the leather straps into place. "Let's test that."

She shifted her weight to her feet, rising up in the saddle a bit. I could feel the rightness of her balance now. The stirrups had definitely been too short for her.

"Much better. Alright, you can sit back down. Keep your heels down as much as you can, and your... um... seat yourself deeply in the saddle."

She wriggled her delightful ass deeper into the saddle, and it was all I could do not to nicker with encouragement. She felt my appreciation and laughed, her voice husky. "I didn't realize that riding a horse had so many similarities to making love."

:Wait until I canter for you.:

"Pick up the reins," Itztli said, his voice deeper than before. "Tighten up a little until you can feel the bit in his mouth. That's how you tell a horse where you want to go, along with shifting your weight or tightening your thighs. It depends on how well the horse is trained, but you can often direct a horse by pushing against his side with the opposite knee. Like you're pushing him in the direction you want to go."

She slid the reins through her fingers until she felt the contact with my mouth. By instinct, I arched my neck, ears flickering back and forth, waiting for her command.

"Watch his ears," Tlacel noted. "He's listening to you. Ready for you to tell him where and when and how fast."

She laughed again and stroked my neck. "Yes. Very much like the bedroom. But sometimes a girl just wants the guy to take over."

If I wasn't a horse, I would have laughed at Tlacel's labored breathing, let alone the way he stumbled over his words.

"There are times you'll want to trust your horse's instincts rather than your own. For example, picking a path down steep terrain, or at night. They have better night vision than humans, and a horse has an instinctual ability to plant his hooves on the safest path."

"Horses don't see well behind them," Itztli added in a voice so deep and raw that I flicked my tail at him. "They spook easily and whirl to check behind them. Or they balk at something they've seen a thousand times. If you feel as though he's out of control, just pull his head around to either side. Force him in a circle. Eventually he'll come to a stop, no matter how spooked he is."

Enough was enough. :*Will you allow me to show off?*: I asked her through the bond, keeping my focus narrow, though I made sure Rik knew what I was up to.

She laughed in my mind, her magic sparkling like starlight through our bond. :Without question.:

:Tighten your thighs and stay deep in the saddle. I'll take care of you.:

I pivoted on my rear left hoof, shoving both twins out of my way, and more importantly, away from our queen. I did it quickly, but so smoothly that she didn't have a problem keeping her seat.

Clear of the twins, I started an old dressage drill I'd used as a young stud to warm up. Back before Desideria had gotten her claws into me. When I'd been young and idealistic. When I hadn't known how heavy my honor would weigh upon me.

I trotted slowly in a large circle, neck arched, picking up each hoof like the ground was hot lava, but so smoothly that she never once lost contact with the saddle. She had no need to post or rise up in the stirrups. Then to really show off, I changed leads, back and forth, giving her a good rocking motion in the saddle, before I leaped, all four hooves leaving the ground. I landed so softly she didn't even jar her teeth.

Rik, Daire, and Ezra rode after us while the twins scrambled to get on their mounts and follow. Mehen and Nevarre circled in the air above us. Xin was his ghostly wolf, and though my eyes couldn't see him, my hell horse was fully aware of a predator quietly scouting ahead. I could smell him, even if I couldn't see him without our queen's bond to point the way.

I settled into a gentle canter, though I couldn't resist

putting just enough bounce in my gait to make sure her pelvis rocked up against the saddle. I circled around the waiting riders, Xochitl and her father on their mounts. The child laughed and clapped her hands. "You were teasing me. You don't need help learning how to ride."

Shara laughed ruefully as I settled into a walk beside them. "If this was any other horse, I would have fallen off in the first five minutes. Where are we going, Xochitl?"

"Papa said I could show you where the Fire Ceremony will be tonight."

I drew to a halt and snorted. I could feel the outer boundary of the nest shimmering a pace ahead.

Our queen felt it too, and though she said nothing, I felt her immediate anxiety. She'd been hunted all her life and had only recently learned of the safety to be found in a nest. Rik rode closer on our left, his knee brushing my shoulder, while Daire and Ezra rode ahead to be sure it was safe. In broad daylight, there shouldn't be any thralls about, and if Keisha Skye was half as smart as everyone thought she was, she'd wait to attack Shara on her own turf in New York City, not in another queen's territory. Keisha couldn't know how strong our queen was, let alone after taking her first sib.

I stepped across the invisible barrier and she shivered, though she kept her voice light. "What's a Fire Ceremony?"

"We turn out all the lights at home and pile up big bonfires, but we don't light them right away. There's drums and dancing and singing, and I get to stay up all night." She scowled. "If I can make it. I will this year."

"I'm sure you will, butterfly." Tepeyollotl's voice rolled

with thunder, even though he spoke to his daughter with a smile. He rode a black stallion almost as large as me, without a single rein or stirrup to control the animal. Evidently ancient Aztec gods had no need for something as trivial as tack. I had a feeling that he'd stride into war the same way: no weapon, no shield, just his formidable presence. The air around him was thick and heavy with danger, like any moment, a hurricane would explode out of him and devastate everything in his path.

"Tell her about the ceremony, Papa. What it means."

"In the old days, we held the ceremony at the end of the fifty-two-year cycle with the hope that life would continue. All the fires were put out throughout the villages, and the priests waited for the signs to confirm the sun would rise again and life would continue. Zaniyah started the tradition of having the ceremony on the modern calendar's New Year's Eve. The intent is the same. Starting a new year, a new appreciation for life, our gifts of fire and sunlight and the promise of spring."

"And death," the little girl added. "Sacrifice."

"We don't sacrifice any longer, butterfly."

"But you used to."

He nodded and looked over at my queen, a wry smile softening the harsh planes of his face. "Our queens make the necessary sacrifice for us now."

Shara's thought echoed in all our bonds. :*It always comes back to blood.*:

Her bond tightened, not with fear, exactly, but preparation and grim acceptance. She would do whatever was needed to protect us all, without hesitation, though she didn't look forward to whatever trial she would face. None of us did. In fact, a giant ball of dread settled in my stomach at the memory of what she'd gone through the last time the goddesses desired a sacrifice of her.

She didn't want to suffer agony again, like when she'd grown the grove in her own nest.

When she'd died.

SHARA

The burn of thorns in my flesh flashed through my memory. I didn't want to die on a heart tree again. Though if the goddesses wanted to grow a grove for House Zaniyah...

I would do whatever they required of me.

Xin's silent, still bond suddenly sharpened in my mind. *:There's something watching from the clump of trees by the grotto. I'll investigate.:*

Nevarre let out a loud caw and circled lower, but even his sharp eyes couldn't see whatever Xin had sensed.

:I can blast the entire area with fire,: Mehen offered, his dragon eager to lay devastation on the land.

:No,: I told him firmly. *:It could be someone bathing who merely wants their privacy. I won't have anyone harmed accidentally.:*

:They have no scent,: Xin whispered as his wolf ghosted through the trees. *:They're almost as invisible as I am.:*

Rik didn't hesitate. *:Shift. Be ready.:*

Daire leaped down off his borrowed horse, shifting

before he hit the ground. Rik shifted into his rock troll, and his terrified horse ran away as he took up position in front of us. Guillaume braced beneath me like he was ready to leap into war or run hard in the opposite direction to get me as far away from danger as quickly as possible. Ezra's mighty bear and Daire's warcat both took up defensive positions in front of me, and Tlacel's feathered dragon surged up into the sky to join the dragon and raven on the hunt. Itztli stayed on my right to guard our flank.

Their concern for my safety made me warm and gooey on the inside... but also irritated me. I had already escaped living skeletons and survived several attempts by other queens to ensnare me, not to mention breaking the geas on Mayte's nest. Surely—

:*I have no doubt whatsoever in your ability and power to save us all,*: Rik rumbled through me, an avalanche of crashing boulders. :*But I won't see you unnecessarily harmed or taxed either.*:

The bushes rustled at the edge of the grotto, and a dark shape suddenly burst from the undergrowth. A dog. They were worried about a dog. The poor thing looked rather thin and scrawny, dirty and black with soot. Though it was rather large. Almost as big as Xochitl's pony.

Xin raced after the poor creature, his teeth bared in a snarl. :*It has no scent. It's not a normal dog.*:

I glanced over at Itztli, my own giant black dog. "A Blood like you?"

"He's not my queen's," Tepeyollotl said. "Nor is he part of her nest. I don't recognize him."

Itztli's nose tipped up into the air, his mouth slightly

parted. :*No, my queen. Not like me. He's not Blood. He's...*: He glanced over at his niece's father. :*He's more like Tepeyollotl.*:

"A god? An Aztec god?"

Tepeyollotl snagged his daughter's reins and started back toward the nest boundary. "None that I recognize. I suggest you allow your Blood to dispose of it to be safe, my queen."

Itztli ran forward to help Xin capture the intruder. They were both mighty Blood in their own right, and powerful predators. But the other dog kept eluding them. Easily. Almost as if—

I whirled in the saddle to make sure Tepeyollotl was successful at getting the child back to safety.

The world disappeared in an intensely painful blaze of light. Tears dripped down my cheeks. My eyeballs felt scalded, my retinas seared. Only one person... god... had been able to do that before. :*Ra!*:

I heard the wings, though I couldn't see anything. Rik folded his arms around me, scrunching me down against Guillaume's withers. :*He's not here for me. He's here for Xochitl!*:

I felt Xin's pain before I heard his yelp. I tasted blood in Itztli's mouth as he crunched mighty jaws down on the intruder, dragging him off my wolf. Nevarre tumbled crazily toward the ground, stunned by the blaze of light. Mehen and Tlacel had been higher and out of harm's way, but my raven...

:*I have him, my queen,*: Tlacel swooped down and caught Nevarre before he could crash into the ground.

I pushed up against Rik and he let me straighten, though he kept his stone body against me. I blinked away the streaming tears and searched for Xochitl. Her white pony lay lifeless on the ground. Her father's mount struggled and flopped helplessly, at least one leg broken. The mighty god of jaguars had indeed shifted into his huge beast. But he could only stand there and roar with frustration as a large golden eagle carried his daughter kicking and screaming higher into the sky.

Away from the nest. Away from her queen mother.

Mayte screamed so loudly in the bond that I winced. All her Blood raced toward us, but they were jaguars too. They'd never be able to catch a bird of prey.

Mehen dived at the giant bird, trying to turn it back. He didn't dare blast it with fire, for fear of hurting the child. The huge bird knew it, too, and screeched out its own warning. It was so big... With one twist of its mighty talons, it could tear the little girl apart, or disembowel her. We were helpless, forced to stand and watch as they flew away.

Helpless, my ass.

I used Rik's shoulders to steady myself as I climbed to my feet on top of Guillaume's broad back. I spread my arms open wide and closed my eyes.

The goddesses had given me a new shape—with wings—for a reason.

It was time for the winged jaguar to prove itself useful.

5

SHARA

Power rose inside me, making my nerves and senses come alive. I heard the steady thump of Rik's heartbeat like a timpani drum and felt the slightest twitch of Guillaume's skin beneath me. My blood hummed in my veins, a rising symphony of goddess retribution.

Xochitl was mine through her mother's bond, and no child of mine would ever be harmed.

I tore open my right wrist and the surge of power made me tremble, my head falling back under the rush. The dark beast inside me swelled closer to my skin. Not scales this time, but fur and feathered wings. My jaguar wound its way through my bonds like a cat rubbing against her human's ankles, and then pushed out of me. Teeth and claws, a jaguar's hunting instincts, combined with the speed and agility of a hawk.

Yes, this was exactly the shape I needed to hunt a kidnapping eagle.

Guillaume shifted his weight beneath me, broadening his stance. I hadn't thought about my weight and size in this shape, let alone a horse's instincts to protect itself from a giant predator.

:*Even if your jaguar decides to eat a hunk out of me, this hell horse isn't going anywhere, my queen.*:

Despite my worry, I laughed in the bond. :*No eating horses. Though I can't promise I won't be tempted to take a nice big bite of you later.*:

I spread my wings and gave an experimental flap. I didn't have time for practicing. All I could do was trust in Isis and let the magic She'd given me do its job. I crouched, gathering my power. Focusing my will. I would leap into the air and fly. I would catch this fucking eagle and rip him to shreds. Xochitl would be safe.

I willed it to be so.

Guillaume lowered his head out of my way. Standing in front of the hell horse, Rik ducked down too like a massive linebacker, his fist braced on the ground. His broad back was higher, giving me a perfect runway.

I exploded forward, leaping onto Rik's impenetrable stone hide. He pushed up as hard as he could, giving me extra momentum into the air. Power surged inside me, fed by my blood, lifted by my love. I soared upward, my wings catching the air perfectly. I ran—but on air.

:*I'm coming,*: I told Xochitl through the small bond I'd formed by giving her my blood this morning. :*Don't be afraid, sweetie. I want you to fight and kick and scream. We're going to make the eagle drop you, and my dragon can catch you.*:

Mayte's bond flashed and burned white-hot in my head as she raced to a Jeep to follow us, her rage and fear so bitter I could taste it in my mouth. :*My baby, Shara. He took my baby.*:

:*And I'm going to get her back.*:

Anguish twisted our bond. :*She's so scared. She's bleeding. She thinks the bird is going to eat her.*:

I didn't want to let my imagination come up with all the horrible scenarios that Ra might have in store for a young, defenseless Aima queen. :*Over my dead body.*:

:*That may be what he intends,*: Rik rumbled in my head. :*This could be a trap.*:

:*How?*: Mayte whispered, her voice breaking into splinters in my head. :*How did he find her? How could he know she even existed? No one but my family knew of her birth until you came, and I know beyond a shadow of a doubt you or your Blood wouldn't have done such a thing.*: She gasped, like someone had shoved a knife through her heart. :*It has to be one of my people. My family. They betrayed me, so they could betray you.*:

I concentrated on my Blood bonds to gauge how far I'd traveled already, and how far ahead the golden eagle was. Leviathan tracked the giant bird from a safe distance. Tlacel had deposited Nevarre to safety on the ground and then surged after me. The rest of my Blood were on foot and following, nowhere near as fast as I could fly, though Guil-

Iaume and Itztli were the closest after Tlacel. And Rik. He'd shifted back and rode my hell horse. He wouldn't be left behind this time because of his rock troll's ponderous pace.

If this was a trap...

I had to be ready to spring it.

Even if Ra intended to grab two Aima queens with one net, he wouldn't find me easy prey. Surely, he'd already learned that lesson when he'd tried to snag me out of my own bedroom in Kansas City. But if not, I'd be fucking thrilled to blast him back to wherever he came from.

TLACEL

After living—no, barely existing—for hundreds of years, waiting to be claimed, my queen had come for me at last.

An incredibly powerful, beautiful, and fascinating queen. Every cell in my body burned to be taken by her. I wanted to prove my loyalty. My willingness to do whatever she required of me.

But the last thing I wanted was to find us tasked with saving my niece. I would rather have faced any danger myself, no matter how dire, than risk harm to a single hair on Xochitl's head.

I cut through the air effortlessly, a sinuous, feathered shape of legend in the sky. Shara Isador made this possible. Her blood. Her power. I wore the flesh of Quetzalcoatl, Great Feathered Serpent, for her, but even with this magnificent power humming through me, I could barely keep pace with my queen as she streaked after the thieving golden eagle carrying my niece away. A black jaguar with wings. I had never seen such a wonder.

She touched my bond and lightning tore through me. :Where do you think he's taking her?:

:Huitzilopochtil's main pyramid was in Mexico City, but it's long gone now, only a crumbled ruin beneath the city.:

One of her other Blood, the big dragon, spoke to us. :He's circling around a small body of water, like he's waiting for you, my queen.:

Realization shot through me and I drew on every ounce of power she'd given me to surge faster through the sky. :The cenote. We must hurry.:

:Why? What is it?:

:Our ancestors thought the cenotes were portals to the otherworld. If he takes her through the portal, we'll never get her back.:

Shara's urgency matched mine and she blurred with a sudden burst of speed.

:It's a trap,: the dragon growled. :He's baiting you.:

:Doesn't matter,: she retorted. :He's not taking her from us.:

A massive fist tightened on my heart. It took me a moment to realize it was our alpha's warning. :You and Mehen are the only ones close enough to protect her until I arrive. No harm will come to her, or I'll rip this organ from your chest and feed it to you.:

:Understood, alpha.:

I managed to gain enough speed to hover at her flank. The eagle circled lazily over the cenote. When he saw us, he let out a triumphant screech.

:Enough of this bullshit,: Mehen growled. *:I'll just bite the bastard's head off and catch the child before she hits the water.:*

He didn't wait for our queen's approval and dove at the smaller bird.

Light blazed from the eagle, a sweeping flash of painful brilliance that seared my eyes even at a distance. The mighty dragon howled with agony and tumbled down, crashing off the limestone wall to splash into the water. The eagle made another circle, and then tucked his wings and plummeted toward the surface.

:Mehen's down,: she told Rik.

Our bonds vibrated with the force of his fury, and an image filled my head of the big man leaning lower over the straining hell horse's neck, willing him to gallop harder.

Light sparkled upward from the cenote like someone had turned on a brilliant spotlight deep below the surface. Rainbows sparkled in the air. As we swooped down closer to the shining circle, I felt its incessant tug like the moon on the tides. It pulled me closer, and irrational fear or not, I didn't think I'd be able to turn my path aside now that it had locked onto me. The portal was activated and eager to allow us to pass, to gods only knew what on the other side.

Steep limestone cliffs clogged with trees, roots, and vines passed as we raced down after the eagle. A black shape lunged up and caught the eagle before it could sink into the water. Mehen, the dragon, roaring with rage as he tore the golden eagle apart.

Xochitl screamed and hit the water, sinking like a stone.

:Can she swim?: Shara asked me.

:Yes, but it won't matter. The portal has her.:
:Rik, I'm going in after her. Tlacel, you'll have to pull me back out. I'll tell you when I have her.:

She tucked her wings tight and dove into the water, shifting back to her human shape as her body moved through the water. She stretched her hands out ahead of her, straining for Xochitl. Seconds later, I broke the surface too. Cool water flowed over me. I kept my eyes wide open, straining to keep sight of my queen. Still in my winged serpent form, I sliced through the water, my muzzle touching her calf. I ought to be able to seize her ankle in my jaws and drag her back out of the water. As long as I stayed close and didn't sink too far through the portal myself.

The water suddenly heated, like I'd jumped into my sister's favorite bathing pool. Golden light flooded the water, so bright my eyes would have been streaming with tears in my human shape. I fought my instinct to turn aside, avert my gaze and protect my eyes. I had to see. I had to be ready to grab my queen and haul her back out.

:She's gone too far,: Rik rumbled in my head. *:You have to pull her back out. Now.:*

:Not yet,: she whispered, straining harder. I felt her fingertips brush Xochitl's hair. *:Almost... Fuck. I missed. She's through.:*

Through my queen's bond, I saw Xochitl staring up at her, eyes wide, mouth open on a scream as she fell out of water into blue-green sky. The world tilted crazily, my equilibrium struggling to right itself in the inverted new world. Shara broke through the water too and flung her hands out to snag Xochitl's hair. She tugged the child up against her and wrapped her arms around her protectively.

:Now!:

I sank my jaws around her lower leg and flung my wings out, arching backward, struggling to stop our momentum through the portal. My wings provided drag against the water, and definitely slowed our progression, but we still slipped deeper into the otherworld. Shara was through to her waist, pulling me closer and closer to the inverted world. The world of Huitzilopochtil. Through my queen's gaze, I saw a golden pyramid rising up so high that it pierced the sun. Streams of crimson ran down the pyramid's sides and trickled across the ground to feed a dark-red river.

A river. Of blood. So many sacrifices. So many deaths.

My queen and niece would add to that bloody river if I couldn't pull them back through.

Soulless sacrifices stood below my queen, moaning with agony and ecstasy both. Golden light blazed from empty eye sockets and gaping mouths. Their skin seemed oddly loose, as though they were completely empty sacks. Their arms wavered in the air, rubbery and slack, though definitely reaching for her. Eager to claim her for their god.

Shaken, I strained harder. Something tore in my wings. Pain splintered through my mind. But I threw myself back. Back to our world, dragging our queen to safety. Darkness filled my vision and I tasted blood in my mouth. I broke something deep inside me. I spun out of control, unable to tell if I was even pulling her back in the right direction any longer.

Blood. Her blood, in my mouth. I focused on her taste, the sweet rush of power. *Isis, Great One. Coatlicue, Mother of the Gods. Grant me enough power to save my queen, and then do as You will with me.*

Something seized my tail and nearly ripped it out of my body. I didn't struggle against the pain but embraced it. I was still alive, and that formidable grip was my alpha. He hauled me out of the portal by my tail, I dragged Shara with me, and she gripped Xochitl against her chest. Rik grabbed our queen and pulled her up out of the water. Choking and gasping, she lifted Xochitl up out of the water, too.

Nevarre swooped down to snag the little girl by the back of her shirt and lifted her toward the edge of the cenote. At least the raven hadn't been killed by the first blast. Hopefully the dragon had fared just as well.

Liquid golden power rippled in the water. :*The portal's still open,*: I gasped. :*Get out!*:

The black dragon surged up out of the water and clung to the side of the cenote. :*I can't fly yet, but I can at least get out of the water.*:

I tried to do the same, but I felt like cartons of broken eggshells floated inside me instead of bones. The current swirled me further away from the sides, toward the center, where a whirlpool sucked the water—and everything in it— down a grim path into the portal.

:*Heal me, and I'll get him out,*: Mehen said.

Rik reared up out of the water and tossed Shara toward the edge of the cenote by the dragon. She gave him her arm, and the dragon closed his jaws around her wrist with utmost care, eyes closed in ecstasy as he drank from her.

She kept a wary eye on me. I sank lower in the water. A dull roar filled my head, like a gigantic bathtub plug had been popped, and all the water of the world was sinking through the drain. The whirlpool widened, sucking me faster in a vicious circle toward the center. I didn't try to swim out. I knew I didn't have the strength. It was all I could do to keep my muzzle up out of the water. :*Get her out first.*:

I looked up at the sky as water closed over my head. So blue. I had saved my queen and my niece, the future queen of my people. That was all I'd wished for. Night fell, black spreading across the sky, death closing in.

Claws sank into me and yanked me up. Not darkness or death, but Leviathan. He let out a disgusted laugh in my head. :*She refused to leave even the scaly chicken behind.*:

Head lolling, I was beyond pain as Leviathan carried me up and out of the cenote. We passed Rik in his rock troll form, our queen clinging to his back as he scaled the limestone cliff. The dragon tossed me down on the ground, and Itztli stuck his bleeding wrist in my face. :*Feed, brother. I can't heal you like she will, but at least let me ease your pain until she's here.*:

It was an indication of how close I must be to death for my brother to be willing to feed me. He'd done well to hide that dread from our queen last night when she'd taken us, but she'd have every ugly secret soon enough. I wouldn't torment him needlessly, but I did send a wave of gratitude to him. :*She's the last queen of Isis. If I die, she'll bring me back.*:

He didn't protest. Clutching my sobbing niece in her arms, Mayte knelt beside me, tears in her eyes. "Oh, brother. What have you done to yourself?"

She laid her hand on my head and her power sparked along my scales. She'd healed me before, but this time... It wasn't her touch I wanted. She released a soft little sigh and pulled her hand away with a wry smile. "Here's our queen now."

Rik cleared the edge of the cenote and Shara slid down beside me. I could smell her blood already, her magic sinking into me before a single drop of her blood passed onto my tongue. Her bond glowed like a soft, glowing moon in a clear midnight sky, shining light on all of my internal hurts, while simultaneously wiping them away. She lifted my head into her lap and pressed her wrist against my muzzle, dripping blood from the dragon's bite.

I opened my jaws and carefully cradled her fragile arm inside my mouth, letting her blood drip down my throat without tearing her skin any further. Her fingers stroked over my head and down my neck, kneading strength and power into my hide. "Without you today, both Xochitl and I would be lost to Ra."

Rik made a low, dangerous rumble, though he didn't take her to task for risking her life, and ours, to save the child. I might be her newest Blood, but with her bond shining in me, I knew her heart. She would never hang back, waiting for someone else to help. Not with any child at risk, and certainly not one she'd taken into her heart like my niece. She'd made Xochitl an Isador heir. She would die for her. For any of us.

Not that we would ever allow that to happen.

The great jaguar god came closer, moving as though something deep inside him still pained him. He dropped a hand on Mayte's shoulder. "I thank you all. I had no idea the sun god would be able to strike us so effectively. It's quite humbling to know that all my immense power means nothing, as I was forced to watch helplessly as my daughter was carried away."

His voice broke, and Xochitl reached up for him. He pulled her up into his arms and Mayte swiped her tears away. "Without you, Shara, we would be lost. But it's my great shame to admit that someone in my household must have betrayed us. Very few people knew you were coming to Zaniyah until the very last minute before your arrival. Before this incident, I would have sworn that all my people were one-hundred-percent loyal, but Bianca feared someone might alert House Skye that we were expecting you."

"Bianca." Shara said the name flatly, her mouth twisting as if she'd tasted something bitter.

"No," Mayte gasped, shaking her head. "I can't believe it. Her family has served Zaniyah for generations."

"Who else knew I was coming? Who else would have the contacts to reach out to one of Ra's believers? Who else knows Xochitl's habit of riding with her father?"

Pale, my sister closed her eyes, her mouth moving as she whispered softly beneath her breath. Her hair lifted, fluttering about her face, her voice rising, though I couldn't understand her words. I knew she spoke in our ancient tongue, but those words were forbidden for my ears to understand.

When she opened her eyes once more, they flashed like cold diamonds. "The spell is cast. We'll know the truth once we return back to the nest."

"What about the black dog?" Shara asked, turning to Rik. "Were we able to capture it, or at least kill it?"

:I have him,: Xin said in our bonds. :I kept him alive for you.:

A grim smile flickered across Shara's face. Cold chills raced down my spine at that look. Retribution. A promise of pain and punishment. Justice. A goddess's righteous fury.

I almost felt sorry for whoever had dared not die when Ra's plan failed.

Almost.

6

SHARA

Wrapped in blankets from the emergency stash in the Jeep, Rik and I rode back to the house with Mayte and Tepeyollotl. She drove, and he bounced Xochitl on his lap. Now that she was safe, she recovered quickly, eagerly telling her parents about what had happened from her perspective.

I'd tried to convince Tlacel to ride with us, but he'd insisted he was healed enough to fly back with Mehen and Nevarre. He'd torn himself up to keep us from sliding through the portal. Broken bones, shredded muscles, bruised and bleeding organs. I kept a careful touch on his bond, watching for any difficulty or lingering pain, in case he needed another round of healing.

I leaned forward and whispered to Mayte, "When will

she be able to call her own Blood? She needs more protection."

"It varies greatly," she whispered back. "The more powerful a queen, the earlier her Blood are called, generally speaking. But it depends on many other factors, too. The nest nurtures her power and helps it come in quicker, which will draw Blood to her sooner, but she may not call any until she's past puberty or even in her early twenties, as you did."

She glanced at the man beside her and switched to our bond. :*I always assumed he'd be enough to protect her from anything, but his powers are limited, too. I never dreamed something would swoop down from the sky and carry her away. I wish I called more than jaguars.*:

:*You helped call my flying jaguar,*: I reminded her. :*Intent is everything. She mentioned a ceremony tonight. Maybe you should try sending out a call for another winged jaguar for an extra layer of protection in the sky.*:

:*Yes. I'm stronger now, thanks to you, my queen. I have the capacity to call another couple of Blood that can help us protect her until she has her own.*:

Xochitl turned to her mother, her eyes bright. "Mama, what do you call a flying horse?"

"There was a horse named Pegasus who could fly."

"Then I'm going to call unicorns that fly like Pegasus. I want Blood who can fly so they can stab any mean bird that tries to get me again with their shiny horns."

Mayte smiled, though I felt the wrench in her bond. A mother's fervent wish that her daughter not grow up too quickly. That she never be in such danger ever again, even though she knew pain and fear and disappointment were inevitable.

Goddess, let her have a great deal of unwavering love in her life, too.

"That sounds like a great plan, sweetie."

I felt the tingle as we passed through the nest, but this time, the energy felt more like a buzzing hive of angry bees. Mayte drove up to the back of the house where a knot of people waited for us. They parted as she parked the Jeep, revealing the consiliarius on her knees. Blood trickled from her mouth and nostrils, her eyes wide and flashing white. She tried to stand as Mayte got out of the Jeep, but flopped and jerked helplessly, unable to rise. Something popped loudly, and her mouth twisted with a grimace of pain.

Mayte's spell was not something to fuck with.

"My heart, please take Xochitl to get something to eat."

Tepeyollotl gave their daughter a playful toss, artfully distracting her from the scene unfolding. "What do you think unicorns eat, butterfly? We should ask Sarah to make some special dishes, so they come to your call quickly."

"Cake!" She squealed with laughter as they headed for the kitchens. "They eat cake, Papa."

Gina came to my side as I got out of the Jeep, and her eyes were tight with concern. "What happened? One minute we were talking, and the next she let out a horrible cry, fell to her knees, and started crying and begging for help as she crawled out here. I tried to help but..." She shook her head.

"My most trusted confidant," Mayte said in a flat, hard voice. "My betrayer."

Gina sucked in a shaking breath. I took her hand firmly in mine to make sure she knew instantly that I didn't doubt her in the slightest.

"My queen," Bianca moaned with pain. "I didn't know they'd use Xochitl. I swear. It was only supposed to be Isador."

"You betrayed Zaniyah. You brought shame to our house by betraying our new queen to her greatest enemy, and then gave them our only Zaniyah heir. Why? Why would you do this?"

"I was trying to protect us! Protect you! I thought she would take everything, and if I could get rid of her first..." Bianca swallowed hard, blood dripping down her chin. Eyes wild, she turned to me for assistance. "Please, Great One, I had no idea—"

I quivered with rage. Great One. That was Isis's name. Not mine. The sky darkened. Clouds boiled on the horizon and thunder rumbled. Lightning tore across the sky, opening it up for a deluge of rain that hammered the crowd, drenching us all. But Isis's rage could not be cooled by rain.

Bianca found her pride and stiffened her spine, raising her voice to be heard over the storm. "You're unharmed. Xochitl is fine. Besides, you can always have another heir. I was trying to save us all."

"You would damn a child to Ra's hell to save your own skin." My voice echoed with Isis's thunder. Wind whipped across the plaza, overturning tables, chairs, and even a few potted plants. "There can be no forgiveness for worms like you."

"There will be no Fire Ceremony tonight." Mayte didn't sound like herself any longer. As I gazed at her, I saw a different shape overlaid on her familiar features, like a blurred photograph of someone caught in motion, or old-fashioned double-exposed film. Her goddess hovered over her, long black hair waving around her down to her knees.

No. That wasn't hair. They were snakes. They hung around her legs, almost like a skirt.

"Perhaps in sacrifice, this worm can find some way to atone for her sins," Mayte said.

Bianca's bravado faded quickly. "No, please. We don't sacrifice any longer."

Staring at Coatlicue's avatar and heir to Her power, I felt certainty shifting inside me. Sacrifice was needed. A great deal of blood. But not all of that blood had to be shed in retribution. I wouldn't interfere with what Mayte needed to do…

But I had a brutal, bloody task to accomplish, too.

The pressure inside me rose, dragging my head to the side. My gaze collided with Itztli's and I remembered the obsidian blade he'd shown me last night. As soon as I thought of it, he strode forward and knelt in the mud before me to lay the blade on the ground at my feet.

"My queen. Use me as your blade. I'm yours."

7

ITZTLI

I came to my queen as willingly as my brother, but not as easily.

My pulse hammered frantically in my throat, and my stomach churned with the sour taste of fear and uneasiness. In the joy of coming into my power last night, I'd managed to suppress the dark stains in my memory, but soon, she would know the truth. Tlacel had already proven exactly how precious he would be in her service.

Now I would prove how monstrous I would be.

Shara looked down at my obsidian blade a moment, and when she met my gaze again, the same blackness filled her eyes, a glittering icy darkness of faceted glass. Hairs rose on my arms. The goddesses walked among us tonight. Coatlicue had already doomed me. If Isis turned me away too, I would beg to be sacrificed along with the consiliarius who'd betrayed my family.

My queen tipped her head back, letting the blanket slip from her shoulders to the ground. Rain sluiced down her cheeks like tears. She let out a soft sigh and met Mayte's gaze. "Would it be terribly inconvenient if you had a large tree in this spot?"

The sound my sister made might have been a laugh, but it hurt my ears. Last night, they'd laughed and splashed each other in the grotto like two maiden goddesses, but tonight, the earth mother's killing devastation roared in their power. "Not inconvenient in the slightest, especially if it's large enough to provide some shade for the courtyard."

"Oh, it'll be large enough, I think." Shara dropped her gaze back to mine and I flinched. She stripped me bare. In a single look, she weighed my heart and began to sift through my mind. All too quickly she would find the poison that remained.

I didn't pull away. I didn't try to hide. I let her have it all.

She cupped my chin, her fingers hard on my jaw. The pressure stirred something inside me. It lifted its head, the monster's interest piqued. Not my giant dog. No, this was something else entirely. Something I loathed with every fiber of my being.

She whispered inside my head. :*What are you protecting me from?*:

She could have pushed that cracked door wide open and dragged my filthy secrets out one by one. Gratitude that she didn't, that she allowed me to face those truths one by one in my own time, clogged my throat. :*It'll be easier if I show you, my queen.*:

Tales of twin gods were common to my people, which made the reality of growing up as a twin much more difficult. In ancient times, when twins were born, it wasn't uncommon for one of them to be killed. Sometimes it was easy to see which twin should be sacrificed, because one would be born with a deformity. For others, like me, the deformity wasn't apparent immediately.

I was the gigantic black dog, like Xolotl, Quetzalcoatl's monstrous twin, and Tlacel was the beautiful feathered serpent.

Thus it had always been since the day I was born.

She slipped deeper into my mind, past my conscious thoughts to actual memories. Reading them like a book, watching flashes of my childhood like a movie.

Our mother had delivered us during the bloody time of Tenochtitlan's invasion and the crumbling of the mighty Aztec civilization. Grandmama and Mayte often said our mother died when Tenochtitlan fell, but that wasn't entirely true. She lived, long enough to deliver Mayte hundreds of years later.

But Mama was never the same after she left Tenochtitlan. After she delivered me.

As a young queen ripe with power, Citla Zaniyah had gone to foster with an older and more renowned queen descended from the Great Goddess of Teotihuacan, and when she returned, she was changed. Silenced. Broken. No one ever spoke of her time there, or who our father, or fathers, were. Though I heard the whispers.

I was so different from Tlacel. He was kind and generous, beautiful and gentle. He would never harm another.

I, on the other hand, had gained the reputation for being sullen, dark, and yes, extremely dangerous. I fought to the death like a starving dog over scraps of refuse. Mama had retreated into her mind, and Grandmama had been busy establishing the new Zaniyah nest and moving our family from Tenochtitlan. But one thing always stuck in my mind.

Mama never had Blood. Not even an alpha. So who, then, had sired us?

When I was older, I asked Grandmama what had happened to my mother. She had only shaken her head and said some things were better forgotten.

Forgotten. Like how I came to be. How I was so different from my brother. As we matured into young Aima males, hungry for the chance to serve a queen, the differences in us had become even more stark and grim.

Grimacing, I pulled back from those memories and focused on Shara. She cupped my face in both her hands and leaned down over me, staring deeply into my eyes. She turned the page in my mind, and I was sharing blood for the first time with someone not family. My first sib, my first lover. Shame clawed at my throat, and I tried to shut the memory away, but I couldn't refuse my queen.

The first taste of sweet, new blood. Her hot skin against mine. Her cries that had quickly turned to screams. Even when she fought me and clawed at my face and arms, I couldn't stop. The pain only inflamed me. I wanted more. I wanted her to shred my skin off in strips. I wanted to cover her in my blood and wear hers too.

They'd had to drag me off her, beating me like a wild animal until sense slowly edged back the red haze clouding my vision. Panting, achingly erect, and covered in blood, I could only watch as she fled from me. That look of horror and fear on her face flashed in my mind constantly, but especially when I fed. Even from family. I hadn't touched Tlacel's or Mayte's blood in over a century. It'd been so long...

I was afraid someone would have to drag me off them, too. That I'd turn into a savage monster and devour the people I loved most in the world. Or, that if they tasted my blood, the same savage, mindless hunger for blood and pain would contaminate them, too.

It was one reason we'd never served a queen despite our age and potential power. Tlacel refused to go without me, and I couldn't bear to feed or risk touching a woman ever again.

:*After that incident with the sib, Grandmama sent us to the same nest where Mama had fostered. She said I needed to know the truth about how I was sired. I needed to understand what I came from, in order to protect us all.*:

We'd gone to the nest of Theresa Tocatl, descended from the Great Goddess of Teotihuacan. Little was known about the goddess, though She was always depicted with spiders. Sometimes as a giant mouth lined with teeth. Her Blood each descended from the old gods.

A jaguar god. A sun god. A quetzalcoatl god. And the flayed god.

After seeing how the latter Blood fed, I knew who my father had to be.

Even now, my mind flinched from the memory.

We Aima reveled in blood, but the Flayed One reveled in pain as much as the blood, and he saved his darker tastes for hapless human women. He could strip the whole skin off his sacrifice with only a small slit in the chest, and he gave the skin to his queen to wear.

Worse, his power allowed him to keep his sacrifice alive and screaming the entire time. He feasted on her pain as long as possible, until she ultimately died. Humans were too fragile after all. Nothing like Aima queens.

Unfortunately for him, drinking pain made him as loose-lipped as a drunk human, and he had told me, in brutal detail, exactly what had happened to my mother years before.

A young queen without Blood. Without protection. With a great deal of power that she didn't know how to wield.

I killed the monster who'd fathered me. I killed them all, even their queen, but the damage had already been done.

:*He tortured her and used her power to keep her alive while they all raped her.*: I whispered, squeezing my eyes shut. :*Tlacel and I were sired by Tocatl's Blood through rape and horror, and I was her greatest horror. The one who tortured her the most lives on in me.*:

SHARA

So much pain and guilt and shame, all for something completely out of his control. He'd carried that needless guilt for hundreds of years, to the point where he hadn't fed or enjoyed the powers he'd been born with.

:*How did you make it through last night? You were able to take my blood, and you allowed me to feed as well. I sensed nothing amiss, and I was looking for a reason not to trust you.*:

A grim smile twisted his lips. :*The goddess sent me a vision of you killing a magical spider without hesitation, and I hoped you could also kill the spider that I carry. The Great Goddess and the Flayed One live on inside me, my queen. I fully understand if you cannot abide such Blood. I only ask that you sacrifice me here, so my blood will at least feed Zaniyah lands, and I beg you to allow Tlacel to continue to serve.*:

I had envisioned the geas on Mayte's nest as a spider, but I'd sensed nothing like that in his bond. Only the giant black dog.

However, I hadn't sensed his reluctance to feed or allow others to feed, either.

His bond firmed with conviction. He knew I would reject him. He braced for his own blade to sink into his heart.

:*If I'm not mistaken, your sister's crown was made to look like human hands and hearts. All goddesses have their dark side of death and destruction, and we are given their gifts as they see fit.*:

His face hardened, his eyes flashing like his blade. :*I begged Coatlicue for centuries to lift this curse from me. Or at least *allow me to die, so Tlacel could have a normal life. But she refused to even allow me honor in death.:*

I softened my grip on his face and lightly trailed my index finger over his lip. His eyes narrowed, suspicious of even the smallest caress. :*Did it not occur to you that your goddess has a purpose for you? That I may have a purpose for you? Despite these dark needs you're worried about?:*

:*I do not wish to be a darkness that only reminds you of how precious and wondrous the light is when it returns. Take Tlacel. Sacrifice me. It's the best option.:*

The goddesses whispered in my head. *Make the sacrifice. Grow the heart tree. Plant our seed in Zaniyah's nest. Another tree in Our grove.*

Would this tree be able to communicate with mine at home? What kind of tree would She grow? How much blood would it require?

I let these questions flicker through my mind, a distraction while I thought about my options. I wasn't eager to die on a heart tree again, but I'd do it without hesitation, if it would protect Mayte and her people. But I didn't feel called to give them my life's blood this time.

I felt called…

To give them *his*.

I hesitated, making sure of Her will. I wasn't even sure which goddess wanted his blood and the promise of his life, whether it was Isis, Coatlicue, Morrigan, or even this Great Spider Goddess I'd never heard of before. Or all the above. The desire for his blood, pain, and ultimate sacrifice swirled through my power. Like an eager drip of blackest ink on crystal clear water, swirling and spreading to stain the entire pool.

He wanted to die and prove himself needed. He wanted me to punish him for the dark gifts he carried.

When my own power would revel in those gifts.

I reached down and picked up his obsidian blade. Straightening, I watched his face, and more importantly, I listened to his bond. He didn't flinch, look away, or pretend surprise that I was apparently willing to take him up on his offer. His bond remained as grim as before, eerily silent except the low, mournful whine of his black dog, pleading for forgiveness when his master could not.

"I require your blood, Itztli, and quite possibly, your life."

"Take every drop of blood in my body, my queen. I'm yours."

8

SHARA

Tipping my head back to look up at the rising moon, I raised the black blade above my head. I wasn't usually so ceremonial, but with the Zaniyah clan watching, I felt like they needed to see my respect for rituals and the goddesses. "Great One, your last daughter offers a sacrifice to You and Your sisters tonight."

Instantly, the rain stopped, as if someone had shut off the heavenly faucets. People whispered around me. Pale, Mayte stared at me silently. She wouldn't dishonor me, or herself, by protesting my decision in front of her people, but I felt the need to comfort her, at least a little. :*This will be ugly, but it's nothing that I haven't already done myself and survived.*:

I made sure Itztli heard that thought as well, but his only reaction was a slight huff of his breath.

:*Do what you must do, my queen,*: Mayte replied softly.

:*Brother, I love you.*:

:*And I love you, sister.*: Sincerity echoed in his bond, a heart-wrenching twist at the thought of not seeing her, or Xochitl, again. He didn't look away from me, though, even as he said goodbye to his twin. :*At last, you're free of me, brother.*:

Tlacel dropped to his knees beside him and looked up at me. "Take me, too, my queen. We came into this world together, and we'll leave it together."

I tipped my head to the side, listening to the distant whispers on the wind. Night fell quickly. "You already risked your life to save me and Xochitl today. This sacrifice is not required of you, Tlacel."

"I won't let him die without me."

I laid the obsidian blade on my left palm and drew a deep cut. "I will decide who lives and dies tonight."

With the scent of my blood on the air, all my Blood focused even more intently on me, automatically drawing closer, a tight ring at my back and on either side of the two men kneeling before me. Mayte took a step toward me, but I shook my head. "House Isador makes this sacrifice for House Zaniyah tonight. This sacrifice will strengthen your defenses and give you a direct connection to my nest in Arkansas, but it takes a great deal of blood and power to complete it."

I let my blood fall on the muddy soil between me and

Itztli. Despite his misgivings about feeding, his nostrils flared, and his eyes blazed with heat. He hungered, and no wonder. He'd never fully embraced his needs, for fear of releasing the dark god's power.

He leaned forward slightly, his eyes locked on my blood that dripped down my fingers. I held out my bleeding palm, but I didn't touch him or tug on his bond. He had to want to taste me of his own accord, or I could never bring him fully into his power.

His lips brushed my index finger, his tongue flicking out to gather some of the droplets before they could fall. His eyelashes fluttered down. His breath caught, his pulse leaping at the immediate adrenaline kick. Through the bond, I felt the heavy pounding of his heart. The surge of brutal desire. He quivered with need, his muscles straining to keep him locked in place on his knees.

My fangs descended, forcing me to open my mouth and bare them to the air, or risk puncturing my own lips. Tiny electric bolts flickered through me at the sensation. My mouth ached, my fangs too sensitive, too bare, needing to be buried. Deeply.

In him.

His mouth twisted in a grimace, revealing his own fangs. A low, rattling growl rumbled from his chest. But then he beat down that sound, locking his lips, tightening his throat, swallowing down the groan of hunger and desire.

Silly man. Did he think he could keep this need from me? That I, last daughter of Isis, needed him to protect me from lust and hunger and blood—the very gifts She gave me?

:*I've lived this long without giving in to need. I can certainly die tonight without it.*:

For a moment, my mind froze. Goddess. Surely, I misunderstood. :*You're still a virgin?*:

His lips curled with disgust and he tried to avert his gaze, but the steady drip of my blood held him transfixed. :*I have never known a woman, since the attempt to take my first sib that ended in disaster. I refused to risk harming a woman like my father did.*:

I looked over at Tlacel beside him, my eyes wide. :*You too? Are you still a virgin?*:

:*I don't go anywhere without my twin. So yes, we're both untouched, my queen, other than the pleasure you gave us last night when you took us as Blood.*:

It was all I could do not to slap my forehead and sigh with disbelief. Two five-hundred-year-old virgins.

Daire snorted in the bond. :*It's going to be hilarious watching you break them in, my queen. If they survive this ritual.*:

Mehen let out a reluctant grunt. :*The scaly chicken did save our queen today when we could not. He can surely survive our queen's darkest lusts, though I ask that you do to me whatever you do to him, my queen.*:

:*And me,*: each of my Blood said immediately in my head, except Rik. He touched the small of my back briefly, the heat of his palm a reminder of his strength. He was there for me. He was protecting me, even from whatever darkness

Itztli managed to bring to life in me. I could throw myself into the abyss and embrace the waiting darkness.

Because my alpha had my back and always would.

EZRA

My queen always made a formidable impression on a man, but Shara Isador holding a wicked-sharp obsidian blade in her hand made the hairs on my nape stand up. Ice dripped down my spine, but I said nothing.

I hoped to goddess I was wrong.

Fuck me. If she started torturing the man on his knees before her, I was going to have to…

My ribcage ached and I couldn't breathe.

I'd seen too much shit go down in Skye's court. How she'd tortured alpha after alpha. Itztli was not Rik by any means, but in any other court, he could be alpha. He had the age and enough power waiting to be unleashed by his queen.

We Aima loved feeding on blood and sex, sure. But the moment she started feeding on pain…

She'd be just another Keisha Skye, and that'd fucking break my goddess-damned heart. I never loved Skye, but I'd been welcomed into Isador. Between Shara and Daire, and yeah, the rest of her Blood, even the bitching dragon, I'd found family I'd never known I missed. The thought of dragging my shaggy ass back out into the wilderness to live the solitary bear life damned near made me lose my mind.

I couldn't be alone now. Not like that. Not after being a part of Shara's court. Her fucking family.

But if she was going to torture anyone, especially a Blood, then I'd have to find the strength in me to leave.

Her blood on the ground sprouted a plant that shot out of the dirt and surged upward toward the shining moon with alarming speed. Woody vines writhed like a nest of snakes, as the center of the bush grew tall enough to touch Shara's outstretched hand. The plant shivered with ecstasy, her dripping blood giving it life like some kind of alien plant, but it curled its vines around the man, not our queen.

The whites of his eyes flashed with surprise, but he didn't fight the entwining plant, even as it dragged him off the ground. When I finally realized what the tree was doing, I almost threw up.

The bush had flattened out into what looked like an altar, with Itztli spread-eagled on top of it.

Someone laid a hand on my arm, making me twitch with surprise. Daire whispered in my head. :*She'd never torture someone like Skye.*:

My heart insisted he was right, but my brain kept throwing up images of bleeding alphas and endless screams. It was horrifying how long Skye had been able to keep a man alive while screaming like that. Alphas, no less.

Despite his assurance, I sensed a heavy weight in his bond, too. A memory that made him feel almost as badly as I was right now. With a wry lift of his shoulder, he gave me the memory of a huge black cobra breaking Rik's bones like nothing, and then pumping him with venom. I watched

Rik's flesh swell and blacken, and then the cobra sucked him dry.

The cobra. Our queen.

:*It was awful,:* Daire whispered, his mental voice shaken. :*But it wasn't done so she could revel in his pain. If Skye had this power, you know she'd be pumping every male she could get her hands on with venom. But that's not Shara. She'll do what needs to be done, even if it's terrible, because she's one fucking badass queen and she'll do anything to keep her family safe. Us. Her Blood.:*

I gave him a grudging nod and turned my attention back to the new Blood on his back, waiting for the knife to sink into him. His face was calm and smooth with acceptance. In fact, he looked up at our queen with relief and reverence. His bond was full of black holes and shadows that gave me the sense of being guarded by rabid dogs. Evidently, he'd been fighting some internal darkness his whole life, and it was apparent, even to me, that he fully expected to die.

He *wanted* to be sacrificed.

Shara turned to face the watching crowd. "This is the beginning of a heart tree, a powerful, sentient connection to our goddesses. I have one in my nest, and I believe it'll be able to connect our two nests. My grove will power yours, and this will be the anchor. If your queen wishes to grow a full grove, she may sacrifice her blood as directed by your goddess."

Mayte nodded. "I will, absolutely. I feel the call already from Coatlicue. We will have a grove here in Zaniyah."

"To bring the heart tree fully to power, a great deal of blood and suffering is required," Shara said solemnly. "I suffered and there was nothing my Blood could do to help me." She touched the circular scar between her breasts. "My heart was punctured by a large thorn. I should have died, but Isis's power kept me alive."

She stepped to the side, making sure the crowd could see the man stretched out on the tree altar. "I would suffer for your heart tree. I would die on its branches and let Isis's power bring me back. But Itztli has volunteered to make the heart tree sacrifice in my place tonight. He makes the sacrifice for you."

Turning to him, she laid her hand on his shin, and even from feet away, I saw the fine shimmer of his muscles up his leg at the small touch. I couldn't help but note that she never promised to resurrect him. She never gave him reassurances that he'd come back, because we all knew how fickle the goddesses could sometimes be. Her power had raised Rik and herself, but someday, it might fail to raise one of us back from the dead. It was a risk we accepted as her Blood. Our life for hers, even if her power failed.

"Are you ready, my Blood?"

"Yes, my queen."

Closing her eyes, she tipped her head back and soaked in the moon's glow. She had a fucking regal profile, the planes of her cheekbones gleaming with dark pearls and opals. The moonlight illuminated her perfectly, like a spotlight. Her breasts, high and full, the swell of her hips, the dark shadow between her thighs drawing my gaze. All her Blood stared at her sex. I burned to stroke her and give her pleasure. I ached to feel her skin against mine. Her sighs of pleasure, her hands on me, driving me harder.

I'd had Daire, and yeah, it'd been fucking great. I'd tasted her pleasure while I was fucking him, and I wanted more, more, more. Of him. Sure.

But I wanted my queen most of all.

I wanted to have her body beneath mine, writhing in pleasure *I* gave her. I wanted to touch her. Taste her. Feel her need. For *me*.

:Soon,: she whispered in my head, making me flinch with surprise. I hadn't realized I was projecting my lust to her. :*I want my bear hooked inside me.*:

My dick swelled so hard that I couldn't hold back a grunt of pain, need, desperation. All the above.

Daire snickered and pressed his tempting body against me, but thank goddess he didn't touch me, or I probably would have spilled right there. :*Who's the big bad bear now?*:

:*Shut the fuck up.*:

The little shit started purring, his chest vibrating against my arm. His dick was hard against my thigh. I looked around quickly and realized all of us were erect.

Even the man preparing to die for his queen.

9

SHARA

I had a feeling that we were headed for another bloody orgy. Not that I minded in the least. But I had to admit, I wasn't too excited about having a hundred or so strangers watching while I fucked my Blood one by one.

I adjusted my grip on the obsidian blade until it felt right in my hand. It was longer than my familiar pocket knife, and much sharper. The glassy edge was so fine that I could easily cut him much deeper than I intended.

Rik touched my bond. :*You'll cut him? Why not bite him?*:

My lips quirked at the heat shimmering in his bond, from all of the Blood. Of course, he'd want me to bite the Blood he trusted the least, over and over, like I'd done to Mehen that first night. :*I'm not so cruel that I'd make a virgin come like that over and over again.*:

He huffed out a low laugh. :*It'd be fucking amusing to watch.*:

Mehen grunted sourly. :*If anyone's going to be bitten over and over, let it be me, not the virgins.*:

:*My queen.*: Itztli's bond vibrated with tension. :*Please, put me out of my misery. Make this quick.*:

Guillaume snorted. :*He doesn't know our queen very well yet, does he?*:

:*Enough,*: I told them all firmly as I stepped closer to Itztli, bound and waiting for his death.

I ran my eyes over him, drinking in the long, muscled lines of his body. He wasn't as heavily built as Rik, but he was stockier than Tlacel, who definitely had a leaner musculature like Xin and Nevarre. I trailed my fingers up past his knee to his thigh. His leg quivered beneath my touch. His cock jerked, begging for my attention.

I skipped over his groin and swirled my fingertips over his stomach, enjoying the twitch and quiver of his muscles as I advanced. He didn't have any chest hair. I touched one of his nipples, and he sucked in a hard breath of surprise.

Naturally, I had to touch him again, rubbing the small nub with my thumb until he let out a low growl that made my lips quirk. I switched to his other nipple, ignoring the dark glare he shot at me. I leaned down to press my face against his chest, breathing in his scent. Smoky chocolate with a kick. Like a rich, delicious hot cocoa spiked with cayenne. I scratched his other nipple with my fang and he jerked his arms against the vines holding him down.

Concerned, I started to lift my head to check his reaction. I was all for teasing and torturing a man with lust, but if he wasn't into it...

:*Don't stop, my queen. Please. Unless you're ready to bury my blade in my heart.*:

:*Not even close,*: I assured him. :*Will it bother you if I bite you again? Or if I fuck you in front of your people?*:

:*Not in the slightest. Bite me at will, my queen.*:

Before I could ask, Rik stepped closer and lifted me up onto the tree. As I settled on Itztli's lower stomach, he arched up beneath me, straining against his bonds hard enough his wrists started to bleed.

Once I caught the scent of his blood, I couldn't wait any longer. I bent down and sank my fangs deeply into his pectoral with my tongue on his nipple.

Roaring, he bucked beneath me with release. I felt a bit of guilt that he still wasn't inside me, and I'd made him come twice now, but not guilty enough to wriggle lower and take him inside me yet.

The tree needed blood. A great deal of blood.

With that thought I lifted my head, letting his blood trickle down his ribcage and splatter the tree beneath him, while I shifted to his other nipple and sank my fangs again. Another wave of release rocked through his body. His blood tasted as good as he smelled, like dark sweet chocolate that blazed down my throat, but the flow wasn't strong since I didn't hit a vein. Just a delicious appetizer to stir my hunger.

I sat upright and licked my lips. Itztli stared up at me, his lips parted slightly, showing his fangs. His nostrils flared, and he worked his hips beneath me. I'd forgotten my left hand was still bleeding. I smoothed my bleeding palm over his chest, painting him with my blood. He hissed and squirmed like my blood was acid that burned through his flesh to the bone. The tree liked it too, jerking up taller with our offering.

Holding his gaze, I lifted the razor-sharp blade to my own throat and dragged the tip of the knife down my neck and across both breasts, leaving a thin red line in its wake.

Then I did the same to him, cutting thin, beautiful lines in his chest. Blood welled on his skin, mixing with mine. His tattoos came alive, standing up more solidly against his skin, like they were chiseled out of rock. Green, gold, red, and blue sparkled like jewels in his flesh, the shapes moving and swelling before my eyes.

Like before, in Isis's pyramid, I could suddenly read the marks, even though I had never seen glyphs like these before.

Flay me, Great One, and I will be your loyal dog for all eternity. My heart is yours.

Oh fuck.

I could only hope She didn't mean flay literally, as in strip off his skin.

He tipped his head back, baring his throat to me, his body straining up against me. His bond thudded with a heavy thrum of need that made my own desire ratchet higher. Everything else faded. The watching crowd. His sister. His brother, who still knelt where he'd begged me to kill him, too. My own Blood. Though I was always aware of them, they stilled and softened in my mind.

This was for Itztli alone, and our goddesses.

Who very much wanted his blood.

And mine.

And most especially, our pleasure.

10

SHARA

Still wrapped tightly around his wrists, the vines shifted his arms closer to me in silent invitation. They wanted more blood, though he'd broken his skin open by twisting against the restraints.

Leaning out as far as I could, I dragged the tip of the obsidian knife up the inside of his forearm, splitting his skin deeper than the thin lines on his chest. Then I switched over to the other arm and did the same, laying both of his wrists wide open to his elbows. Thick, ruby blood glowed in the moonlight. The tree shuddered with him in its grasp, mirroring his reaction. I suddenly wondered if the tree would somehow climax with him next time. If the goddesses would feel his—our pleasure—through the tree.

The resonance deep inside me confirmed the thought.

Isis, Coatlicue, and Morrigan would feel our pleasure as the trees feasted on our blood.

No wonder they wanted the heart tree grown in both groves.

I twisted around to reach his legs. His erection brushed my stomach and breasts as I reached out to cut both of his thighs down to his knees. I wasn't sure where the tendons and muscles were beneath the skin, so I had to hope the goddesses guided my hand, or would at least help me heal him back to full strength.

I'd feel terrible if I caused him to walk with a limp, or gave him long-term pain from a badly healed injury.

:*Please,*: he whispered in the bond, his voice trembling. :*Let me feel your touch just once.*:

He still thought I was going to kill him. Maybe I would. I wasn't sure how far the goddesses would take this sacrifice. But I fully intended to make sure he enjoyed it as much as possible, and more importantly, that I would do my best to heal whatever damage I caused.

But I could certainly make sure this virgin knew the touch of his queen before he died.

I wrapped my bleeding palm around his dick and pulled him through my fist. His hips jerked and he groaned like I'd plunged the blade to the hilt in his abdomen.

:*Yes, please.*:

I thought he wanted more of my touch on his dick. What man wouldn't? I pumped him a bit harder, but he groaned and tossed beneath me.

:*The knife. Please. I'll come as hard as when you bit me.*:

For the first time, I hesitated, my stomach trembling with a sudden flood of anxiety.

He *wanted* me to stab him. To bury his own knife in his body.

He wanted it enough to beg, something that wouldn't come easily to such an old, powerful Aima male who'd contemplated trying to overthrow my impressive alpha just nights ago.

His erection was as big as ever. His bond, wide open to me. The pain from the cuts had fired his lust to new heights.

Pain. Blood. The memory he'd shared flickered through my mind, how they'd had to beat him to subdue him enough to get him off the sib he was trying to share blood with.

Pain aroused him. Even deadly pain, like a knife sinking into him.

I'd been fully prepared to share some rough, bloody lovemaking with him, but he really did want me to kill him, or at least come close to it.

Goddess.

How the fuck did I come to terms with killing him while I fucked him? Every single time? And what would the rest of my Blood think?

:*We think that you're queen enough to give him exactly what he wants most of all,*: Rik answered in my head. :*If he takes pleasure in it, who cares?*:

I cared. :*He doesn't want to be a darkness just to remind me of the light. How can I stab him like that when making love? It's...*:

My brain wanted to say, *"It's horrible,"* but my body had other ideas.

So many things were "horrible" to my human sensibilities. Tasting blood. Especially menstrual blood, but Rik and Daire had reveled in my period every chance I'd given them. Biting, sinking teeth deeply into flesh. Poisoning Rik and ultimately killing him. Watching Rik squeeze off Mehen's air while he fucked my mighty dragon into submission.

Goddess, that had been so hot that even now the memory was almost enough to make me come. And it hadn't been horrible, not in the slightest, though my brain floundered, trying to point fingers at what Itztli requested of me.

He requested it.

He consented to it.

He needed me to sink a knife into his body.

Even if I didn't fully understand why or how he could feel pleasure in it.

Holding his bond so I would sense the slightest hesitation or negative feeling, I cut him again, this time on his biceps. I felt the searing cut sliding across his skin, separating tissue. A white-hot branding iron tore through him, and the immediate surge of need poured through his body.

The dungeon door in the basement of his mind flew open, revealing his deepest, darkest desires.

Flayed. Stabbed. Cut open. The images flickered through his mind. While I rode his cock and screamed with release. I shuddered with dread, my mind flinching at the horror. But

I didn't pull away. I sat with his image in my head, adjusting to it. I'd taken him. I'd claimed him for my Blood.

It was my privilege and honor to take care of them, as they took care of me. They fed me, blood, power and body, whatever I needed. Without hesitation, they'd lay down their lives for me. How could I turn away from Itztli's need, even if that need was something that made his own stomach churn with hatred and dread?

He hated this need. He hated himself. He was so sure that I would feel the same hatred, that he'd rather die than allow this monstrosity, as he believed himself to be, to taint me in any way.

I rose up enough to slide backward over his cock. Ever so slowly, I pushed him inside of me, enjoying the way he gasped and shuddered, his hands twisted, reaching for me despite the vines holding him in place. He looked up at me, his eyes black blazing pits of desire, his face stark in the moonlight.

Seated deep within me, he sucked in a shuddering breath and closed his eyes. He relaxed, all the tension and fight bleeding away, his face softening. When he finally opened his eyes to meet my gaze, his eyes were haunted with regret. Not because he regretted making the decision to allow me this sacrifice.

Instead, because now I must go through with killing him. He didn't want to cause me pain or sadness, even if it was to put him out of his misery.

Swallowing a hard lump in my throat, I tightened my

muscles and ground my clit against him, pushing my desire higher. I rocked on him, driving my hips harder. I let my head fall back on a ragged groan. Desire coiled inside me ever tighter. Pushing me closer to release.

He panted beneath me, his hips rising to meet mine, an involuntary rocking motion as old as time. :*Thank you, my queen.*:

The first wave of climax rolled through me. I closed my eyes. *Isis, Great One, guide me.*

:*Thank you, my Blood.*:

Without opening my eyes, I plunged the blade into his body.

MEHEN

Well, fuck. I wasn't the only Blood she'd stabbed now. Though I hadn't been Blood when she stabbed me with her pocket knife to keep my dragon from draining her dry.

The Blood beneath her let out a mighty bellow of release, his back arching so hard that he pushed them both up off the tree's branches. No one watching would mistake that sound for a scream of pain or denial or fear. Not with his hips jerking and spasming beneath her.

I wasn't sure where she'd actually stabbed him. It didn't matter. She could have sliced and diced his liver for all I cared. Isis's last daughter would heal whatever damage she'd done, and Itztli had certainly enjoyed it.

Though the big bear looked a bit queasy. Daire pressed

against Ezra, his arms around his waist, comforting him. I waited a minute to see if I felt a surge of jealousy or rage that the purring, sassy cat I'd fucked was cuddling up to another. Shockingly, I didn't care. How could I? As long as our queen fucked me again, or at least asked me to her bed again, I couldn't care less who else Daire fucked.

He had been mine, and likely would again, but only because I was hers, and we all belonged to her.

The gasps from the crowd made me focus on Shara again. She jerked the blade through the man beneath her and reached down, working her hand inside him. And yeah, I suddenly felt a bit queasy myself. I found myself closer to Daire and Ezra, sandwiching the cat between us.

Guillaume grunted with disgust. "Pussies. Our queen should carve you open next."

"That's easy for you to say, since you're the fucking headless knight," I retorted.

The ancient Templar knight smiled, and you could have knocked me over with a feather. I would have sworn the grim man's face would have shattered into a million pieces before he'd ever make a joke or grin. "We're all headless knights. Now he's heartless too."

Indeed, Shara lifted her bloody hand above her head, gripping a lump that very well could have been a heart.

It thumped and jerked in her hand, still very much alive.

She stepped down off the altar and the tree surged upwards, growing higher and taller as we watched. Branches thickened and spread out above our heads, sprouting leaves in seconds.

"Wondrous," the other queen whispered, her voice shaking with both reverence and sobs. "Our very own world tree, like the legends of creation. But at such cost."

Mayte stepped closer to her other brother, who was still kneeling on the ground, and wrapped her arms around his shoulders.

"It's what he wanted." Tlacel's voice sounded like he'd swallowed slivers of glass. "His torment is over."

"Yes." Shara's voice echoed with power, a deep, silent thrum I felt in my bones. "His heart grew this tree for you. His heart's desire is now mine."

The tree towered above us, taller than the heart tree she'd grown in her nest. There, she'd used her blood to grow a whole grove. Here, only one tree stood, powered by her blood and Itztli's sacrifice.

I stared at the thumping heart. All of us did. I held my breath, waiting for it to cease beating. He had to die. He didn't have a heart.

Yet his organ continued to beat steadily in her palm.

"Itztli," she called in that deep goddess voice. "Come down from our tree and take what's yours."

I couldn't see the other Blood any longer—the tree was too high. The trunk was big enough that it'd take two or three of us to reach completely around it. Wood creaked and cracked above us, as if a strong breeze moved swept through the branches. A dark hole opened in the trunk, groaning and complaining as it widened into a doorway.

Itztli stepped out of the trunk and dropped to his knees before our queen. Blood dripped from the open wound in his chest. Bone glistened in the moonlight, ribs cracked and pushed open. His eyes glittered like facets of obsidian.

"My queen."

She leaned down and pressed her lips to his in a gentle kiss. Then she shoved her hand into his chest, giving him back his heart. He seized her arms and pulled her closer, clutching her as his body thrashed.

"There," she whispered against his lips. "It's done. Now take your reward, Itztli."

She turned her head, offering him her throat. He lunged up and sank his fangs into the side of her neck. Leaning back on his heels, he drew her down on top of his thighs, locking her tightly to him.

Her hunger rose, drawing us all closer to her. Her blood burned. Her desire called us to her need. But one burned hotter than all of us.

Tlacel, the only Blood who'd never given our queen pleasure, or, at least, had never been in her bed. He waited, still on his knees, though his eyes blazed with joy that his brother still lived.

Shara looked at him over her shoulder. "Itztli would very much like to taste pleasure in my blood."

The man moved closer and dropped to his knees behind her. He lifted his hands to touch her, but hesitated, his fingers trembling.

I wanted to make a snide comment, but the words wouldn't come. I was fairly certain I'd probably trembled with wonder like that the first time she'd taken me.

He finally smoothed his palms down either side of her delicate spine and settled his hands on her hips. She arched back against him, encouraging him with the glide of her body. As he slid inside her, her breath caught on a moan that echoed deep in the pit of my stomach. My dick was hard enough to cut diamonds, and I'd wager all of us were on the verge of spilling, just from the glorious sound of welcome and hunger she made.

Even Rik. I glanced at our alpha, not surprised to see him the closest to her, his erection as painfully large and throbbing as mine. As all of ours.

Flames suddenly shot up into the night, making the Zaniyah clan gasp and mill around like anxious sheep. I'd noticed the large stack of wood for a bonfire earlier, but after the deluge, it shouldn't have caught fire.

The silent Blood materialized between Guillaume and me, making even the knight jerk a hand toward his closest blade before realizing Xin wasn't a threat. "I believe one of her gifts is fire."

Daire nodded. "Yep, her first gift. She used it to burn up a master thrall when it was just me and Rik."

The crowd's mood shifted from fearful and grief-stricken to celebratory in moments. Drums started up and people danced around the large fire. Someone brought out vats of wine and tequila, and a cheer went up.

No, wait, that was just Tlacel, shouting out his release. *Then* the cheer went up.

The twins helped her stand, each holding on to her hand

like she'd sprout wings and fly away if they didn't keep a solid grip on her.

My eyes narrowed, my teeth bared.

The hell if they were going to control who she turned to, or when. I felt her need still burning, far from sated. She hadn't even fed much yet, and after that demonstration, and the battle with Ra's minions...

Oh, fuck. Of course.

She came closer to Xin, her eyes glittering like hard diamonds in the moonlight. "He's still alive?"

"Yes, my queen." Xin shrugged one shoulder. "Barely."

She turned to Mayte. "I need a place that's private enough for an interrogation."

"Of course. You can use the room below the house, where you saw Xochitl the first time. Do you need me or my Blood to show you the way?"

She smiled at Xin and shook her head. "No, my wolf knows the way. I trust you'll take care of your traitor yourself?"

Mayte looked down at the woman curled in a fetal position, covered in mud as she'd struggled to crawl away. Whatever spell Mayte had used on her was a brutal one. The woman's arms and legs were bent at unnatural angles. Each time she tried to flee, another bone cracked.

Our queen would do well to learn this spell. I had a feeling she'd need every trick in the bag when she went after House Skye.

She came closer, her gaze meeting mine. "Are you sure that I'll go after Skye?"

I nodded without hesitation. "It's what I'd do."

"Why?"

I gave her my most dragon grin without shifting into Leviathan. "Because I'd be fucking tired of her bullshit."

Shara gave me a slow, glorious smile that dripped with vicious anticipation. "Exactly right."

11

SHARA

Letting my gaze move over each of my impressively aroused Blood, I let out a sigh of regret. "I'd very much like to see to each of your needs, but something tells me I need answers from our unwanted guest first."

Rik picked up the blanket I'd dropped and jerked his head slightly at Itztli, a silent command to get out of his way. They might have objected before, but this time, they let go of my hands and stepped back without argument.

Rik wrapped the slightly soggy blanket around my shoulders. I shivered at the dampness, but it was better than being completely naked. He didn't pull me in against him or make any other possessive move. My alpha was above such displays because he was fully confident in his place.

I leaned against him and wrapped my arms around his waist anyway.

"Xin, Nevarre, Mehen, Guillaume—take the prisoner down to the room," he ordered. "The rest of us will dress and join you momentarily."

"I've got him stashed over here." Xin turned and headed into the night. "Just outside the nest boundary. Mayte's Blood gave me some rope to tie him up."

As he moved away, my skin prickled like I'd stumbled into a nest of fire ants. "Stop!" I barked out, my heart racing. He stopped immediately and started to turn toward me, his mouth opening.

Instinct took over. The shrill siren in my head wasn't something I'd ever ignore. I drew on my blood and envisioned a shield rising above us. A giant dome, like a billion-dollar football field. I pushed it out as far as I could, nearly to the nest boundary itself, straining to make it stronger. Higher. I didn't want anyone inside this nest hurt.

Mayte's bond swelled inside me, spilling lush green power into mine, buoying me higher. :*What is it? What's wrong?*:

I couldn't answer, other than sending her a sense of urgency. I didn't know what was going to happen, or how, only that it would be bad.

The heart tree that I'd just grown with Itztli's sacrifice grounded me. I reached through its roots and felt my grove at home respond. The earth energy of my ancient trees poured into me, and I let my power blaze higher. Fire whipped to the heavens. Moonlight shimmered like beautiful opals in the air.

Then Nevarre added his gift of Shadow, Morrigan's thick blanket of darkness. Fire and moonlight, green jungle and shadow braided above us.

Automatically, my Blood started to shift. Their instinct was to protect me. Leviathan crouched, wings unfurling, ready to soar into the sky with a roar.

I screamed at them through the bond. :*No, stay low! Don't fly!*:

An explosion lit up the night a few paces outside of the nest—where Xin had been leading us. A golden fireball ballooned toward the nest, solar power so hot it melted rock, disintegrating everything it touched. The ground rocked beneath us. Rik swayed and stumbled, clutching me against him. People screamed.

The golden wave of power hit the nest and cut through Mayte's boundary like butter.

I braced for impact. Rik, my rock, shielded me with his body. Guillaume's hell horse and Daire's warcat pressed close to me, too, and the rest of my Blood made a defensive ring around us, just in case my shield failed.

Liquid gold slammed into my shield. Power crackled and sizzled in the air. My hair shot out like I'd stuck my finger in a light socket. My ears rang and the fine bones of my face ached like someone had slammed me with a bat. Repeatedly. My eyes streamed tears, even though I'd squeezed my eyes shut without even realizing it.

The shield sagged, bowing under the massive weight of the golden bomb. In slow motion, I tried to lift my right arm toward my mouth, fighting to get my wrist close enough to tear open again. Blood. I needed more blood.

The warcat locked my wrist in his mouth, pressing hard enough to break the skin. With more blood, my power shored up the shield. I didn't try to fight the golden wave, for fear it would only gain strength from me. Panting with effort, I concentrated on holding the shield firm and allowed the solar power to flow over it. Feet planted wide, head back, I strained to hold back the blazing might of the sun god.

Finally, the golden blaze dissipated into the night.

Rivulets of sweat tracked down my face and chest. My knees trembled. I ached deep inside. Stress fractures, maybe, as if I'd fallen off a horse onto the rockiest ground imaginable. I forced my eyes open and lifted my head to look around.

The heart tree still stood, though the very highest branches were a little scorched, and a few smaller limbs littered the ground. Mayte blew a kiss to me and then turned to round up her people and see if anyone was hurt. Groups started moving around, checking on the houses and outbuildings, but everything seemed okay.

"Amazing," Rik whispered, shaking his head. "You're incredible, my queen. To hold off an attack like that... What made you suspect anything amiss with the prisoner? Xin, did you feel anything off with him?"

Xin sat back on his haunches but kept his head low. :*Not at all. Forgive me, alpha, my queen. I sensed nothing in his scent that led me to believe he was a ticking time bomb. If I'd brought him into the nest…*:

Yeah, that would have been bad, to say the least. If I hadn't been able to react quickly enough, we could have had several casualties. Exactly as Ra intended.

"Did he say anything to you while you were guarding him? Was he some kind of Blood to Ra? Do the gods even have Blood like that?"

:*He remained a black dog until Mehen killed the eagle, then he shifted. He told me if I didn't release him, he'd take me and everyone with me to hell.*:

"Hell? That's the word he used?" My words slurred, and I had to concentrate to make the words string together. "That seems like a weird thing for the sun god's minion to say."

Rik swept me up in his arms and started for the house. "You need to feed long and hard, my queen."

"Rest," I mumbled, fighting to keep my eyes open. "Home."

Either he was extremely fast, or I passed out momentarily, but the next thing I knew, he was settling me into bed and kissing my forehead. "Tomorrow. I can't wait to get you home and rested up."

I made a low hum of agreement. I didn't have the energy to say the words, but I made sure he knew what I was thinking.

Hot flesh pressed against me. Skin and blood and sweat. Too many dicks to count.

He huffed out a laugh and drew me closer. "As you wish, my queen."

12

SHARA

In the dream, I stood on top of a pyramid, but it wasn't Isis pyramid that I'd seen the first night when Rik and Daire had found me. This pyramid was made of large blocks of weathered gray stone. Instead of sand dunes stretching into the distance, I saw the lush green jungle that I smelled when I tasted Mayte's blood. The rooftop was flat, with a low wall of carved stones along the edges. Sinuous feathered serpents with gaping jaws raced along the top of the stones.

Great Feathered Serpent, like my Blood, Tlacel.

"Are you well pleased with my gift to you, Daughter of Isis?"

I turned toward the voice, musical, lovely, and echoing with power, just as Isis' did.

This goddess sat on a carved jade throne that rose above her in the shape of two large serpents, facing each other with mouths gaped, fangs bared. Her hands rested on two massive jaguars, one black and one gold. They panted softly with their distinctive grunting growl, their eyes shining eerily in the night.

Her face was painted blue, her dark hair long and thick, curling over her bare chest. Her breasts were heavy, her stomach soft and rounded, and even from several feet away, I could see the stretch marks. She was the embodiment of Mother Earth, and she'd nurtured many.

She wore a thick white sash around her waist with one long end that hung down in the front to cover her genitals. Something moved in the thick shadows that hung around her. The dry rustle and strong musky scent told me what wound around her ankles and knees.

Snakes.

The same ghostly shape I'd seen hanging over Mayte tonight. I clasped my hands together and bowed at the waist, but kept my gaze locked on hers. I don't know why. It just felt right. I wasn't terrified, like I'd been when I first met Isis. Reverent, absolutely. Grateful for all They had given me. But not scared.

"Thank you, Mother of the Gods, for my twins."

She smiled and gestured for me to come closer. "They've already proven themselves loyal to you, but they offer much more. They're as close to my sons, Xolotl and Quetzalcoatl, as you are to Isis."

"Why give them to me, rather than giving twin gods to your daughter? She needs protection for Xochitl."

"Mayte's a healer. While this world needs healers more than ever, you are the warrior we have selected to end the sun's tyranny. Your twins burn for war and destruction and death."

One of the snakes stretched upward, winding around her knee. It was small and rather cute, a brilliant crimson color without the deadly king coral stripes, scales glowing like fiery rubies. It seemed offended at my thoughts and hissed at me, its tongue flicking out like it could taste me.

My cobra queen stirred, her scales slithering inside me, making me shiver. I wouldn't be surprised if my eyes were slitted now.

"So many gifts," Coatlicue whispered as she stroked her index finger down the small snake's head. "Such cost."

I swallowed, pushing the cobra back down inside of me. "I'll pay that cost to keep my Blood and Mayte's family safe."

Coatlicue let out a low, sighing breath that sounded like a mournful wind. "So many lost. Queens wiped out before they could come into power. Entire Houses devastated. We call for blood, daughter. We call for an end to our queens living in fear, on the run, or trapped in their nests. We want our daughters to have many children as in days of old. A time when children ran the nests, learned our ways, and lived with love anywhere they chose."

The lost little girl inside me nodded, aching for the childhood she'd never had. A chance to grow up in a nest, knowing full well what she was, without guilt or shame or regret. With a loving mother, who hadn't been banished from living Aima memory in order to give birth to me.

"I have a powerful gift to offer you, but beware. I am Mother, which means I give birth, yes, but I'm also a destroyer. I am the womb and the grave. I defend my children vehemently, but I punish them even more harshly if they abandon my ways. Huitzilophochtli..." Her voice broke and tears of blood dripped down her cheeks. "He was my son. Ra's influence contaminated him, twisting and ultimately consuming him, as he consumed many sun gods before him, until only he remains. My son is no more."

She leaned forward, pinning me with Her gaze. My nape prickled, and my nerves quivered with sensation, as if an invisible breath swept over me.

"The Great One made you the queen of resurrection. I would make you a divine queen of death, the sole carrier of a grave so great that not even a god could withstand your power. In exchange, I ask for only one thing. That you kill Ra, and release Huitzilophochtli's soul so he may return to me in Aztlan."

I didn't answer right away. She didn't offer these gifts lightly. I'd be a fool to rush in without thought. A divine queen of death. That sounded... terrifying.

I would much rather be a queen of love and sex, pleasure and laughter, hope and lightness. Not grief and death. As Itztli had told me, it would suck to be a grim reaper of death, only so people appreciated my passing with relief that they were still alive.

I didn't want to be the kind of queen who sacrificed a Blood on an altar and cut his heart out of his chest, something I had already done before Her gift. How much worse would this gift of the grave make me? I'd already killed with my gifts. I certainly hadn't been sorry that I'd destroyed Greyson, the master thrall who'd killed my mother, nor his minions. I would have killed the golden eagle myself today if I could have caught it before Mehen snagged it in his jaws.

I would have interrogated the dog we'd captured after the attack. And yes, if I'd had to cut off a few body parts to get him to talk about Ra's plans for Xochitl, or me, I would have. Gleefully.

I was already a fledgling monster, and I hadn't even had the awful pleasure of dealing with Keisha Skye yet, let alone Marne Ceresa.

"You may indeed find it necessary to kill other queens," Coatlicue said softly. "But that is not why I give you this power. You would find it easy enough to kill another queen without my grave. But not a god, and certainly not Ra himself. He absorbed all the other sun gods before and after him, taking their power for himself, and using the lifeblood of countless queens to fuel his obsession. He would enslave all women, but especially our queens. His purpose is why there are so few Aima queens still living. All queens are under constant attack. You may find it best serves your needs to ally yourself with them, rather than kill them."

She laughed softly and sat back in Her throne, still petting the snake that slithered up Her thigh. "Though, I admit I would likely kill them, too, and be done with their convoluted plots."

I stepped closer, eyeing the jaguars on either side of Her. They started purring, so I knelt at Her feet between them. They both rubbed their heads against my shoulders, and the black one lay its head in my lap, playfully rolling over and begging me to scratch its stomach. "What's the cost for this power?"

"A life for a life." She reached out to cup my cheek, Her eyes glimmering with regret. "It cannot be your own life, either. I know your heart, child. You would willingly die to save another, but it cannot be paid by you. You won't have the choice of who pays the cost. If you call upon my grave to kill, it will claim another one you love at great cost to you."

My throat swelled shut with tears, shredded with agony at the thought. Who would die? One of my Blood? My heart bled at the thought. Gina? Winston? Mayte? "I can't bear it."

"You must, if you accept this gift. But I will tell you truly that if you do not kill Ra, then he will kill many more. You will lose loved ones. You will die in great pain, and everyone you love will suffer. The only difference is that you will not have the responsibility of knowing that someone died because of your power."

"If they die, can I resurrect them?"

She shook her head solemnly. "My grave is beyond even the Great One's resurrection. It must be so to ensure Ra's death."

Tears trickled down my face, and I bit my tongue and

lips, shredding my own flesh with my fangs. "Can you tell me who you'll take?"

Silently, She shook Her head again.

The cost. So steep.

If I lost Rik...

Goddess. I couldn't breathe at the thought.

Daire. Guillaume. My grumpy dragon. My silent, ghostly wolf. My poor, tortured dog.

I choked on sobs, splattering Her with my blood.

She shivered, Her eyes flaring with hunger. "Decide, child, so I may send you back unscathed. You've aroused my hunger, which is never wise."

Decide reverberated in my head.

If I said no, then many people would die, probably myself included. If I said yes, only one person was sure to die, but I'd have to live with the knowledge that they'd died because of me for the rest of my very long Aima life.

If I didn't use Her gift, Ra would have more time to hurt and kill people. Maybe the very same people I loved. Maybe he'd attack Zaniyah again, and I wouldn't be here to pull Xochitl back from the cenote. Maybe he'd get to Winston, mostly alone at my nest while I was away on Isador business, like this trip.

My loved ones could die in countless different ways, indirectly by my hand because of my indecision.

Or *one* loved one, indirectly by my hand, but wholly my responsibility to bear.

My chest ached like Itztli had shoved his fist into my

ribcage and yanked out my heart this time, but I nodded. I had to protect as many as possible. Save as many as I could.

I thought She would give me blood like Isis had done, but instead, She seized the snake curling up Her thigh in Her fist and yanked it free. By the grimace on Her face and the fresh blood trickling from Her lips, it hurt Her to do so.

The snake hissed and writhed in Her grip. It struck Her forearm, leaving bloody holes in Her flesh, but She didn't release its coils. She moved Her hand closer to me, and the snake turned its head to glare at me.

I tipped up my chin and willed my tears to dry. I was the last queen of Isis. My mother and father had both died so that I might live. They had paid the ultimate cost to create me.

I would not flinch from my duty.

Even if it bared fangs and hissed with fury to be torn from the Mother of the Gods.

The ruby snake lunged at my face, and this time, She let it go. It sank fangs into my cheek, its small body winding around my neck. It hurt, but nothing like how badly my heart already ached. Shaking, I waited while the snake bit me a few more times, and then grudgingly settled around my throat like a collar, its head over my right breast.

Coatlicue leaned forward and enfolded me in Her arms. "There, my child. It's done."

But it wasn't over. It would never be over. Dread would hang over my heart until I knew which one of my loved ones would die.

SHARA

I woke, sobbing.

Rik pulled me toward him, but I jerked free of his arms and sat up. Moonlight shone through the balcony doors, gauzy white curtains dancing in the gentle breeze like ghosts. Or shrouds.

Fuck. Was everything going to remind me of death now? Would I be able to smile and laugh without remembering that I was going to be sobbing over someone's dead body?

Sensing my mood, he didn't wrap me in his arms, but sat beside me, silent and comforting, my rock in the worst storm. Which only made me cry more. What if it was him?

"I'm not going anywhere, my queen."

I choked on another wracking sob. "You don't know that. I could lose you. I could lose any of you."

He didn't press for answers. Maybe he'd seen enough of my dream to know what the goddess had given me. Or maybe he already knew me so well that he didn't have to ask questions. He read my heart and soul without effort. He always had.

My other Blood drew near, as silent as my alpha, but just as determined to soothe my wounded heart. They knelt around the bed, not reaching for me or making demands on my person. Just present. Steady. Unquestioning in their desire to be near me and do anything I asked.

"Even if I ask one of you to die for me?"

"Yes," "aye," "without fail," they said, one by one.

"I can't do this," I whispered, slinging tears aside angrily. "It's not fair. I love you too much to ask any of you to die."

"You won't have to ask," Rik replied, his voice ringing with surety despite the soft, soothing rumble of his rock troll. "You never have to ask for anything, my queen. We know. We live to serve, even if that means dying."

"I will die for you, my queen." Guillaume offered me one of his blades over his arm. "Now. This very moment. Cut my heart out like Itztli's. I'm yours."

"I won't be able to bring you back. This grave will be final."

He stared back at me unflinchingly. "It doesn't matter. I'm still yours. Kill me if it will ease your heart. I die gladly for you. I've had a very long life. It's no hardship to leave now, if it makes your choice easier. Your power is great enough to take even the headless knight to the grave."

"It's not my choice." My voice broke, my heart shredded to ribbons. "It could be any of you. I can't control it or make the choice. It's in the goddess's hands."

"Where it should be." Rik lightly touched my collarbone. "Any of us will pay the cost for you. Without question."

I looked down where he touched me. A glittering red snake was embedded in my flesh. From a distance, it might look like a tattoo, but I could feel the tiny snake coiled around my throat, its scales settling into my skin, becoming a part of me.

Death. A part of me. A constant reminder of how much I had to lose.

I looked at them one by one. My fearless knights. My

deadly beasts. My protectors. My warriors. My killers. My loves.

Tears splashed on my chest. I couldn't breathe with the pain stabbing through my heart. Instinctively, I tried to draw away from the pain. I tried to harden my heart so it wouldn't hurt so badly.

Itztli shook his head and reached out to take my hand, pressing a kiss to my knuckles. "Please, my queen, don't make the same mistakes that I did, or that my mother did. Don't wall yourself off from everyone. Don't cut us out of your heart to avoid this pain. I know your pain is great. I know what it costs you to love us, but that love saved me. It saved Tlacel. It saved Xochitl. If you do not love, who will you save? Why save anyone at all?"

"I don't want to be the darkness," I whispered, forcing each word out, even though they sliced like razor blades. "Is that not what you said? I don't want to lose anyone to remind me of how much I love the rest of you. I already know that. I don't need the reminder."

"I was wrong. I was lost in darkness and thought your light would only remind me how damaged and unworthy I am. But you came into the darkness with me, not to shine light on all my sins, but to stay with me. To love me, even in that darkness. You weren't afraid to face what you saw inside me, no matter how hideous. That monstrosity is still there. I'm still dark. You're still the greatest light of love that I've ever been graced by the goddesses to see. But I'm not forgotten and lost in my darkness any longer, because you're still here with me."

Tlacel pressed his face against my calf in the same spot where he'd bitten me to pull me out of the portal. "Stay here with us, my queen. Even though it hurts."

Daire inched onto the mattress and curled around me to put his head in my lap. Guillaume sheathed his blade and held my other hand, his thumb lightly stroking my palm. Nevarre pushed in around Ezra, opposite Daire, so he could put his head on my other thigh, his hair sliding over my skin like silk. Mehen wrapped his hands around my left knee. Xin sat by my dragon and tucked up against my side.

My alpha didn't move. He didn't have to, because he was already right beside me. So close that all I had to do was tip my head to the side, and I could rest on his broad chest, his heartbeat loud in my ear.

They stayed with me, touching me, offering solace and comfort while the moon crossed the sky. They said nothing else but held me as I cried.

Even though we hadn't completed the Fire Ceremony, the sun rose again. Dawn always came. Even if I wished it wouldn't.

13

RIK

I would give my queen my last breath. Every drop of my blood. I would suffer unimaginable pain to ensure her safety.

But I could not protect her from the vision she'd received from the goddess.

Pale and listless, she refused to feed, even though I felt her hunger gnawing through her bonds. She'd taxed her power mercilessly yesterday, first saving the child, completing the ritual with Itztli, and then throwing up the shield to turn Ra's attack aside. Any other day, I would have declared this trip an impressive victory.

She'd gained a sib, two old, powerful Blood, a new goddess patron and Her gift, an Isador heir, and, of course, she'd dealt a hefty blow to Ra. He'd lost two powerful avatars and two queens had slipped free of his traps.

Shara was more powerful than ever.

But her heart had taken a serious blow. As dawn broke, she insisted we prepare to leave immediately, and I feared she might need weeks or even longer to recover.

I didn't know exactly what the goddess had shown her in the vision. But I read the sorrow in her heart, the tears in her eyes, and her dread that one of us would die.

I didn't have the heart to tell her that I'd kill one of her beloved Blood myself if that would ease her suffering.

She hurt, but only because she loved us so well.

For once, we had to wake Gina to ensure the plane was readied and Winston expected us back earlier than planned.

As we were carrying luggage to the waiting car, Mayte came racing down the steps dressed only in a robe. "You're leaving? So early? What happened?" She took one look at the dark circles under Shara's eyes, and gripped our queen's hands in hers, pulling her close. "Shara, what's wrong?"

"I spoke to Coatlicue last night." She released one of Mayte's hands and reached up to pull the neckline of her blouse aside enough to bare the new snake coiled around her throat. "Do you know what this is?"

"No. I'm sorry. Did She give it you?"

"I know that mark," Tocih, Mayte's grandmother, said as she joined us, wiping her hands on her apron. "Coatlicue called you last night to Coatepec."

"If that's a pyramid carved with the Great Feathered

Serpent and a jade throne made of massive snakes, then yes."

Tocih nodded. "Snake Mountain. Did She tell you of the cost?"

Shara swallowed hard and averted her gaze, nodding. The older woman threw her arms around her, startling her. Wide eyed, she gave Mayte a questioning look, but then patted her grandmother's back awkwardly.

"The gift of the grave is a heavy burden to bear, child. My mother bore Coatlicue's serpent but failed to use it. In the end, it devoured her, and the one she was destined to kill went on to destroy our people."

"What?" Mayte exclaimed. "You never told me this story. Who was she supposed to kill?"

"Hernan Cortes himself. In the end, she was afraid of the cost. She couldn't bring herself to use the grave, and he destroyed us. Tenochtitlan fell. House Zaniyah was decimated. Rather than losing a single beloved, she nearly lost our entire family." She sighed heavily, shaking her head. "When Citla came home from being fostered at House Tocatl a shell of my bright, beautiful daughter, I prayed and fasted for days, begging Coatlicue to bestow the mark on me."

Mayte let out a shaking breath. "You hardly ever talk about Mama."

"Because I failed her. I sent her in good faith and they…" Tocih lifted up the corner of her apron and dabbed her eyes. "They broke her, and they didn't care. Theresa knew I wasn't strong enough to punish them. The only way I could have given them the retribution they deserved was if Coatlicue gave me Her grave, but I understand why She did not. I had so few loved ones. If I'd lost you, dear child, Zaniyah would be no more. We wouldn't have Xochitl now. And if I'd lost either of Citla's boys, our queen's Blood would not be complete. At the time, I failed to understand Her reasons, but in the end, She had a purpose. A great purpose indeed."

Tocih reached out and seized Itztli's hand, tugging him close enough to pat his cheek. "Instead, She gave me you, Itztli. You claimed retribution for House Zaniyah when I could not."

I watched as my fellow Blood, the one I'd trusted the least, broke before my very eyes, crumbled against his beloved grandmother, sister, and twin, and then slowly rebuilt himself into a fine, gleaming blade as sharp as the obsidian blade on his waist.

His heart, powered by our queen's love.

She made this possible. She protected Zaniyah. She'd restored Xochitl to her mother. And she made Itztli whole again, even though it cost her greatly. Surely, she couldn't regret the pain when she wrought such miracles with her love.

Tocih looked back at my queen and hardened her voice. "Be sad for a time, yes. It's your right. But don't let this dread task our goddesses have set in your path destroy you, or you'll lose everything. You won't lose one beloved, but all of them. If you fail to love, and deny the light and hope They have in store for you because you're afraid of losing someone, then you've already lost the most important thing in this world."

Some of the turmoil eased in Shara's bond, and I breathed easier myself.

Three generations of Zaniyah queens walked outside beside my queen. The child, Xochitl, watched as her great-grandmother, mother, and Shara each cut themselves on Itztli's obsidian blade and held their hands over the blood circle protecting the nest. With Shara's additional power added to the blood circle, their defenses anchored deeper than ever in the bedrock, grounded by the massive heart tree she'd grown with Itztli's sacrifice.

A whole flock of bright green and red birds had taken up residence in the new tree. The black hole remained in the trunk, and the birds swarmed in and out of the tree's core. Hopefully the tree wouldn't be susceptible to rot and disease with its heart exposed to the elements.

Mayte hugged her brothers, her cheeks damp with tears, but a smile on her face. She took my queen's hands in hers and kissed both of Shara's cheeks. "Thank you, Your Majesty. It's an honor to serve House Isador. If Zaniyah can be of assistance to you, call on us day or night."

Shara mustered a smile. "Did you deal with Bianca?"

Mayte's smiled sharpened, her eyes glittering with malice. "Indeed. Why do you think the birds swarm inside the tree? She'll feed the heart tree you gave us, and I managed to hide her punishment from innocent eyes at the same time."

Nodding, Shara drew her queen close in a hug, her face

tucked against Mayte's neck. She stroked Shara's back, and I felt her hunger rise another notch.

"Yes," Mayte said immediately, tipping her head aside. "Please. Let me feed you one last time before you leave."

"I don't want to make you come in front of everyone," Shara said with a rueful grin tugging the corner of her mouth. "At least if we're not going to take full advantage of my bite."

"I can make the bite for you," Tlacel offered. "We've fed from each other many times."

I listened to Shara's bond, but she didn't feel any jealousy that her Blood would touch another woman, not when they were brother and sister. Though it surprised me when she shook her head.

"No. I want Itztli to make the bite for me."

It might have seemed like an insignificant gesture, but the light shining in his dark eyes said otherwise. He had denied himself most of his life for fear of hurting others, even his family. With Shara's bond solid inside him, he felt no hesitation as he sank his fangs into his sister's throat, and then stepped back so our queen could feed.

She drank until Mayte made a soft, lazy sound of contentment, her hands sliding down Shara's back, pressing their lower bodies closer. Shara's hunger still blazed, the small amount she'd taken barely even an appetizer, but she licked the wound and lifted her head. "Thank you, my queen."

"Your Majesty," Mayte slurred, her eyes heavy lidded.

"Safe journey. If I may be of assistance, call me at any time, and I'll come to your aid."

Shara started to pull away, but Mayte tangled her hands in her hair and tugged her down for a soft, lingering kiss.

With a reluctant sigh, Shara lifted her head. "I must go."

"I know. Will you come again? Soon?"

She met my gaze, her bond still shadowed and cold, not with grief, but determination. "I think we'll be paying a visit to New York City soon."

Mayte's breath rushed out. "Oh, Shara. Be careful. Draw on my power as often as you need to. Everything I have is yours."

Shara looked over at the dancing little girl, chasing butterflies in a beautiful dress. "No. You must protect her above all else."

As if she sensed the attention, Xochitl turned and waved at us, her smile bright. "Goodbye, Your Majesty!"

"Goodbye, Princess of Unicorns."

Shara remained silent in the car, though she dropped her head against my shoulder. We transferred to her jet and she immediately kicked her shoes off and cuddled into my side. I dropped my arm around her and just held her, letting her soak in my warmth and assurance. All would be well. I would make it so.

She finally looked up at me, her eyes dark, but not as haunted. She didn't say anything. She didn't have to. I held my hand out and Guillaume slapped a blade against my palm so I could make a cut on my throat for her.

Her mouth tightened for a moment. I felt the war inside

her, a flood of rage and tears. Vicious determination to keep us all safe, fighting the hopeless fear that even the last queen of Isis was not all-powerful against the grave.

With a sigh, she settled against my chest and pressed her mouth to the cut. Her hunger rose, and she dug her fingers into my shoulders, pulling me closer like she wanted to crawl inside me and hide from the world forever.

"You will never have to ask, my queen. For anything."

:That's what I'm afraid of.:

14

SHARA

Coming home to my nest after being away was damned near a religious experience. I'd enjoyed Mayte's nest and it had felt secure.

But *my* nest…

Layers of tension and alertness that I hadn't even been aware of, fell away from my shoulders. My trees whispered a glad greeting, the gentle rustling of their leaves a soothing balm to my nerves.

Surprise. For you. Welcome home.

The whispers drew my gaze to the heart tree, now surrounded by large boulders mixed in with the thorny bushes that ringed the rose tree. I took a step toward the new landscape to explore, but Winston opened the door and called to me.

"Your Majesty, I was going to call you, but then Gina texted of your imminent arrival. A package arrived for you."

I wasn't sure why he seemed so anxious, if his voice was quivering with nerves or excitement. Until I realized it was New Year's Day. No postal service would be delivering packages today. "Who's it from?"

"Rome," he replied, his eyes wide. "Marne Ceresa herself."

Of fucking course. I'd barely even been home a minute, and all the plots came tumbling back to ensnare me again. With a scowl, I stomped back toward the house. Whatever surprise my trees had in store for me must wait.

Winston met me at the driveway and led me down to the guard's station at the gate that blocked the front public entrance to the property.

Frank McCoy, my head security guard and one of my human servants I carried a blood bond with, gave me a worried nod of welcome. "Sorry, Your Majesty. I didn't know if I should say anything when you first arrived or not. I thought you might be asleep."

I did have the annoying habit of sleeping on Rik while traveling. Even the first time I'd seen my home, I hadn't been able to wake up long enough to look around.

"A sharp black Mercedes drove up about fifteen minutes ago. The rear window rolled down and an older man held the box out and said, 'A special delivery for Her Majesty, Shara Isador.' I didn't know what else to do, so I took it, but I didn't think you'd want it carried into your nest until you took a look at it."

Nodding, I studied the box. It looked like an old-fashioned hat box, beautifully decorated with white and black damask paper and a baby-pink bow. "Did you get a good look at the man?"

"I'd know him if I saw him again. White hair, goatee and mustache, neat and trimmed, black suit that looked like a million bucks. He wore black leather gloves, too. That gave me pause. If he had to wear gloves to touch the package, I definitely didn't want to take it up to the house until you saw it."

"Gina, do you know who that might have been?"

Eyes wide, she stared at the package like my massive cobra was about to crawl out of it and strike us all down.

"Gina?"

She gave herself a shake. "Sorry, yes, that was probably Byrnes. He's Marne Ceresa's American consiliarius."

"American, as in she has more than one?"

"Yes, she has seven consiliari in total. Few outside the Triune have ever spoken to her directly, but deal with one of her consiliari instead."

"Any guesses what she might have sent me?"

Gina grimaced and shook her head. "None whatsoever. She's not known for sending bombs or threats or anything like that. She plays the game with brutal precision. This is a deliberate move on her part. Any gift from her will have layers of meaning and intention behind it."

"Hopefully something won't try to kill me as soon as I take the lid off."

"That's not her style. If she decides to kill you, it'll be a grand spectacle to show the world how brilliant and clever she is."

I picked up the card lying on top of the box. In beautiful calligraphy, my name was written in the center of the card, with *Marne Ceresa, Rome, Italy* in the upper left-hand corner. The stationery itself was thick, gorgeously expensive, and smelled of sweet lavender. The envelope was closed with an old-fashioned black wax seal, stamped with what looked like an ancient Roman coin and a curly wand. Something was written in Latin around the edge of the coin, but I couldn't read it.

I cracked the wax seal and pulled out the small square of heavy card stock. A single sentence swirled in the same elegant script. *I look forward to making your acquaintance.*

I met Rik's gaze and he gave me a silent nod of assurance. My Blood were ready for anything. They circled me, braced for attack in any direction.

Taking a deep breath, I removed the lid and handed it to Gina. I pushed back several layers of tissue paper and found a decorative mirror. It was roughly the size of a nice, large dinner plate, though its gilded frame was ornately carved in whorls and leaves. I carefully reached in and picked it up, surprised at how heavy it was.

"A mirror," Gina breathed out. "Of course. I've heard rumors that she secretly communicates with her consiliari face-to-face despite their distance from her seat in Rome, but I wasn't sure how."

That almost made me drop the fucking thing. "She can see me through the mirror?"

"I think it has to be activated first, though I admit, I don't know if she controls the activation, or if you do."

Tlacel didn't turn his head away from guarding to look at me, but said, "I know someone who can help with mirror magic. Tepeyollotl. One of his names means Smoking Mirror. Our people used mirrors for divination and communication with the otherworld."

I touched Mayte's bond, and she immediately filled my senses so strongly that I could smell the sweet spicy scent of her flowers.

:My queen?:

:Would Tepeyollotl be willing to discuss mirror magic with me?:

I'd barely sent that thought and Gina's phone rang. "Yes? Of course."

Smiling, she held the phone out to me. I handed the mirror back to Frank and accepted the phone. "Hello?"

"Sorry, I didn't have your number, and I'm carrying Bianca's phone until I hire a new consiliarius," Mayte replied. "Tepeyollotl will be here shortly. I sent the call for him to attend me at once. Are you well? Did you have a quiet trip home?"

I didn't want to insult her, but after Bianca's betrayal, I wasn't taking any chances. "Are you where you can talk securely?"

"Yes." I heard a door shut. "I'm in the library, alone."

"I'll be right back," I said to Frank and Gina, giving the mirror a wary look. I stepped outside into the sunlight and lowered my voice, in case Marne could eavesdrop through her gift. "I had a package waiting on me from Marne Ceresa. It's an antique mirror, and the note only says she looks forward to meeting me. I want to know what I'm getting into before I try to use it."

"Had it been there long?"

"Frank said about fifteen minutes."

Mayte sighed. "She probably had someone watching for you to land, so she'd know exactly when to send the package."

"She wants me to know she has eyes on me."

"Exactly."

I sighed. "I don't know that I'm cut out for these kinds of cloak-and-dagger bullshit games. I'm sorry to say I'd almost prefer Ra's blatant attacks. At least I know how to defend myself. I'm not used to thinking a dozen plays ahead."

"It takes experience, but Gina gave me the impression she was used to Triune politics."

"She is, or at least she was, but she's been out of the game ever since my mother abandoned the nest over twenty years ago. I trust her implicitly, but I need a better grasp of how to play the game myself."

"I'm hopeless myself, I'm afraid. House Zaniyah has deliberately stayed out of the game for generations. What about your Blood? Were any of them raised in a Triune house?"

"I don't think so, but I'll ask."

:I learned a great deal in House Devana before I fostered with

House Skye,: Daire piped up. *:I'm still young, but Triune politics are one of my gifts.:*

It made me smile to think that Daire was considered "young" for an Aima. *:How old are you exactly?:*

:Sixty nine.:

I snorted, shaking my head. I was a mere babe then.

"Here's Tepeyollotl." To him, she said, "She needs to know how to work mirror magic."

"My queen." His voice boomed through the phone with the power of a hurricane. "Mirror magic is a powerful tool not recommended for the uninitiated."

"I don't have a choice. I received a mirror as a gift from Marne Ceresa, and I'm sure she wants me to contact her using it."

"I see. Is it activated? If you can see a normal reflection, then it's not. If it's smoky or clouded, then she activated it, and the portal is open."

"Wait, portal? Like the cenote? It isn't smoky, so I guess it's not activated right now."

"When activated, a mirror creates a connection to another place. If the mirror was big enough, and the magic strong enough, a person or thing can pass through."

Holy shit. Thankfully, she hadn't sent me a full-length mirror. I'd be tempted to break the glass and prepare for the seven years of bad luck to be safe. The last thing I'd want is to wake up with Marne Ceresa crawling out of a mirror. "It's only about the size of a plate. Is it safe to take the mirror into my nest, then? I don't want her having access to the inside of my home."

"Since it's small, the risk should be minimal. A queen like her would know your justified fear of such a possibility. There are also precautions you can take to be sure it doesn't activate without your wish."

"Yes, please."

"Cover the mirror with a cloth. If it activates, she will not be able to see anything, though depending on her magic, she may be able to hear. I've also seen them put into a basket and covered with salt or coffee."

"Coffee? Like beans, or liquid?"

"Beans, preferably dried, roasted, and ground. They absorb negative energy better that way. Both salt and coffee have a purifying effect and can be used to cleanse a mirror if you suspect another's magic is interfering or contaminating your connection. It shouldn't have any effect on the original coding, other than to make it stronger and clearer. Water has a magnifying effect. If you dropped the mirror in a pool of water, say the grotto, and activated it, the entire pool could become the mirror. According to legend, that's how humans were able to open cenote portals themselves."

"Fuck that shit," Guillaume muttered.

Yeah, no kidding. "How do I activate it?"

"Blood."

I blew out a sigh. "Of course."

"Just a drop on the surface of the mirror is enough. The magic is set by your intention, and hers, of course. I'm guessing she coded the mirror she gave you to one in her nest, so they can act as receivers or senders. Her magic sets and defines the connection between the two mirrors. When you drop blood on the mirror to activate it, it'll notify her that you wish to make the connection. I would assume she can alert you the same way, and the mirror will chime or otherwise draw your attention to it when she wishes to speak to you."

"If she doesn't want to speak to me, then I can't activate it on her side?"

"Generally, no, but anything is possible with enough blood and power behind it."

I shivered at the thought. I didn't want to find out how much blood would be required to overpower one of Marne's own mirror spells.

"The single most important thing to remember: when you wish to close the connection, you must wipe the blood away. If you forget, the connection will remain viable, and she may be able to manipulate the mirror at will."

Rik sent an immediate order through our bonds. :*I charge anyone present with our queen when she's using the mirror to check and verify the blood is wiped away in case she forgets.*:

:*Understood, alpha.*: They each replied.

"Do you have any other questions, my queen?" Tepeyollotl asked.

"If I decide I want to break the connection so she can't contact me through the mirror at all, how do I do that?"

"Break the mirror into pieces and bury or destroy the shards. Beware, there may be a great deal of energy released when you destroy the connection. This is where the saying comes from that implies bad luck results from breaking a mirror. Care must be taken to be sure a magically-charged mirror is disposed of correctly."

"Can she change her appearance in the mirror? Like show me something that isn't true?"

"Of course, if she has enough power to do so. She may choose to conceal or mask her appearance, but so can you."

Again, if I had the power, or, if I offered enough blood to raise that amount of power. "Thank you, Tepeyollotl. You've been extremely informative."

"It's my pleasure to serve my queen's queen."

I hung up and stepped back inside the guard shack.

:Thank you, Mayte.:

:He was able to help?:

:He was of great assistance.:

I felt her smile in the bond and then she slipped away. I handed the phone back to Gina and reluctantly took the heavy mirror back from Frank. The surface was slightly bubbled with impurities from age, but I could see myself clearly. Without blood… it looked like an old mirror you could find in any antique shop.

Carefully, I laid the mirror back in the box. "Well, I guess we need to pick a place to store it. Do one of you want to take charge of it?"

Tlacel took the box from Frank. "I will be honored to mind the mirror for you, my queen."

"If I may make a suggestion?" Winston waited for me to nod before continuing. "I'm guessing you'll want to keep it close—but not too close. Off your master bedroom, there's a small room that would be perfect for a private study. It's a bit dark and gloomy, since there aren't any windows, but perhaps that would be best for such a potentially dangerous item."

True. I hadn't thought to ask Tepeyollotl if the mirror should stay out of the sun, but I would guess light reflecting off the surface could be painful, especially if I was trying to use its magic.

That made me think of something else. Eyes narrowed, I thought back to how Ra had opened a window into my bedroom in Kansas City. How he always used bright flashes of light to stun us during an attack. "Do you think Ra is using a form of mirror magic?"

"It's very possible," Rik answered as we made our way back to the house. "When you shattered the portal in Kansas City, the explosion was tremendous. I'm guessing that would be very much like what Tepeyollotl described when breaking a magical mirror."

"But there wasn't a mirror on my side that he could use, not like this."

"Maybe he's powerful enough he doesn't need one," Guillaume replied.

Great, just fucking great.

Winston hurried ahead of us to swing the impressive front door open for us. "Let me show you the newly renovated rooms, Your Majesty. I hope you'll be most pleased."

"I'm sure I will." Inside, plastic stretched across the large doorway that led to the dining room and kitchen.

"We've started work on the kitchen, which should be ready in a few more days." Winston led us upstairs, speaking over his shoulder. "The contractor says five, but I'm guessing it'll be more like ten. Did you want to pick out the appliances, Your Majesty?"

"Honestly, no, I'd have no idea what to pick. I trust your judgment implicitly."

His cheeks colored, eyes sparkling with pleasure. "Of course, thank you, Your Majesty. We left the grand fireplace untouched, other than some minor sprucing and cleaning. It's perfectly functional. The fireplace in the sunken living room still needs some masonry work. Depending on the weather, we may need to wait another few weeks or longer to ensure they have easy access to the roof."

"Of course, not a problem."

At the top of the stairs, he paused and gestured up at the gorgeous stained-glass windows. "The artisan examined the windows and declared them mostly sound, though she recommends that a few sections be re-leaded. In the spring, we'll have them very carefully cleaned, both inside and out."

He turned to the landing. Like Mayte's house, one door led to the master suite, and other rooms and hallways led off to the right. He swept open the French doors to the master suite. "Your library, Your Majesty. It was mostly cosmetic in here. Some paint, deep cleaning, and new draperies. We found some true treasures hidden away on the shelves, including some beautiful first editions."

I wanted to twirl like Belle when the Beast showed her his impressive library. Mine wasn't quite as grand, but the twelve-foot floor-to-ceiling shelves were filled with books. Another fireplace and stone wall made the room warm and cozy, with plenty of comfortable leather chairs and sofas for reading and lounging. "Incredible, Winston. I can't wait to…" I caught myself and sighed. So far, I'd done nothing but run from one fire to another, including urgent trips to Venezuela and Mexico.

Rik gave me a heavy-lidded look, his sensual mouth curving enough to reveal just a hint of fang. "You need some down time, Shara. Rest and relaxation and lots of reading."

Daire stepped closer and flashed his adorable dimples. "You should let us take turns reading to you."

"I get to read to her first." Mehen butted in, literally pushing Daire aside to get to one of the shelves. "Fucking hell. A first edition *Les Trois Mousquetaires*! That's *The Three Musketeers* to you cretins. Let me read this one to you first, my queen."

"Sure, but if you read it in French, I won't understand it."

"I'll teach you. I'll read and translate it as we go. By the time we finish, you'll be an expert in French."

"Or we'll all die of boredom," Daire muttered.

Mehen let out a very draconic hiss of displeasure, and they continued the banter as we walked to the private staircase in the back of the library. I braced for sadness to flood over me at Daire's casual words, afraid the joy of seeing my manor house coming together would be tainted by the fear about who might die, and when.

But in my nest, surrounded by my loved ones, I couldn't be sad. Not when they teased and laughed and tried so hard to please me down to the most insignificant details.

"There are a few things still outstanding, so it's not perfect, yet, Your Majesty. But I thought you would rather be here since you'll have more space than the guest house." Winston pushed open another set of French doors and stepped back, waiting for me to go inside my new master bedroom.

Oh. My. Fucking. Massive. Bed. Alert.

The largest bed I'd ever seen sat in the middle of the room, loaded with so many pillows that it looked like a puffy cloud. We'd have to try it to be sure, but it certainly looked like it would be large enough for all of us.

Finally. I'd be able to sleep with all my Blood near.

One whole wall was lined with large windows that looked out over the river far below. Rugged Arkansas mountains rolled into the distance, carpeted in a thick forest. I could only imagine how gorgeous all of the trees would be this spring when the leaves started to come in.

"This isn't the final bed," Winston said, wringing his hands. "It's being shipped from the East Coast and won't be here for another week. This is the best I could do. I ordered two California kings and pushed them together."

I threw my arms around his shoulders and kissed his cheek. "It's absolutely fabulous. I love it! Thank you, Winston."

I turned back around and wanted to jump up and down and clap my hands like Xochitl exclaiming over her unicorns. The ceilings soared incredibly high, two full stories to be exact. The raw rafters gave it a rustic, old world look that I adored. Another gigantic fireplace lined the exposed-stone wall. White sheer curtains hung at the windows and cascaded down onto the thick planks of the original hardwood floor. In the summer, I could open the windows and let the breeze and fresh air flood the room.

"I can't believe it. Honestly. It's exactly what I pictured in my head."

Winston dabbed at his eyes with his handkerchief. "I'm so pleased, Your Majesty. So very pleased. Come this way, and I'll see if the new bathroom meets your specifications." He led me to a set of two doors. "We took the liberty of reclaiming space from one of the guest rooms to make a walk-in closet."

He opened the left-hand door and flipped the light on. I made a choked sound of surprise and amusement. This "closet" was bigger than my entire tower bedroom in Kansas City. Built-in shelves and racks lined the walls, with a cushioned ottoman in the center of the room where I could sit and try various shoes on.

"There's no way I'm going to ever have enough clothes to fill this much space."

Daire snorted. "Wanna bet? I could fill this in an afternoon."

There was another door tucked in the corner of the closet. "This is the small room I was talking about." Winston opened the door and turned on that light for me to peek inside. "The contractor was going to tear it out and make the master bath even bigger, but one of the walls butts up to the chimney from the dining room fireplace."

It was dark without any windows, but I was well used to

that. I'd chosen my old bedroom deliberately because it didn't have any windows—which meant fewer ways for the monsters to break in. If only I'd known the greatest monster already lived inside of me.

He'd set up a desk, several lamps, and an inviting chaise lounge draped with a soft, fluffy shawl. Perfect for cuddling on a rainy day, reading a book, or… talking with a fearsome queen.

Tlacel set the box on the desk. "Should I cover it as well, my queen?"

"No, I think the box will be fine for now. Thank you."

We stepped back out and Winston showed me the show-stopper bathroom. More windows framed a bathtub large enough that easily six of us could use it at once. Fresh, white marble floors were accented with lapis, emerald, and ruby mosaics. He opened a cabinet beside the tub to show me an array of bath salts, candles, and fluffy, thick towels.

"Gorgeous. I mean it, Winston, this looks like an expensive spa. I love it."

"I'm so pleased, Your Majesty. If there's anything you need, anything at all, please let me know and I'll have the contractor make adjustments." He took my hand and inclined his head. "I'm at your service, Your Majesty. I'll leave you to rest from your trip. I'm sure you're exhausted. When you're ready to eat, have one of your Blood come down to the kitchen. I have a space readied, so I can heat up food at a moment's notice."

"What about the clothes we took on the trip?"

Gina patted my shoulder and followed Winston to the

door. "Not to worry, we have a crew assembled to take care of laundry needs. The car has already been unloaded, and we'll bring your things up later."

"You'll find some robes, pajamas, and loungewear in the closet," Winston called back over his shoulder. "Plus a few other things that Gina had delivered from your Kansas City house. We'll get your closet filled in no time."

As I walked back into the bedroom, Rik pulled the twins aside. "Do you two want to have guard duty together, or split up?"

"Together," they both said without hesitation.

He nodded and then looked at the rest of my Blood. "Everyone on guard duty except for Ezra, Daire, and Guillaume. Check the grounds thoroughly, and then hit the shower and food as you want. Stick close."

He didn't have to tell them why. They all felt my hunger. I'd fed from Rik on the plane, but only enough to get home. I hated to destroy the gorgeous, brand-new bedding with a bunch of blood stains. I hoped Winston had hired a fucking stainmaster to get all the blood out of my laundry.

They all filed out, still joking and talking among themselves. I couldn't help but smile. Mehen was still rhapsodizing about finding the Dumas set in the library.

Once it quieted, I sat on the edge of the bed and turned my attention to Daire. "Should I use the mirror now? Or wait a bit? I don't want to insult her—but I also don't want to appear too eager to do her bidding."

Daire plopped down beside me on the bed and rolled around like a cat marking its territory. "She knows you've been traveling, and I'd hazard a guess that she even knows that you have a sib, and maybe even that you had some problems with Ra. You're a new queen, with a new nest, so you're going to need some time to prepare for a visit, even via mirror magic. I say take your time. Completely ignoring her would be rude, but if we wait until tomorrow, I think that's perfectly acceptable."

"I agree, my queen," Guillaume added. "If you had a prior relationship with her, then she might expect a quicker response. Or she could have specified her expectation in the note. She left it open for a reason, and Marne Ceresa has a reason for everything she does."

Some of the tension eased in my shoulders and I took a deep breath. "Okay, good. I'll worry about her tomorrow then." I looked at Rik. "Do we need to ward these windows or set up any extra protections? I know it's inside the nest, but all this glass still makes me leery."

"The glass won't be a problem." His voice deepened to a low rumble that strummed deep inside me. "Though if you will rest better, we'll salt the window sills."

"No, that's fine. As long as you're not worried."

"Not in the slightest. This nest is solid and secure. You selected well, my queen."

I looked at my magnificent Blood one by one. Showing them my appreciation for their incredible physiques, I didn't hide my rising desire. "Yes, I did select very well indeed."

Rik tugged his shirt over his head and tossed it aside. "Are you thinking the same thing I am?"

It was a rhetorical question, but sometimes it was nice to

actually say things out loud rather than use the bond all the time. It was definitely more of a turn-on. "If you're thinking that I should feed on Daire while Ezra shows me his hook, then yeah, we're on the same page."

Ezra growled roughly. "About fucking time."

15

DAIRE

The memory of Ezra's hook made my purr rumble like a jet engine taking off. The thought of him giving that hook to Shara…

While I fed her…

Damn near made me blow my load before she could even start.

Ezra shoved me to get me moving. "Get her fucking jeans off, D."

Which meant I should strip in record time first, so I could help her.

By the time I moved closer to her, she'd already tossed her blouse aside. The glittering scales of the snake around her throat drew my attention. It fascinated me, but not necessarily in a good way. Not after her cobra queen had pumped Rik full of poison.

Her arms came up to cross over her breasts, a shyness coming over her that I hadn't seen since our first night together. When Rik and I had found her a few miles away, fighting off a dozen thralls with nothing but a board with some rusted nails in one hand and a pocketknife in the other.

My throat ached with regret that I had made her feel unsure of herself. I leaned in and dropped kisses along her shoulder until my mouth touched the red snake.

It was definitely coils and not her skin against my mouth. It even moved slightly. Chills raced down my spine, but it didn't move again.

"It bit me," she whispered, her fingers touching her cheek. "When She gave it to me. I don't think it'll bite again, at least not until it's time to kill Ra."

I rubbed my lips against her cheek, seeking to take away the memory. "I didn't see any marks on you after the dream."

She sighed heavily. "There are marks, but they're invisible. More like dark blots. Stains. I don't want to think about it or I'll cry again."

I unbuttoned her jeans and helped her pull them off, then her panties. She scooted backwards on the bed, lifting her gaze to find Rik. "You'll be close too, won't you?"

"Of course, if that's your wish."

"And G. I think I could drain you all and barely put a dent in this thirst."

Guillaume had stripped off his clothes, but he still had some work to do removing all the leather harnesses and sheaths for the blades he kept concealed all over his body. "I'll be ready and waiting for you, my queen."

Ezra and I both started toward her, crawling across the mattresses. It was bigger than it seemed—and took a ridiculously long time to get to her. I was snickering by the time I managed to touch her, because it was hard to do the sexy beast crawl for that long without looking like an idiot.

"Fuck me sideways." Ezra finally flopped down on his back, pretending exhaustion. "This is one fucking big bed."

She laughed and bent down to rub her face against his chest. "I know. I can't wait to see how many of you can sleep with me now."

He reached up and hooked his arm around her shoulders, but he turned his sultry brown eyes on me. "Get busy warming up our queen, D. I want her motor purring as loudly as you."

She threaded her fingers through the thick mat of chest hair and gave him a playful tug. "Can I purr, do you think? If I'm not shifted?"

I rubbed against her, a soft glide of my body against hers, inviting her cat out to play with mine. "You can do anything you want because you're Shara fucking Isador."

SHARA

I hadn't felt like Shara fucking Isador since that dream on Snake Mountain, but with my two Blood stroking my skin, I was starting to feel less shaken and scared of how much I had to lose, and more like myself. A badass vampire queen who wanted to revel in her hunger for blood and sex.

"Yes," Daire drew the word out with a pleased hum. "Revel in me, my queen."

The mattress on either side dipped slightly as Rik and Guillaume joined us, moving closely enough to step in if I asked for them, their eyes dark, cocks hard and eager. It made me remember what I'd wanted after pushing Ra's blast aside from Mayte's nest.

Too many dicks to count.

I rolled Daire beneath me and mounted him in one deep lunge that made us both groan. So good, to have him deep inside me. Beneath me. Purring. Swirling his hips. Rocking me like Guillaume's delightful canter.

Ezra straddled Daire's hips and rubbed against my back, giving me more sensation. His furry chest and thighs, his solid weight. The rasp of his beard against my shoulder when he kissed my throat.

"You are one fucking fine queen, Shara. I could eat you up."

"Be my guest."

Edging closer, so his dick rubbed against my buttocks, he sank his fangs in my throat. He growled against my skin and locked me against him. I arched against him, my body eager for more. I wanted him deep inside me too.

:Not the hook, sweetheart. Not in that fine ass, at least not the first time. Let D finish, and then I'll give you what you want.:

My other two Blood braced on their knees on either side of Daire, offering up their bodies to me. I took a cock in either hand and dropped my head back against Ezra, soaking them all in. My Blood, my men, my dicks. All four of them. Touching me. Loving me. I would take them all inside me at once if I could.

My hunger licked inside me like an inferno. Daire sat up, offering his throat while he squeezed and molded my breasts in both hands. I struck hard and his hips jerked up on a shout of release. Shaking as he spurted inside me, semen and blood both. I gulped him down, gasping as he pushed me to climax too.

Panting, he nuzzled up against me, his arms sliding around both me and Ezra, pinning me against the other man. Eyes closed, I simply breathed them in, soaking in the textures of muscle and tendon, the throb of erections against my palms. Guillaume was so thick I couldn't close my fingers around him, and Rik wasn't far behind.

Ezra licked my throat and raised his mouth to my ear. "You haven't felt my dick when the hook is released. It'll feel like Rik and G both are shoved inside you."

A groan tore from my throat and I arched back against him. "Sounds good."

He pushed into me gently, and at first, he felt like a normal man. Nothing strange or different at all. He thrust several times, giving me a little grunt each time he pushed inside me. Deeper, lower, harder with each thrust. And yeah, it was good. Fucking fantastic. I loved a good, hard fuck. I wasn't going to break, and some of the guys were a bit too... reverent... when they touched me.

I loved that too, but sometimes, I just wanted to fuck. Hard.

I wanted to feel like I was breaking from the inside out. Like I was being reshaped into something new.

Ezra was the furthest from reverent any of my Blood could be.

He fisted his hand in my hair and pushed me down with Daire beneath me, shifting me lower to improve his leverage. I squeezed my hands tighter, refusing to let go of Rik and G, though the angle made my shoulders ache.

It was a good ache, and it matched the growing heat in my pelvis perfectly.

Ezra growled again and nipped my earlobe hard enough I gasped. "Get ready, sweetheart. I'm going to fucking blow your mind."

He sat back upright, but kept one hand fisted in my hair, my head shoved against Daire's chest. Ezra's other hand gripped my hip so hard I'd probably have fingerprints in my skin. Breathing hard, he pushed deeper, grinding against my buttocks.

And something exploded in me.

I jerked with surprise, pulling my hair in his grip. Daire squeezed me tighter, holding me while I twitched and moaned. "Oh fuck!"

Ezra roared, leaning harder against me, his forearm digging into my back. I fought their grip, trying to escape the sensation. It was fucking fantastic, but also too much.

Too full, too large, too everything. Too fucking good to survive.

Relentless, Ezra pushed even deeper, sending another shockwave tearing through me. It didn't even feel like a climax, but a motherfucking category one-hundred hurricane. I sank my fangs into Daire again out of desperation. I probably almost ripped the guys' dicks off, but for the life of me, I couldn't let go of them.

"When you've had enough," Ezra ground out, "sink those wicked fangs in me, sweetheart. I'll even make it easy for you."

By easy, he meant that he let go of my hip and wrapped his forearm around my neck, hauling me up off Daire. My poor warcat was dazed out of his mind, his eyes spaced, panting so hard he couldn't even purr. Sets of my fangmarks dotted both pectorals, some neat, some jagged and torn from my thrashing.

But I hadn't had enough yet.

Not by a long shot.

Twisting my arm around, I pulled Guillaume closer by his dick and sank my fangs into his thigh. He bucked against me, his come splashing my shoulder. Instantly, his essence sank into my skin, my body devouring him as readily as his blood.

Sweet dessert wine. His rich, delicate blood was so at odds with my dented and battered Templar knight. I drank from him until he wavered and tumbled down beside Daire.

Ezra shifted his forearm up closer to my mouth, either to make it easier for me, or more likely, because he wanted to tempt me into ending our locked position. He still felt impossibly large inside me, as though his dick had swelled to the size of a baseball bat. It hadn't—even though my sensitive walls insisted he was too big. Too wide. Too much.

I fucking loved it.

I fucking loved the sweat pouring off him, his ripe scent of grizzly bear and pine needles filling my nose. The tickle of his body hair, very much like fur.

Rik damned near shoved his thigh into my face, more than eager for me to bite him again, even though I'd fed from him on the jet. But I'd do one better than that. I twisted in Ezra's grip, ignoring the pull on my hair, and inched my face closer to Rik so I could take his cock in my mouth.

He shuddered in my grip but didn't pull away. I had to be ever so careful. I didn't want to shred his dick with my fangs, and they were big enough to do some serious damage. I could heal it, sure, but what man wanted his dick injured and bleeding? If Ezra had been thrusting, I wouldn't have been able to do it, but with his hook solid in me, neither of us were moving very much. We didn't have to.

I licked the head of Rik's cock and pressed my tongue against the tiny slit. Traced the delicate layers of skin around his cock head with my tongue, and ever so gently scraped my fangs on his tender shaft.

My fearless rock troll rolled his hips slightly, pushing his dick further into my mouth. A silent gesture of exactly how much he trusted me. Even if I hurt him, he'd let me do it. He'd have no regrets, even if I'd be devastated later.

He kept up those tiny thrusts, a gentle, slow rocking of his hips that matched the slight stroking of Ezra's hook inside me. My hair was damp with sweat. Mine. Theirs. Guillaume and Daire both stared up at me, their eyes blazing with heat, lips parted to show me their fangs. Their dicks were spent, but already stirring, and their hunger was certainly not sated. It'd never be sated.

Neither would mine.

I pulled back enough to let Rik's dick slide out of my mouth and sank my fangs into his thigh. He roared and heaved against me like tectonic plates were tearing apart. Mixed with the familiar powerful taste of his blood, the hot splash of his come pushed me over the edge again.

I finally took pity on Ezra and released Rik so I could jam my fangs into my bear's forearm. He bellowed and jerked against me. "Sweet fucking goddess, finally."

He felt like a hot flood inside me, wave after wave of his release filling me. For the first time having sex with one, or many, of my Blood, I felt rather sticky when we all tumbled down onto the mattress.

Panting in a sweaty pile with my Blood, I closed my eyes. This. I had to remember moments like this. No matter how badly the fight against Keisha Skye or Marne Ceresa went. No matter how soon I had to strike Ra down and risk the cost of Coatlicue's red serpent of death. This love made everything worth it.

I could only wish that if one of us had to die, that I could go with him to whatever afterlife Isis had planned for us.

"Never," Rik murmured against my ear, tugging me up

on his chest. "You must live. You must continue Isis's line. Think of your surviving Blood, my queen. Think of how they would suffer if you walked away to the afterlife and left them suffering without you."

"I know," I whispered, my heart cracking into a thousand pieces. No, actually, it was only a few pieces. Nine for my Blood. Gina, Winston, and Frank. Mayte. And Xochitl. Fourteen.

My family.

The curtains at the window billowed out, even though the windows were shut and there was no breeze. As if a ghost lingered near the glass, always keeping watch over me.

It had to be my mother, Esetta Isador, her name forbidden to anyone still living. She'd often left me signs that she was with me. If she watched over me, then I also had to count Typhon, father of monsters, the god who sired me. Selena, my aunt who raised me as her own outside a nest, alone and powerless, with her human lover, Alan Dalton. They all four died so I might live. Seventeen pieces of my shattered heart.

All so I could be here. Wrapped in sweaty muscle and fuzzy chest hair and listening to my purring warcat.

"May we join you, my queen?" Nevarre asked.

I smiled at the rest of my Blood, who waited at the door for permission to join me. "Please. As many of you as will fit."

They all moved at once, jamming together in a knot of

eager, belligerent men. Each wanted to be the first to reach me, in the hopes that maybe I'd take him next.

Mehen finally broke free of the pack and leaped for the bed. Only he had the extremely bad fortune of landing on the crack between the two large mattresses.

Since we were in the middle of the room…

Nothing held the two mattresses together.

He slipped down into the crevice spreading between the mattresses. With a yell, he scrambled and flailed, grabbing at the bedding, but instead, he seized a handful of Daire's hair, and pulled him down on top of him.

"Get the fuck off me," Mehen growled.

Daire was laughing so hard that he couldn't breathe. "I can't. The bed ate us."

It took Itztli and Tlacel both to haul Daire up out of the tangle of bedding between the mattresses. Mehen crawled out from the space with as much dignity as possible. While the other Blood shoved the two halves back together again, he watched, arms crossed, nose in the air.

"Leviathan, king of the depths, is not eaten by beds. No. He destroys beds. He breaks them into kindling."

"No, that was me," Rik said, laughing. "The first time I shifted into a rock troll. We should keep track of how many beds we destroy in our efforts to please our queen."

My Blood crowded close while Rik pulled me up onto his chest, very carefully avoiding the crack so the bed couldn't eat us, too.

Mehen stood defiant and arrogant at the edge of the bed.

My lips quirked, and I held my hand out to him.

He lunged for me, snatched me up against him, and tried to roll me beneath him.

Though my alpha refused to let go of me. Not that Mehen minded fucking me on top of my alpha.

Not at all.

16

SHARA

My grove had been extremely busy while I was away in Mexico. I stared in wonder at what Morrigan had wrought.

At the base of the heart tree, the ground had cracked open and fallen away to create a deep, hot mineral spring. Lined with smooth stones, a pool bubbled and steamed, inviting me to step down into the water for a nice long hot soak. Rose petals from my heart tree covered the surface, releasing their delicious scent into the air. Almost like Mayte's flowery scent, but thicker and less sweet, like the difference between a cabernet sauvignon and a crisp, light moscato.

The tree itself looked damaged with a deep gaping hollow in its trunk, but then I noticed the flash of brilliant feathers inside. Quetzals. They were flying in and out of my tree... like the ones in Mayte's nest.

A portal, between the two heart trees. My mind raced with possibilities, though I didn't step into my tree in order to find out if I was right. I didn't want to smell whatever was happening with the traitor Mayte had disposed of in hers.

Rik gave me a hand as I slowly stepped into the water. "When you admired the Zaniyah grotto, I had a feeling you might find your own surprise when we returned home."

It was smoking hot and oh so good. I had to step down incrementally until I was in up to my neck. Closing my eyes, I leaned back against his chest. "Intention, I guess. I need to be careful with random thoughts. I don't want to accidentally wish ill on someone and regret it later. Surprises like this, though, I absolutely love."

Daire sat on a boulder beside us and dangled his feet into the water. "Are you ready to talk about how to deal with Marne's mirror call?"

I blew out a sigh. "Yeah, we need to talk through a strategy. Guillaume said she doesn't do anything without a plan, so I can't afford to wing it. You said that Triune politics were your gift. Do you mean like a power? A strength? Or just something you've always been interested in?"

"Both." He quirked his lips, flashing his dimples. "I'm easy to talk to. I'm easy to get along with. Mom and our queen always said I was too amiable by far. So I built that as my reputation. It's my greatest strength. The Triune game gets tricky when other people know you well enough to start playing to your weaknesses. If I said I'm too amiable by far, what do you think my weakness likely is?"

"That you're naive and too trusting."

"Exactly. I allow people to believe that I'm naive and too trusting. It's what they expect and it matches my strength. You'd be surprised how much people will tell me, hoping to mislead me, or worse, hoping that I'll mislead others because I won't see through their lies."

I frowned. "I don't like lying to anyone. Even Marne."

Omissions, sure. My life wasn't anyone else's business and I didn't have to correct their ridiculous assumptions. But I didn't like the idea of deliberately lying to someone, especially if I meant to bring them to justice.

"Then we use that. We make sure your reputation is that if Shara Isador tells you something, it's not a lie or an exaggeration. But then you have to follow up on it. If you say you'll kill whoever tries to hurt one of your Blood, then you'll need to act on that when someone does."

His words alone were enough to trigger my anger. Nobody had better try to get to me by hurting one of my Blood. "That won't be a problem."

"Think about what Marne Ceresa knows about you. You were lost and never raised in a nest. Most queens will assume that you don't know how to deal with the finer details of court life, let alone the Triune. But you've already proven yourself more than capable by claiming a sib and deflecting House Skye's attempt to absorb you."

"If she's heard about Ra's attacks, then she'll be even more impressed," Rik added. "You're a new fledgling queen, dealing with Ra and the most powerful American queen. Marne will know you have plenty of power to spare, and either you're damned lucky to escape so far, or you actually know your stuff."

"So, what you're saying is, it's too late to play stupid."

Daire huffed out a laugh. "Which would be a lie anyway, and Shara Isador doesn't lie. If you go into this meeting with Marne pretending to be stupid and unskilled or weak, then she'll know you're playing her for a fool. The queen who broke Keisha Skye's geas and claimed House Zaniyah as an ally cannot be clueless."

Guillaume and Nevarre climbed down onto the ledge beside Daire, though neither sat down. "All clear, alpha," Nevarre said. "I didn't see anything for miles in any direction."

"Good. How are the twins fitting in?"

Guillaume shrugged. "Fine, though they're a bit standoffish. They have each other, so they don't need camaraderie with us."

I concentrated on their bonds and found them walking the edge of my nest with Xin. He was his ghostly wolf and Itztli was a huge black dog, but Tlacel walked with them like a man taking his pack on a walk. They weren't talking like friends, but they were comfortable together. My silent wolf often ran alone, so I was pleased that he had company, and his silence made him a welcome partner for the twins.

I turned toward Guillaume, propping my arms on the ledge, and he immediately squatted down. "How many queens have you known?"

"In the biblical sense, or received introductions?"

I arched a brow at him. "Both, I guess, but I don't want the details. You know I'm a jealous queen."

"Many queens, but they're all dead now, thanks to Desideria. She ruled as the highest Aima queen for centuries. The other two Triune queens are Marne Ceresa and Jeanne Dauphine. I personally met Marne Ceresa three or four hundred years ago but would not say I know her at all. I've certainly never *known* her."

He waggled his eyebrows, making me snicker. "I've never heard anyone mention Jeanne."

"Most queens refer to her as the Dauphine. She's one of the oldest queens, and certainly powerful, both in our courts and the world's. Her less powerful line founded the ruling family of France centuries ago, though her Aima court became more and more secretive as the French monarchy grew in prominence. She was rumored to be a close friend of Desideria's when they were young queens, but they became bitter enemies once they both gained seats on the Triune. As Desideria's reputation grew, the Dauphine withdrew, though she still holds a Triune seat."

"What's the point of holding a Triune seat if she's not actively doing anything for Aima queens?"

"Power. She holds great power, so much that no one can unseat her, even if she chooses not to interact with any other court. However, I wouldn't make the mistake of thinking she's not actively doing anything. She absolutely does still act to influence events to her wishes, but from a distance so great that by the time the deed is done, no one realizes it was a whisper from the Dauphine that started it."

"Influence, too," Nevarre added, plopping down beside Daire. "Even if she hasn't been seen for hundreds of years, every queen still knows of her. A whisper from the Dauphine is enough for even Marne Ceresa to pause and consider whether she wishes to continue her course or not."

"Did you ever meet the Dauphine?" I asked Guillaume.

He shook his head. "No one from Desideria's court would have been allowed anywhere near the Dauphine. Especially me."

"Where's her court, her nest?"

He shrugged. "No one knows."

My eyes widened. "Wow, really? From her name, I would have expected somewhere in France."

"Rosalind Valois is descended from the Dauphine and does claim Paris as her home. But she's nowhere near as powerful as the Dauphine."

All these names were starting to blur in my head. "Rosalind is Keisha Skye's sib and lover?"

"Yes. They both covet Desideria's Triune seat and have been jockeying back and forth for decades. They finally allied, hoping that would put one of them on the Triune, but it still wasn't enough."

"Who determines which queen will take that seat? Is it a vote from the Dauphine and Marne?"

"If only," Nevarre snorted. "Though getting even those two to agree on anything would be a feat indeed. The Triune decides."

"But they are the Triune."

"Ah, I see your confusion," Guillaume said. "Sometimes I forget that you weren't raised among us, my queen. Forgive me for this minor history lesson, but I think it will help. The Triune was originally three courts of three queens each. A Triune of Triunes, a perfect number. Over thousands of years, we lost one court entirely, and the other two courts diverged and sided more against each other. Skolos is typically ruled by queens with darker gifts, and the other court simply became known as *the* Triune, though even the dark queens are still part of the original Triune that Gaia founded. Each of the original three courts had a relic from the Mother that symbolized their power and their connection to Gaia. We often call those relics the Triunes too, since there were three of them, and they represent the true power of Aima courts. As a queen calls her Blood, so each Triune calls its queens to take a ruling seat."

Rik grunted softly. "That's way more than I ever knew, and I grew up in a nest, though House Hyrrokkin has always been isolated and remote."

"You and Daire are still babes," Guillaume said. "And Keisha Skye, for all her efforts at gaining a seat on the Triune, has never fully understood what that means exactly, nor how it's achieved. Your home queens did you no favors by fostering you with House Skye. A Triune seat is not something to be won. It's a blessing from the Goddess, a great blessing. But you know what they say about great blessings."

"They can also be a curse," Daire said.

The more they told me, the less I wanted any part of it, and I'd already dreaded having any dealings with Marne Ceresa. "The one court that was lost—what happened to it? Did the other Triune queens destroy them?"

"It was lost before my time, so even I'm not clear of the details, but it's my understanding that they lost their relic. Either it was stolen or destroyed, and their court was broken. As a result, the remaining Triune and Skolos relics were hidden away by their queens to protect them. Since Desideria died, the Triune relic hasn't called forth a queen for the third seat."

"Does Marne have the Triune relic?"

"It's possible, but I would suggest it more likely that the Dauphine has it, and that's why she disappeared entirely. Desideria certainly didn't have it."

The wheels started turning in my head, slowly, like they were coated in molasses, but definitely moving. I stared at a huge map draped in a cloak of fog, that was slowly starting to thin enough that I could make out the shadow of trees and hollows between mountains. "Marne is a Triune queen. She understands how she was called to the take her seat. Yet she strings Keisha Skye along like it's something she can personally guarantee her."

"Ding, ding, ding," Daire said, nodding. "That's Marne's game. That's her angle. She plays other queens against each other, while maneuvering them on the board in a way that hopefully aligns them on her side, rather than the Dauphine's."

"Or Skolos's," Nevarre added. "When they split from the Triune, they fell off most queens' radar as insignificant."

Leviathan plummeted down from the sky, shifting into Mehen at the perfect moment to land on his feet and walk the last few steps to the new grotto. "Which is a mistake. The Gorgons and Krakes have always been the stuff of nightmares. I should know."

"What's *my* angle? I don't want her to read me like a book."

"That's not the right question to ask," Daire replied. "She's going to read you like a book. It's what we do. The question is, what book do you *want* her to read? Deep down, what do you really want? Ignoring all the politics and games."

Looking at them, my throat tightened. "This."

Rik took my hand and kissed my knuckles. "A home. A family. Blood that you love, and who love you in return, so much that we'd gladly do anything you asked."

"Yes." The word was harsher than I intended, but only because I fought back the surge of fearful tears. I resisted the urge to touch the ruby snake around my neck. "Plus, safety for Zaniyah."

"It's more than that." Mehen shook his head. "You don't give a fuck about the Zaniyah clan in general." He slipped into the pool with us, submerging completely despite the heat. He came up slinging water like a dog. "Why them, and not Keisha Skye?"

"Because Keisha tried to hurt me already."

He shrugged. "Mayte hurt you by not telling you about the geas."

"But—" I wanted to say that was different, but even I knew that didn't make sense. Mayte had hurt me. She'd lied to me. She'd hidden everything until I dragged the truth out of her.

Yet I still gave her my blood, made her daughter my heir, and took her to my bed.

"Let me say it another way," Guillaume said, drawing my attention back to him. He danced one of his blades across his fingers, twirling it like a pencil. "Any other queen powerful enough to free Leviathan would have put him down like the rabid monster he is and saved herself the trouble of breaking him to her Blood. But not Shara fucking Isador."

Mehen swam around me, a dark, lithe shape in the water, flashing emerald scales. "Why did you save me, Shara?"

"I dreamed you."

He swept back around, making me jerk my head around to keep sight of him. "So? Nightmares don't mean a motherfucking thing. I had nightmares for centuries."

I was starting to get irritated. Not at them, exactly, but at my failure to figure out what they were trying to tell me. "I wanted you, okay? So I took you."

He swept toward me in a rush of water and pushed me back against the boulder, lifting me up out of the water so we were eye to eye. "You wanted *me*, when I would sooner tear you limb from limb and gnaw marrow from your bones than suffer Triune politics and queen commands."

I gripped his nape and squeezed hard enough that his upper lip curled in a snarl. "Yes, I did."

"You took *me*."

"Yeah."

"Shara fucking Isador doesn't lie, and she *takes* what she wants. She takes what she wants because she wants to fuck it, claim it as hers, and bend it to her will for all time. Even Leviathan, king of the depths."

"Even the headless knight," Guillaume whispered. "Long-time hated and feared executioner for Desideria Modron, with the blood of a thousand Aima on his hands."

"Even Morrigan's broken Shadow, the son whose family lost the grove and was rejected by his own queen for that failure," Nevarre whispered. "Who died, helpless to save even a minor druid witch who'd taken him in when no one else would."

Ezra crashed through the underbrush in his grizzly form. *:Even a grumpy bear that everyone hates because he can't be fucking bothered to mind his tongue for anybody or anything. Except you, my queen.:*

Xin and the twins were right behind him. My silent wolf —who was an invisible killer. Tlacel, my beautiful, graceful feathered serpent who'd given himself massive internal injuries to save me and Xochitl.

My tortured black dog, Itztli. Though I'd healed him after sacrificing him on Zaniyah's new heart tree, he still bore a long brutal scar on his chest to remind us both of what I'd done to him. He didn't have to say anything. All he had to do was stand there with his fingers lightly touching the obsidian blade on his hip, with a brutal scar over his heart.

"Okay," I whispered, nodding. "I get what you're saying. I take what I want. Even Blood other queens would use as weapons, or Blood other queens would kill outright, or simply reject because they're too dangerous."

"If you use that as your angle…" Daire gave an artful toss of his head that drew my attention to his hair sliding over his shoulders and down to his waist. "What's your perceived weakness?"

I looked back at Mehen and grinned. "I take Blood because I want to fuck them. So I probably fuck. A lot. And it gets messy, bloody, and yeah, dangerous."

He leaned in and inhaled deeply, his mouth on my throat. "You're obsessed with fucking monsters, aren't you, my queen?"

I laughed and looped one arm around his neck and the other around Rik, who was never far from my side. "That'll be an easy thing to sell to Marne Ceresa. Because it's true."

Mehen sank his fangs in my throat, making me arch against him. *:Because Shara fucking Isador never lies.:*

17

SHARA

Daire was right. Once I knew how I wanted Marne to perceive me, setting up for our first face-to-face via mirror magic was easy.

I let Rik pick out a sexy negligee and a long, elegant black silk robe. I deliberately tied the belt loosely, letting the robe gape open and flow with my movements. The hint of lace beneath the robe was provocative without revealing anything. We left the bed rumpled with blood-stained sheets and all.

So much blood.

A clear indication of how, and how much, I fed. How much power I wielded as a result. Without making a single demonstration or statement.

As I'd done during the final Zaniyah procession, I used

Rik as my seat and support and leaned back against his chest, cradled by his massive thighs. Daire shifted into his warcat and laid across my thighs, his head in my lap. His purr was a thunderous roar. I wasn't sure how much she'd see through the mirror—if she truly had to see our reflection in the glass, or if her power extended to the rest of the room. To be safe, I sent everyone out of the immediate vicinity except for Gina, Guillaume, and Mehen, my two oldest Blood who knew Triune politics inside and out.

Guillaume wore black jeans and a simple white long-sleeved shirt. Anyone who knew him would know that he wore a dozen blades beneath his clothes.

:Fifteen today, my queen.:

Someday, I was going to have to strip him slowly and count every single blade.

:It will be my great pleasure, my queen.:

My dragon lay on the floor around the bed, so big that he provided a perfect back rest for Rik. For now, Leviathan kept his head low. Hopefully he'd be mostly hidden and out of sight—until I wanted her to see him.

Tlacel knelt on the bed before me, holding the mirror so I could see my face reflected on its surface, within easy reach. "Ready, my queen?"

I looked over at Gina, poised with pen and paper. "I'm ready. I'll write down every word that she says."

I took a deep, centering breath and cleared my mind. "Let's do this." I punctured the tip of my index finger on my fang, waited for the blood well up, and pressed my fingertip to my reflection.

My image blurred and stretched like I was looking at myself on a funhouse mirror. Then it went gray and fuzzy, smoky like Tepeyollotl had said. I didn't hear anything like a chime, or even a warning when the great queen herself attended me.

One minute, the surface was fogged over like I'd taken a really hot shower, and the next, I was looking at a very striking woman's face. Platinum blonde hair was artfully piled on her head in a glorious up-do. Her face was classically beautiful with high cheekbones, a small, pert nose, gorgeous blue eyes, and perfect skin that gleamed like she dusted herself with crushed pearls and diamond dust. She might be over a thousand years old, but she looked like an incredibly rich, beautiful woman, thirty or forty years old.

:Age before beauty,: Guillaume whispered in my head. :Allow her to speak first.:

"Shara, I'm so pleased to meet you at last."

Her tone said she was truly delighted to meet me—light and eager and warm. But her eyes remained untouched, cold, assessing, and all-seeing. Her pupils weren't slitted, but she reminded me of my cobra.

:She didn't use your House name. So match her casualness. Don't give her respect if she doesn't give you any.:

"Marne, I presume? Thank you for your beautiful gift."

She inclined her head slightly, enough to be barely polite. "Are you settling into your new home?"

I didn't need Guillaume to tell me that was a deliberate message that she knew where I lived and that I had established a new nest. I kept my voice light, as if her snooping didn't bother me. "Oh, yes. We're doing some wonderful renovations. I can't wait until the whole manor house has been completed."

"I hear you have Timothy Winston to attend to your household affairs." Her voice was a smug, purring know-it-all, and I hated it. "Gaining his services was quite the coup."

:*Sorry, I don't know much about him prior to him coming to your service,*: Guillaume said. :*You'll have to ask Gina.*:

Since I didn't know Winston's backstory, I let myself appear ignorant, because I was. "Really? I didn't realize his services were in such demand, though I completely agree that he's a fabulous addition to my staff. We're keeping him quite busy, I'm afraid."

Marne smiled. "We? How many Blood have you managed to call?"

She said "managed" with a polite lilt that made my hackles rise, implying whatever number I said would be sneered at. I refused to be baited. "Nine."

Her eyes flared, but it didn't seem genuine. If she knew exactly when to deliver the package to the house, then she would have seen how many Blood were with me at the airport. Her surprise had to be that I came right out and told her without trying to cover it up. "So many? Already? My, you've been a busy girl."

"Not as many as you, Your Majesty." For the first time I acknowledged her power and her position of authority. "You have, what, a hundred Blood? That's what I was told, at least."

"Oh? By whom?"

"Guillaume de Payne." I said his name as if I had no idea who he'd been before he came to me. As if I didn't know she'd ordered that no queen feed him, so he'd be forced to come to her.

She laughed softly. "That old hell horse is still alive? Miracles do happen."

I felt Guillaume's rage in our bond, but he remained silent and out of sight.

I smiled. "Yes, they do. But you already know that, because I'm sure you saw footage of the Christmas Eve Miracle in Venezuela."

She lifted one shoulder in an elegant shrug. "So they say. It was probably faked footage anyway."

I made my eyes wider and kept my voice light and almost childlike. "Oh? That's odd. Because I have Leviathan right here."

Her eyes tightened slightly. "You have Leviathan, king of the depths? In your Blood?"

Leviathan lifted his head, curled his long, sinuous neck around Rik, and put his muzzle against my thigh. He let out a rumbling hiss with a plume of smoke, his eyes blazing with hatred and malice.

Staring at him, her face smoothed to a blank, unmoving mask, without even a single wrinkle about her eyes. Such a perfect visage told me more than anything that she was concealing her true reaction. She didn't have a tell, other than a perfectly blank response.

:*Tell her that Clarissant Avalon tasted delightful,*: Leviathan said in my mind. :*One of her closest cronies, who had designs on bringing me to heel and making me her slave. I made her last a long time while I tried to break free of my prison.:*

:Did you actually eat her?:

:Damn straight. She wasn't strong enough to free me. None of them were.:

I'd known other queens had tried to free him and failed, but the reality of how close I'd come to dying… I made myself smile slightly at the other queen as I stroked his spiny head. "I'm afraid my king was very destructive before I managed to tame him. He says that he ate Clarissant Avalon and enjoyed her very much."

Marne met my gaze and the tiniest glimmer of emotion flickered in her blue eyes, though it was gone before I could be sure what it meant. "A headless knight who's killed more Blood and queens than any other living Aima. A murdering dragon. A warcat. Whatever your alpha is. Given his Hyrrokkin heritage, I'm guessing some kind of giant. You have a penchant for monsters, don't you, dear?"

She meant to insult me, but I smiled widely and nodded. "Yes, I do. I can't seem to help myself. They're so…" I let my eyelashes flutter down over my eyes and I bit my lip enough to hint at the size of my fangs. "Sexy."

"Then you and Keisha Skye may get along much better than I anticipated."

:Give her some resting bitch face,: Rik suggested. *:She insulted you. Greatly. There is no comparison between you and Skye.:*

I met Marne's gaze and leaned forward slightly, letting her see the way my face hardened. The promise in my eyes. "The thought of what she would have done to my alpha if he hadn't come to me first makes me want to order Leviathan to crunch on every single bone in her body, one by one, while she screams—exactly as she's tortured alphas for years."

"Decades." Marne smiled, one delicate brow arching in a subtle reply that said, *"as if anyone cares."* "What's the difference between you and her again?"

"I gleefully fuck my monsters. I don't torture and kill them. What I'm going to do to Keisha Skye is called retribution. Here's my fair warning to you and the Triune: I fully intend to exact justice on Keisha Skye."

Marne let her head fall back on a trill of laughter. "You think that you, a half-human child of an outcast queen, is going to take on the most powerful queen in the Americas and deliver retribution?"

Stroking Daire's fur, I waited for her laughter to subside. He rumbled louder and rolled over slightly, his tail tapping back and forth along my legs. Not to be outdone, Leviathan slithered closer. He hooked his front leg over my thigh and tugged on me, trying to open my thighs wider.

Despite his care, his claws pierced my skin. Blood trickled down my thigh, which Daire was all too happy to lap up, even though the dragon snarled at him.

Marne quieted as she took in our tableau. A dragon and a warcat fighting over my blood, which I let them have without a care. When she met my gaze again, I smiled, letting the rising heat shine in my eyes as my Blood tasted me. "What makes you think my father was human? Or that my mother was Selena Isador?"

:*Now,*: I told Daire. :*Wipe the mirror clean.*:

He whipped around and lunged at the mirror, and yeah, the way she jumped back, even though he couldn't touch her, amused me to no end. With a quick swipe of his tongue, my blood was wiped from the mirror and the clouded surface cleared to reveal my face.

"Well, fuck," Guillaume said mildly, his blue eyes dancing with amusement. "You just kicked the lantern over in a barn full of last year's hay."

Closing my eyes, I lounged back in Rik's arms and opened my thighs. :*Shift back first,*: I told the guys. "That was my plan. Let's see if it works."

18

RIK

At long last, we were able to give our queen the restorative rest that she needed so badly. As the days passed, we kept everything quiet, easy, and as low-key as possible. She slept for hours at a time, only to wake up, enjoy a good fuck and a deep feeding with whoever was in her bed, and go right back to sleep while Mehen droned on and on in French. We brought every imaginable food to her so she could feast without even getting up. As when we were in Kansas City, we had picnics in her massive bed, only instead of takeout pizzas, we devoured aged cheeses, delicate fruits from all over the world, the finest wines, fresh bread, antipasto platters, muffins, cakes, bagels...

Nevarre even made her Scottish scones with clotted

cream, which she loved so much her eyes rolled back in head and she came. Though Daire was busy between her thighs at the same time.

When she finally caught up on her sleep and restored her reserves, we switched to watching movies. Winston had a stadium-sized television screen installed in the bedroom, and instead of movie-theater seating, she lounged on us. The bed finally arrived, and it was even bigger than the two kings pushed together. Bonus—it didn't slide apart when we got too energetic.

Most importantly, we made her laugh, and we never once talked politics. She didn't even ask to see the legacy, as if she wanted no part of new powers. Yet.

Marne's mirror never chimed, or if it did, we didn't hear it, since Shara had buried it in both salt and ground coffee. She'd also surrounded it by an extra salt circle to be safe. Mayte's bond remained quiet for the most part as she hunted for a new consiliarius. Ra didn't attack us. Keisha Skye was a distant memory.

I held Shara's bond in the forefront of my mind constantly. I was in her mind and body and spirit. While she definitely healed and restored her energy, she was preparing, both mentally and spiritually, for war.

My queen was planning something, but it was so deeply buried and convoluted that even I didn't fully understand what she had put in motion. We sat on planet Earth whirling at thousands of feet per second, but couldn't feel a fucking thing.

Until we screeched to a crashing halt with a few simple

words.

"I would like to go to New York City."

Without batting an eye, Gina pulled out her phone. "When, my queen?"

"Next week. Could we go to Broadway? I've always wanted to see a live musical or play. Anything is fine."

"If you wait until February, you could also go to New York Fashion Week. That would be a fantastic way for you to meet some designers…"

"No. I need to go next week. Any day after Sunday should be fine."

Gina slowly lowered the phone, realization dawning on her face.

Sunday…? I tried to do calendar math in my head, but my skull felt like it'd been stuffed with cotton.

"Holy fucking shit," Daire breathed, his eyes flying wide.

"What?" Mehen retorted.

I could only stare and hope my tongue wasn't lolling like a dog's. My brain shut off out of necessity. All the blood in my body had raced south. Already, I felt the surge of hormones in answer to the promise of her need for me. My nostrils flared, seeking her scent, eager to detect the slightest change in her body temperature or readiness.

"Her period," Daire choked out. "She'll be breeding."

Eight Bloods' heads swung my direction.

"You're shitting me," Mehen replied. "Next week? And you're going to travel into Skye's territory, rather than holing up in your nest to fuck your alpha's brains out?"

She huffed out a soft laugh. "Don't I always fuck *all* your brains out? I don't need to stay in my nest to do so, either. But yes, next week I should start bleeding, and I must be in New York City at the height of my period."

Gina got up and hurried out. "I'll be right back. Let me get my tablet. It'll be easier to plan on."

I cleared my throat so roughly that it felt like I'd swallowed razor blades. Yet I could only manage a garbled, "Why?"

"The power, surely," Guillaume said with a grimace. "Though I'd rather you not expose yourself when you're vulnerable like that. Rik won't be at his best."

"No," she whispered, shaking her head. "Rik will be at his absolute best. He'll be obsessed with me. Wholly focused on me and pumped with alpha power. I will be stronger, but that's not why I'm waiting to challenge Keisha Skye until next week."

"It's a message," Daire said.

Even though she only wore one of my old soft cotton T-shirts and a pair of panties, she tipped her head up, her shoulders back and proud, and I could see the fucking crown on her head. "Yes. I can breed. I don't need to resort to dark magic or torture to try and have a child. I care so little about having an heir that I'm not even staying home in my nest, but traveling to my enemy's territory for some R&R."

Gina came back in and sat down beside the bed. Typing rapidly, she was quiet for a few moments and then looked up at Shara. Her eyes flashed, her mouth a hard line of determination. If our queen was going into battle, so was she. "I've got my immediate staff online and ready to implement your plans immediately."

"Thank you. Can they hear me?"

Gina nodded and turned the tablet around to show Marissa and Angela pressed closely to the camera, waiting for their orders.

"We're going to New York City because I want to see a musical or play. *Hamilton* would be great, but if we can't get tickets…"

Angela looked away, typing rapidly. "I can get them. No problem. How many?"

"Fourteen."

"Done. Best in the house."

Gina whistled softly, and the other woman stared at her with her mouth hanging open, shocked that she'd gotten *Hamilton* tickets so quickly. Angela chuckled at their reactions. "I have a friend who owed me. Big time."

"I would say so," Gina drawled, shaking her head.

"Great. We're going to see *Hamilton,* and as a courtesy, we'll notify Keisha Skye, right?"

Gina nodded. "Yes. Typically, you would notify any queen in the home region if you wished to visit."

"This is going to sound like a really weird and unconnected question, but what's Winston's story? Marne Ceresa said it was quite a coup that I'd managed to get him to come work for me."

"Winston worked for your mother…" Gina paused, her face going blank.

Which told me she meant Shara's real mother. The

woman who'd raised her had been her aunt, but no living Aima could say Shara's mother's name aloud.

"Yes," Shara said gently, prodding her to continue. "He worked for my mother."

"In London, before you were born. We were all there. Winston could work for the Queen of England if he wanted. That's how good his pedigree is. Instead, he chose to stay with House Isador, even when Selena left the nest. Other queens tried to hire him away from Isador, since there wasn't any queen left, but he refused. You'd have to ask him why yourself, but I can only assume that he had decided to work for Isador, or no one."

"Was Keisha one of the queens who tried to hire him?"

"Every queen tried to hire him, so yes, she did. He refused, as politely as he refused Marne Ceresa."

Shara smiled. "I knew I loved that man, for many reasons, but this one takes the cake. Would he mind making a call to Keisha Skye's consiliarius for us?"

Gina blinked rapidly. "He would do anything for you. But why..."

Shara smiled and it made the hairs prickle at the base of my neck. "She sent her lowest Blood to try and convince me to join her nest. She doesn't know that I love Winston dearly, so I'm asking my butler to tell the queen of New York City that I intend to visit her town. *After* he refused to work for her."

The last Templar knight smiled broadly. "That'll fucking piss her off."

Shara nodded. "That's the general idea."

SHARA

The plan was starting to come together. It was strange, because I didn't know *exactly* what I needed to do. It just was there, in my head, as if it was waiting for me to tap it. I had a feeling the goddesses had been busy planting seeds in my head while I'd been sleeping and making love with my Blood.

It'd been a delightful few weeks, but I couldn't enjoy many more… until I dealt with Keisha Skye once and for all. Every day that I delayed in bringing her to justice was another day that a Blood suffered in her ruthless obsession to have another child.

Marne Ceresa hovered on the edge of my awareness, too. I'd have to come to some kind of deal with her eventually, but my war wasn't with her. It was with Keisha, and then Ra. But I'd take the war to Rome if she wanted to fuck with me or my Blood.

Leaning back against Rik, I met each of my Blood's gazes, and then focused on Gina, who'd pulled a chair up to the edge of the mattress.

"I need to know the implications of killing a queen. What happens to her Blood, nest, and sibs? Are there any repercussions from the Triune? Anything else along those lines that I haven't thought of yet."

"You can do whatever you want as queen, though there are always repercussions." Gina leaned forward and took my hand in hers. "For all her faults, Keisha has a giant network of people who depend on her for their livelihood. Losing their queen will be a huge blow, both economically and socially. She's a prominent member of society, both Triune and human. No offense, my queen, but you're an unknown. They know nothing about you or how you'll handle their businesses, problems, and families. Some of them may not have had much of a choice in the queen they serve."

"People like me, Daire, and Ezra," Rik said, stroking his big palms up and down my arms. "People sent by their queens, trapped by familial loyalty and treaties who would love to escape her, but can't. They'll be thrilled to be free of her, but they need to know what to do. Where to go."

"If you get all of her sibs to swear to you…" Guillaume knelt beside the bed and held out his scarred hands to me. I slipped one hand into his but held onto Gina, too. With Rik stroking me, and them holding my hands, I felt grounded, steady, and focused. "You will rule America. You will be *the* American queen."

"That's not—"

"I know," Guillaume broke in. "That's not why you're doing this. But maybe this is why your goddess set you on this path."

"Nature abhors a vacuum," Gina added. "Killing a major queen of America's largest city will create a massive vacuum. We can't leave those loose ends dangling without a plan, or you may find someone even worse than Keisha Skye stepping in. Chaos would be worse than Keisha's rule."

Chaos. Mother had said I was to be controlled chaos in the world. Isis wanted me to shake things up—but remain in control too. Which to me, meant I had to have a plan.

I nodded, even though my stomach tightened with dread. Taking House Zaniyah as sibs had been one thing. Taking a house the size of Skye… It was terrifying and overwhelming. "How many people are we talking?"

"We haven't been in her court for over a year," Daire replied. "But I'm guessing she has at least a thousand sibs now. She's been actively increasing her base for a very long time."

Xin nodded. "She probably gained a hundred sibs when my queen left San Francisco."

"That's only sibs," Gina added. "Like you, she has many humans and weaker Aima scattered all across the globe who work for her house in some way. She will have properties in all the major cities. She will have staff and offices that need to know who to report to and how. Plus, all her finances will need to be accounted for."

My head pounded. Rik slid his hands up to knead my shoulders, easing the tension straining up my neck. "I don't care about her money. I have more than I could possibly spend now."

"Yet it will be yours. If you take the queen, you take her house. If you take her house, you take her legacy."

"Legacy wealth—or legacy power?"

"Both, if her goddess finds you worthy."

Rik made a low rumble like distant thunder. "Which She will, without question."

"Who's Keisha's goddess again?"

"Scathach," Rik replied. "She's best known from the

Ulster Cycle for training Cu Chulainn. She had a training facility on the Isle of Skye."

"Keisha's a warrior?"

Daire huffed out a laugh. "Not at all. She loves to *watch* fights, the bloodier the better."

"Like duels? Or what?"

He nodded. "Mostly hand-to-hand combat. She even has a cage built in her nest like the Ultimate Fighting Championships."

"I need to know as much as possible about her nest too. How many Blood does she have? What happens to them when I kill Keisha?"

"What do you want to happen to them?" Daire asked. "We know you're not going to claim them all as yours, if any, so we'll probably have to kill them."

At first, I thought he was being cheeky, but for once, my warcat was actually serious. "I'm not going to kill them all. I mean, if they fight us, and someone gets killed as a result, that's one thing. But execution? Just because they served Skye? I won't do it."

"Blood need a queen, or they'll turn," Rik said. "Remember Greyson? Even when a new queen is found quickly, the bond doesn't always take. Sometimes it's kinder to kill them all cleanly, and some may very well ask for death."

My stomach quivered. I'd been fully prepared to kill Keisha, but I hadn't realized I might have to have her Blood killed too. It seemed so wasteful and horrible. If I died…

"We would all be dead too." Boulders crashed in Rik's

voice. "We would not allow you to die and still live ourselves."

"But—"

"No, Shara. There is no other option. In fact, I'll make the formal request. Guillaume, if the worst happens and our queen falls, yet I still live, I order you to kill me."

"On my honor, I will do as you ask, alpha."

"And me," the rest of my Blood said one by one. Even Mehen. Though he scowled at me. "You'd best not fucking die, my queen."

I swallowed the lump trying to choke me. "I don't intend to anytime soon. How soon after Keisha's gone will I have to find her Blood a new queen?"

"It varies greatly," Guillaume replied. "Some, like me, have gone for decades or even a century and more. Others can't make it a week. It depends on the Blood's strength of will, how strong the old bond was, and how strong the future queen's call is. Your call was so strong that I would have crossed oceans of time to find you."

"She had twenty-six Blood when we left," Rik said. "Twenty were female, six male. Ezra, what was the count when you left?"

"Wes was killed in the ring; the male alpha, Conall, was barely alive; and you know how Kendall ended."

"That leaves twenty-two, assuming the alpha is beyond your healing," Rik said. "If you'd even want or be able to heal him after what Keisha does to them."

His tone didn't change, but I felt his tension straining against my back. I still hadn't asked him exactly he'd seen in

Skye's court. How did Keisha torture the alphas? Did I need to know in order to defeat her? I didn't see how, and it would only upset him to drag out those old nightmares.

So, I changed the subject. "Should I assume that she knows how many Blood I have, and who they are?"

Gina grimaced and nodded. "I'm afraid so. Bianca betrayed us to Ra. We have to assume that she passed along other information, too, and she had full access to our guest list before we ever arrived. If Ra knows something that might hurt you, we have to assume he'd share that information with the other queens. He wants to sow chaos and discord among the Aima courts. If he can weaken you without striking you himself, he will."

"She'll know that I have Blood who are famous for killing other queens and alphas."

"Which means if we do a formal procession, she would pair Xin and Guillaume with her best killers," Rik said. "If she lets them inside at all. Honestly, she'll probably refuse to let them inside her nest."

I blew out a sigh. "That's what I'd do if I were in her shoes."

Guillaume didn't move a muscle, but in our bond, I felt his hell horse pawing the ground and snorting flames. Blistering cold rolled from Xin, dropping the temperature around him enough that Nevarre shivered and rubbed his arms.

"So Mehen will probably be refused entrance too."

"Fucking hell." He threw himself down on the bed and

glared up at the ceiling with disgust. "I was looking forward to spreading mayhem in New York City."

"What about you, Ezra? Do you think she'll let you back inside?"

"Definitely, because she'll want to make sure I'm punished. Same with Rik and Daire. If she somehow manages to outsmart you, we'll be made examples of."

Even my rough and tough grizzly bear looked queasy.

Horrible images flickered through Rik's head in rapid succession. A man, screaming, as he was slowly disemboweled. Castrated. Fingers removed. Hands. Feet.

I swayed. My face felt too tight, like the skin across my cheekbones had suddenly dried and shriveled up. Breathing hard, I pushed those images out of my head.

I pressed back against him and he wrapped me tighter in his arms.

:Sorry,: he whispered in our bond. :I would rather spare you the gory details.:

"How will you kill her, if you don't have Guillaume or me to call upon?" Xin asked.

The trees whispered in my head. Blood. Fire. Blood. Fire.

My best weapons.

19

SHARA

Winston flew to New York City with us, so he could meet the staff at the house and ensure their service was up to his level of expectations. Now, more than ever, I was aware of what immense wealth could do. The Isador property we arrived at had once been a small, but posh, Park Avenue hotel situated on the edge of Central Park.

Even after extensive renovations, the gorgeous marble floors, high ceilings, and gold-leaved plaster friezes spoke of old-world wealth. A blonde woman dressed in a very elegant black pant suit whispered quietly with Winston for several moments, and then stepped closer to me.

She dropped into a curtsey. "Your Majesty, welcome to your New York City home."

"Thank you." I held my hand out, intending to give her a polite shake, but she took my hand and bent even lower, pressing my fingers to her forehead.

"It's such an honor to meet you, Your Majesty. When Winston called to let me know to prepare the house, I wept with joy that our Isador queen was coming to town."

I imagined it must have been a fairly rare occurrence for any queen to come to New York City with Keisha Skye's centuries of rule. "What's your name?"

"Magnum, Your Majesty. For the duration of your stay, we'll be at full staff. All of your clothing orders have been carefully unpacked and are hanging in the master bedroom for your approval."

The nicest thing about being rich—I could shop without ever stepping foot into a store. Gina had placed a few phone calls, and Alice Wong, the designer I'd met in Dallas, Texas, had shipped several new gowns ahead. With our measurements in hand, Gina had also called several other designers and had probably emptied racks in dozens of stores to make sure I had a wide selection of clothes to choose from, both for myself and my Blood.

All for a few days' stay so I could catch a Broadway play.

And kill a vampire queen.

We stepped onto an old-fashioned elevator with brass-plated doors and buttons. Rik had already sent three of my Blood up to scout ahead, and now he stepped in close to me, bumping me with his body. He slid a hand around my waist, spreading his fingers out to cover as much of my abdomen as possible. He dipped his head and rubbed his nose in the hollow behind my ear.

Yeah, my period had started yesterday and was going full force today. My alpha couldn't keep his hands off me.

Itztli and Tlacel stood between me and the new woman. Neither of them looked at me, but I could feel the tension simmering in their bodies. They were fully aware of me and my need.

Mehen's green eyes tracked my every movement, narrowed with anticipation. If Rik gave him an inch, he'd have me flattened against the wall of the elevator this very moment, audience be damned.

We stepped off the elevator into a marbled foyer, which opened up to a large room with walls made almost entirely of windows, giving spectacular views of Central Park on one side, and the impressive skyline on the other.

I couldn't help but stare at one particular building only a few blocks away. Keisha Skye's nest was in the largest residential tower in Manhattan. One-bedroom suites had easily sold for a million dollars before she bought the building twenty-some years ago. There were over one hundred units in the building, many of them two and three bedrooms. I couldn't even guess enough zeros for the sum she must have paid for the entire building. Let alone the amount of money she must have put into renovations to combine apartments and blow out walls. Rik said the entire top floor had been renovated to combine four penthouses into one, providing her with jaw-dropping views.

Most of the other floors remained apartments, that she'd been filling with sibs.

So many vampires living right here in the heart of Manhattan.

We'd barely stepped off the elevator, when one of the other staff whispered to Magnum, and then came to me with a monogrammed envelope bearing a swirling S.

"Your Majesty." She bowed even lower than Magnum had and held out the card. "This arrived moments ago for you by courier."

I smiled wryly. "Just like Marne. They want me to know they're watching me."

This envelope didn't bear a waxed seal. I pulled out the single sheet of thick paper and read it aloud.

"Shara Isador, I formally call upon Triune law and demand recompense for the Blood you've stolen from House Skye. You may repay this debt in person at House Skye's court at your earliest convenience. The Blood known as Leviathan, Wu Tien Xin, and Guillaume de Payne will not be granted access to House Skye. In addition, the presence of Alrik, Daire, and Ezra Skye will be required to gain access to House Skye. I, Keisha Skye, demand satisfaction."

"Only six Blood." Daire snorted with disgust. "I fucking hate being called Skye again."

"That's more than I expected her to let me take in." I sighed, looking around at my men, all of them furious, glaring, or in Itztli's and Guillaume's cases, testing the sharpness of their blades. "Gina, what Triune law is she referring to?"

My consiliarius was already on the phone with her staff, but she lowered the phone to say, "Blood for Blood, or at least an equal amount of blood they carry."

"What does that mean?"

"It's a stretch, because they weren't her Blood when they left. But she's claiming their value as Blood from her house. She's probably also going to claim value for Kendall, since he was Blood, and we did kill him, though you have not gained any benefit from the Skye blood he carried."

"So, she's wanting the equal amount of my blood to buy theirs?"

"In effect, yes. It's meant to be a law that specifies an exchange of Blood between queens to solidify an alliance. She'd intended to give you Kendall. Under this law, she could have demanded an equal Blood from yours in exchange. If this case went to a Triune queen, she'd have to weigh the amount of Skye blood that each of your three Blood now bear, which you would repay in kind, if you weren't willing to uphold the Blood exchange."

"You're not fucking giving her your blood," Rik retorted, dragging me closer to him. "Not for me. Not for any of us."

"With any other queen, it could be handled reasonably," Gina said, shaking her head. "Any queen can call her blood out of anyone she wishes and leave them without a trace of her power. We call it Cleansing, and it's especially important for ailing queens to do before they die, so their Blood are freed before her death. However, we all know that's not what she's after. She doesn't want her blood back—she wants yours instead. Let me do a little research and study the precedents to come up with the best defense."

"Does it matter, if I intend to kill her?"

"Yes. She invoked Triune law. Killing her before this debt is resolved could draw the Triune's punishment. The last thing you want is Marne Ceresa ordering your execution because you broke Triune law and then killed the queen before she could bring the case before the High Court, even if that's not Keisha's goal at all."

I blew out a disgusted sigh. "This is all really a ploy to keep me from walking over and killing her before she can hurt anyone else. In that light, it's a very smart play."

"Indeed," Gina said grimly. "She's been playing the game since long before you were born, my queen. The whole reason she sent young Aima males out in search of lost queens was to draw them to her and trap them into becoming her sibs. She planned to demand Blood recompense when she allowed them to leave. Why don't you take a look at the gowns Alice sent while I talk to my team?"

"This way, Your Majesty." Magnum led us down a short hallway to an imposing twelve-foot-tall wooden door. Fanciful animals were carved on its surface, including dragons, gryphons, and even a phoenix rising from the flames. "I hope you will find it satisfactory."

She pushed the heavy door open, and even though I was prepared for grandeur, my jaw still dropped in awe. Most of the ceiling was a giant skylight, illuminating the entire room in soft light to frame a massive bed that was only slightly smaller than my custom bed at home. The marble floors were warm golden honey inlaid with large onyx circles. As in the other rooms, the walls were mostly glass.

Racks of clothes waited for us to examine, even more than I imagined. Daire dived in with a whoop.

Magnum walked over to another set of doors. "Your sauna, whirlpool, and master bathroom, Your Majesty."

"Thank you, Magnum. The suite is lovely."

"You're most welcome, Your Majesty. This home has been languishing for more than twenty years waiting for our lost queen to return."

I turned back to search her face. "I've only been lost five years."

Her face blanked, like everyone when they thought of my mother, but her throat worked, each word forced out like she'd swallowed something thick. "A woman. Beautiful. Dark hair, like yours. Her mocha skin glowed like she'd swallowed the moon. She owned this house and oversaw every single renovation herself. I knew her well, though I can't seem to remember her name. Do you know her?"

My eyes blurred with tears and I nodded. *Esetta Isador. My mother.* "Yes."

"She said this house was to be her daughter's sanctuary away from home, a place of safety and joy in the midst of danger and sadness." Magnum cleared her throat, her eyes as teary as mine. "She was heavily pregnant the last time she came. When she left… she was not."

"I was born here," I whispered, my eyes flying wide. "Where? Could you show me?"

"Of course." She led us back out to the elevator and a

second massive door, though this one was ebony wood carved in snakes and a large tyet, knot of Isis. "Most of this unit was absorbed into the other, except for this one room. She was the last to enter this room. When she left, she ordered that no one enter it until the lost queen returned. I have kept the door locked ever since."

She held out an antique, large key made of iron. My fingers trembled as I took it and inserted it into the lock.

"Should we wait outside for you?" Rik asked.

I shook my head. "No. You're as much a part of this as I am. Without you, I wouldn't have made it here."

Even though the door hadn't been opened in decades, the lock clicked smoothly, and I pushed the heavy door open. A single light flickered on automatically, but the room was still so dark that I could barely make out anything but black marble veined in gold and a small pool built into the floor.

Rik jerked his head, and Mehen, Guillaume, and Nevarre entered the room first, though I wasn't far behind. The room didn't have any windows, so nothing could have gotten inside. Very much like how I'd grown up, hidden from the monsters.

Magnum hovered outside the room. I gestured her inside with us. "Was she here long?"

"Many times over the years for renovations. Then usually a few days around Samhain. The last time I saw her, she arrived in late September and stayed through the first of November."

My birthday.

My heart ached so badly I couldn't breathe. "Did she leave me here? Or take me with her?"

"Another woman arrived, her sister, I believe, but she came and left in secrecy. I never spoke to her or knew her name. She stayed only one night and left with the baby. I never saw her again." Magnum cried silently, fat tears trickling down her cheeks. "I heard..." Her voice broke and she turned aside, averting her face. "Sobbing. All night, after her sister left. And the next morning she left, alone, and I never saw her again. She looked shockingly weak and pale, but she wouldn't allow me to call for help. She whispered something, and I fell asleep. When I awoke, she was gone, as well as most of my memory."

My poor mother. She had given me to her sister immediately, and then left.

To die alone.

I squeezed my eyes shut. *Oh, Mother. I'm so sorry. I wish I could have known you.*

"Shara, you need to see this." Guillaume's reverent voice drew me to him against the far wall.

From a distance, it looked like the wall had been papered, but up close, I realized it was actual hand-painted papyrus. Painted by my mother, in her own hand.

Her last words to me.

"I need more light."

"Here." Magnum hit a switch and rows of lights clicked on all around the room to illuminate all four walls, each painstakingly covered in papyrus and hieroglyphics.

"Can you read it?" Guillaume asked.

I stepped back and scanned the walls quickly, looking for where to start. The shorter wall including the door had a large pyramid with the crescent moon hanging over the top of it, so I started there. "Blood of Isis. Upon this House She builds Her future."

I moved to the next wall. This one was painted with a large volcano, with streams of lava flowing down its sides. Underneath, a man's chest and upper body rose up out of what looked like a nest of large serpents, heads flowing out along the ground in place of legs and feet. "Lo, Father of Monsters, look down from Heaven and see what we have wrought."

The third wall was one long passage. "We loose chaos upon the world. She brings blood. She brings magic. She brings justice. She walks with paws, slithers with scales, and flies on mighty wings. She cries out with flames and the dead rise to do her bidding. The grave is hers to command."

That sounded too much like my dream of Coatlicue. I swallowed hard, pushing away my fear of which loved one I would lose, and stepped to the next wall.

"What she takes, she loves, and what she loves, she keeps for all time. Blood flows from the Mother through the Great One to our Daughter of Chaos. Burn with fire. Kill with shadow. Bleed to punish those who have turned aside from the Mother. Rise, Daughter, and blot out the cruel Sun. Fly, oh dark wings. Run, oh silent feet. Bite, oh wicked fangs, and mark the souls of your dead. Walk the ways cloaked in Shadow seeing all. Rise."

Mehen grunted sourly. "Well, that's as clear as fucking mud."

This door had been locked at my birth—yet she described me so well it was scary. I did burn with fire. I did only take Blood that I loved, and once they were mine... I wanted to keep them for all time. I certainly flew on dark wings, whether as the wyvern or the winged jaguar I'd gained in Mexico. But marking the souls of my dead... Did she mean like I'd bitten Rik as the cobra queen? Or something else? Did I have to do that to each of my Blood? Kill them... to mark them as mine?

Shaken, I turned around to look at the sunken tub in the floor. It was big enough for several of us to fit in comfortably, like a whirlpool, but I didn't see any jets. I laid my hand on the low tiled wall and my ears roared. A vision from the past filled my mind.

Two women knelt naked in the water, both dark haired and dark eyed. Mom, the woman who raised me, had her hands on the other woman's rounded stomach.

My mother. I hadn't ever seen her face before. It was like looking into a mirror in thirty years, if we were human and aged normally. Gray streaked her hair at the temples. Lines bracketed her mouth and eyes, pain and exhaustion sapping her strength. I didn't see great power shining in her eyes or written on her face, but I wouldn't, at this point. She'd already given up her Blood and her power.

To have me.

All I saw on her face was wonder and love, even though I

was killing her. She still smiled. "She's almost here. You must take her far from our world."

"No. She needs you. She needs her mother."

Esetta gritted her teeth and leaned forward, straining. Blood swirled in the water. "She needs. Her freedom. Take her. Away. Let her fly."

She pushed and strained, screaming with effort as I tore my way through her body. Yet she laughed with relief and clutched the squalling newborn to her breast. She held me. She let me nurse. She kissed my fuzzy head and whispered secrets to me.

She looked up and stared into my eyes as if I was there by her side, even though she held me as a baby. "Someday, you'll come here and see where you were born. You'll see how much I love you."

She handed me to her sister. "Go. Take her. Take her now before I change my mind and damn us all to his fiery hell. Go!"

Mom fled with me clutched against her chest and the woman who birthed me sagged in the water, barely able to hold on to the side of the tub as she tried to climb out. Blood dripped down her thighs and pooled on the black tile. She hunched on her knees, her back shaking. I reached out to touch her, but my hand flickered through her image.

"Shara," she sobbed. "My baby."

Tears dripped down my face, my throat locked down with grief.

As before, her voice echoed in my head. Achingly familiar, because even though I'd grown up without her in my life, she had always been with me.

"Ra and his minions have distorted our power to the point that all women, whether Aima or human, have lost control of our bodies. Our power, our very lives, are at stake. They judge us amoral, twisted, and deviant, when the very acts of sex and giving birth show our connection to the Mother. She lives on in every woman, whether we choose to have children or not. We create love in the world. What greater magic can there be?

"And so Ra hates us, but he will hate you especially, daughter of mine. You were conceived in darkness and born here, where the Sun never shines. Always work your greatest magic in complete and utter darkness. Embrace that darkness. Embrace your nature. Revel in your hunger. Love your monsters. Because you are the beloved child of a god and a queen of Isis who died to set you free.

"Beware," her voice thinned as if she whispered from a great distance. "You are not the only child born in darkness and kept in secrecy."

20

RIK

I carried her from the black-marbled bathroom and tucked her into bed. She clung to me, crying, but it felt as though the tears cleansed an old, nagging grief.

Daire started to climb onto the bed with us, but she shook her head. "No, I'm sorry. Not this time. I need to speak to Rik alone."

"Of course, my queen." He leaned down and kissed her forehead and filed out with the rest of the Blood. Someone had turned down the blinds, and the room was dark and cool.

I closed my eyes and sank into her bond. I was not a jealous alpha, but I had to admit, having my queen to myself was a rare luxury that I would remember well. Even if foreboding chilled my heart.

Despite her tears after seeing her birth, she was braced for war. She wasn't closed off from me—she would never lock me out of her heart and mind. Yet she wasn't easy and open to read right now. I could easily guess what troubled her.

We were here to kill my former queen, who tortured alphas. My queen was many things, including fearless and powerful, but she could also be tenderhearted, especially for those she loved.

Before she could ask, I said, "Yes. Use me as bait. She'll want an alpha to make an example of, and I'm strong enough to last until you can find a way to kill her. Let her take me."

"No."

"You can heal me," I insisted. "I trust you implicitly. If you can't heal me, then I'm still relieved to spare your other Blood the same fate. You will kill her, I'm sure of it."

She jerked upright and glared down at me, tears glittering on her cheeks like diamonds. "You think that's why I wanted to talk to you? To ask you if I could risk your life to kill Keisha?"

"It's not?"

She blew out a long breath, shaking her head. "Despite knowing my heart inside and out, you couldn't be more wrong. I will kill her, and I won't have to offer you or any of my Blood up as bait, either."

Eyes narrowed, I searched her bond for answers. She gleamed like fresh, hot steel straight out of the forge, showering me with sparks. "How?"

"By giving her exactly what she wants."

I started to push up in protest, but Shara planted her palm on my chest. I could have ignored her, of course, but my body melted to her every touch and desire. If she wanted me to stay flat on my back, then so be it. "You can't give her your blood."

She swung a thigh over me and straddled my lower stomach. Arching a brow, she shrugged out of the elegant emerald green silk suit jacket that Mehen had picked for her to wear to New York City. "Oh, really? I can't?"

"She's not going to be as easy to kill as Greyson. She won't blindly take your blood like he did."

Shara pulled the ivory shell over her head and tossed it aside. She'd gone braless. The sight of her naked breasts stilled my tongue—so I could put it to better use. I leaned up and nuzzled her breasts, breathing in her scent. She always smelled divine—literally. But when her hormones raged, and blood spilled from her center, I couldn't think of anything else. Her scent permeated my senses, rich, thick blood calling me to insanity.

"I tried something new this time." She looped her arms around my shoulders and leaned back into my hands, letting me support her so I could lave her nipples and feast on the softness of her skin. "I think it worked. No tampon—but I didn't bleed everywhere either."

It took a few moments for her words to sink into my brain. I closed my eyes and let my senses flow through her bond, gliding through her body. All her bonds gleamed in the corner of my mind, glowing red streams tangled around her heart. Deep in her abdomen, something else glowed.

I sank lower, reveling in the way our souls rubbed and melded together. Her power made it possible for me to look inside her body and search for any illness or injury, or in this case, liquid moonlight that caught the menstrual blood flowing from her core.

Her scent still flooded my senses, ripe with hormones and need, but the blood itself stayed contained rather than leaking over her clothes. Smart. But I couldn't help but miss the very visual sign of her fertileness. Since it was difficult for Aima queens to breed at all, we'd been conditioned to respond to the sight and smell of menstrual blood. It was a biological compulsion bordering on the strength of a meth-head's drive for that next hit. One taste of that power-laden blood would fucking blow the top of my skull off.

So much blood, pooled in one place. Waiting.

"What I wanted to ask you..."

She waited until I blinked and tugged my gaze up to her face. "Yes, my queen?"

"When we are presented to Keisha, will any of her people try to feed on you? To try and cower us, or prove her dominance over me?"

"Generally, no, but House Skye likes to push boundaries. Since this is a fight between two powerful queens, her Blood may very well try to make an example of us. If one of them feeds on your alpha, a former sib, that automatically puts the Skye stamp on the rest of your Blood."

She nodded, a small smile quirking one corner of her

mouth, but her eyes remained locked to mine, watching my reaction. "I thought to warn them not to feed on any of my Blood, especially my alpha, or I would see them dead."

I smiled back with appreciation for my queen's wicked sharp wit. Of course, if she warned them not to do something, Keisha would very likely do it out of spite. "An excellent idea."

"You said you didn't care for anyone to feed on you outside of my bed, and I don't want to put you through undo pressure. If you don't—"

I grinned and lay back down, giving her a bump with my hips to remind her I was fully at her disposal. "It will be my great pleasure to let one of those fuckers sink fang into me and taste my cobra queen's poison."

"Who else has fed from you since I poisoned you?" She leaned down and pushed her hands up beneath my shirt to stroke my chest. "Daire, right? Anyone else?"

"No, but it'd only take a few minutes to envenom them all, except Guillaume, of course. Your headless knight won't need any poison, though."

"If you don't mind—"

"Never. Ask me anything, my queen, and it's yours."

She pushed up to stand above me and unbuttoned her pants. "Then I ask that you allow me to give you the blood you hunger for the most, while the rest of my Blood taste yours."

SHARA

The thought of allowing him to taste my period blood still squicked me out—but not as much before. How could it, when his eyes blazed with hunger?

He locked his hands around my ankles. "Are you sure? I don't need or require anything from you, my queen. I'll gladly give your Blood my last drop if that's what you need."

"I'm sure."

His hands convulsed on me, a shudder wracking his big frame. "I wouldn't wish to cause you any unease, and I know—"

"Rik," I broke in. "I'm sure. Why else do you think I used my power to come up with a better way to contain my blood? So I could give it to you, if you wanted it."

"I want." He licked his lips, his eyes so hot the silk should have disintegrated off my body. "I want every drop."

I let the silk pants slide down my body, pushed the black lace panties down to my knees, and kicked them both off. As I started to lower myself to my knees, he reached up and caught me around the waist, lifting me up his body so my knees slid up over his shoulders. He flattened his tongue against me, slowly tracing his way down my body. Locking his mouth over my opening, he thrust his tongue inside me to taste the magic I'd used to contain the blood. Groaning against me, he squeezed me harder against him, working his mouth against me.

:*Call your first Blood, and give me every fucking drop.*:

:You heard him.: I said through the bond to no one in particular.

Shuddering with pleasure, I let the magic dissolve. He reared up beneath me, quivering as the blood hit his system. An explosion of power surged through our bond. He thrust his tongue deep and growled inside me. His hunger roared through me, his hands hard on my hips. I jerked in his grip, drowning in sensation. His hunger, pleasure, and ultimately, his need, to sink deep inside me. My pleasure, rising higher, threatened to throw me to the moon and back.

Mehen joined us on the bed. :I decided we should go by age.:

Of course, because that allowed him to go first. He wasn't even going to be allowed inside Skye's nest, but it wouldn't hurt to make him poisonous too. He flashed slitted dragon eyes at me as he sank his fangs in Rik's biceps. His bond flooded me with flames, as if he could taste my blood through Rik. He pressed closer to us and wrapped one arm around my hips, so he could touch me too.

Itztli came in next, his eyes glittering like his obsidian blade. :Alpha—:

:Yes,: Rik said immediately. :I can feed you both while our queen feeds me. I can feed you all.:

Now that the initial rush of blood and magic hit him, he focused more on technique. Which meant I was quickly moaning and jerking in his grip. I'd fucked one of the Blood while feeding others before, but I'd never seen them feeding off each other. Two mouths, locked on my alpha. It was hot, yeah, especially when they both touched me too.

But I had to admit, I'd rather be feeding them than watching them feed off Rik.

As soon as the thought registered, Mehen surged up to sink his fangs in my throat. Tlacel slid in beside his brother, wrapping his arms around us both as he bit Rik's forearm.

:How much do we need to take?: Itztli asked.

:As much as you want,: Rik replied in the bond. :One drop of our cobra queen's poison is enough to kill.:

Xin and Nevarre crowded in on the other side, both of them biting Rik's other arm.

Climax poured through me, making them all groan. Rik sucked on me harder, working his entire face against me. Gasping, I opened my eyes and looked at them. My Blood. Four heads crowded around Rik, while I rode his face, and Mehen fed from my throat. They'd positioned themselves on purpose, so I could see them. So I could enjoy the way they fed from my alpha.

Itztli and Tlacel lifted their heads as one and turned to me. I offered them my right arm and they drank from my wrist and biceps, just as they'd done Rik, though they moved aside to make room for Ezra.

Which left only Guillaume and Daire. Silently, I held out my other arm and Daire came to me, sliding up against Mehen with that delicious rumbling purr. He cuddled into my wrist and bit me. Guillaume pressed against my back, also straddling Rik. I had a moment of hesitation, worried that we were all on top of him, but then he pushed me to another climax and I didn't care.

Because he didn't care.

He gripped my buttocks, pulling me down harder on him. Drowning on my blood. My pleasure. They all were.

I flew so high I lost sight of my Blood and this new bed we were bloodying so thoroughly. I lost sight of everything. I flew through a night sky on silent wings, cutting through the air effortlessly. No stars blinked in the sky. No moon.

Utter darkness.

How I had been conceived. How I had been born.

Panting, I slowly became aware of the bedroom once more. My Blood all cuddled around me, crammed into the bed. It was large… but not that large for ten full-sized adults. Luckily, they didn't care about lying on top of each other.

As long as they could get a hand or mouth on me at the same time.

21

SHARA

Hamilton on Broadway was the most amazing thing I'd ever seen in my life that didn't involve my Blood. We dressed up like we were going to the Oscars, and I dragged Winston, Angela, and Marissa along too. Stepping out of the long black limousine into the crush of fans all eager to make their way into the show, I felt like a movie star. For the first time in my life, I wasn't hiding.

I was out in the open, in Keisha Skye's home territory, as if I had nothing better to do than go see a musical, despite her summons.

It felt pretty fucking amazing, I had to admit.

I'd never done anything remotely as public like this. After Dad was killed because we stayed too long in the park,

I'd taken more and more of my classes at home with Mom, until I was completely homeschooled by the time I hit high school. We certainly never went anywhere after dark. It wasn't safe. It'd never been safe.

The lonely, lean years on the run were so far behind me that I could hardly remember how miserable it had been. The constant toll terror had taken on me, unable to rest for fear the next attack would come. No one to count on. No one to talk to. No one to help me.

Now I had an entire army of people eager to help me, whether that meant opening up a vein, or quietly maneuvering a cadre of financial advisors and attorneys to prepare for an extremely hostile takeover of the most powerful vampire queen in America.

I didn't sleep that night. I didn't need to. I had glorious music flowing through my mind as Gina went over my alternatives to address Keisha's claim.

"She wants recompense for Blood, specifically, but the actual Triune law as written says blood for blood. An equal measure of your blood to balance the Skye blood she claims you stole from her house."

"What if I gave the Skye blood back to her?"

Gina frowned, studying the ancient, thick book that smelled of dust, like it'd been forgotten on a shelf somewhere for centuries. "I suppose... Ah, here. Yes. 'A queen may reject the Blood'—in this case, it specifically says Blood, capitalized—'and return the house's offering to nullify the implied alliance.'"

"I don't want to send my Blood back, obviously. I just want to send back her *blood* out of my house."

"I don't think you can do that."

"But if I can, will that satisfy the law?"

Gina re-read the passage, her mouth moving slightly. "Yes, I believe so. Because she set the precedent first of switching blood to Blood, I don't see why you can't then switch Blood to blood in return. But I've never heard of a queen being able to pull another queen's blood out of anyone. Her blood won't respond to your will."

"You said there's a Cleansing that queens do before they die."

"Yes, absolutely, but that's your ability to cleanse *your* blood. I don't think you'll be able to do the same to hers."

"If I can't, then worst case, I offer her my blood to equal hers. How would the appropriate amount be determined?"

"If this case went before the Triune, they would be able to magically measure the queen's blood and demand an equal amount."

"Since neither of us are Triune, how do we establish the appropriate payment, then?"

"Exactly. It's a trap for you, because you have to depend on Keisha's satisfaction. We both know that the only thing that will satisfy her is for you to become her sib, or for you to die."

"I'm not dying anytime soon, and I sure as hell won't become her sib. Is there another way to test whether or not an Aima bears a queen's blood, even a drop?"

"Of course. Their blood won't respond to her magic."

"Like when you call blood to you to bathe your body in power," Rik clarified. "Our blood is yours to command and will come to your call. If she can't call any of our blood to her, even a drop, then she has no claim on us."

"If she tests your blood, even as alpha, would it respond to her?"

He grimaced. "Yes. She couldn't force me to do anything against my will, because your bond is too strongly in me. But she could command my spilled blood to come to her, if she still has any hold on me at all."

"And if she took my blood…"

"She'd be able to do the same to you. She'd be able to call your blood, as well as ours, and strengthen herself at your expense."

"But have I ingested her blood through you, then? Does she already have her blood inside me?"

Guillaume shook his head. "Queen to queen has to be direct, except in the case of Marne Ceresa. She has the ability to give a small amount of her blood with a specific spell as bait to bring a queen to her. Like that human in Kansas City. No other queen has that ability to my knowledge."

"And if Keisha did have that ability, she would have forced you to her nest already," Rik said.

I turned to Guillaume. "Could I borrow a blade a moment?"

He flicked his wrist and one of the blades dropped down into his palm. "Be my guest, my queen."

I took the blade and lifted my gaze to Rik's face. Without

hesitation, he offered his arm, wrist up, even though he had no fucking clue what I wanted to do to him. I made a small cut on the inside of his wrist and took his hand in mine, turning his arm to allow his blood to drip onto the table.

The slow drip was arousing and hypnotic. Each tiny plop reverberated in my head. My hunger rose. The scent of his blood made my fangs throb. But I made myself watch for several long moments, until a small puddle of blood had gathered on the table.

I lifted his wrist to my mouth and licked the small cut shut. He cupped my cheek, slid his fingers deeper into my hair, and cradled my head, inviting me to feed long and well.

I pushed my hunger down and focused on the pooled blood. I'd fed earlier, and certainly had plenty of time to feed again to be sure I was at full strength. This was more important.

"What are you looking for?" His voice rumbled slightly like a distant thunderstorm.

Without my power, I sensed nothing unique or different about his blood. Obviously, I hungered for him. I could smell his blood and almost taste it in my mouth. But I couldn't separate out the molecules of my blood from hers. It was impossible. It was just... blood.

I punctured the pad of my thumb with the blade tip and allowed my blood to well up. Power shimmered inside me, eagerly rising to my command. Rik massaged the back of my head, still holding me. I heard the slightest inhale from Guillaume, and each of my Blood's focus sharpened on me. Their senses ready, waiting for my slightest need.

Focusing on the small puddle of Rik's blood, I looked through power-enhanced eyes. His blood glimmered with a richer, brighter hue that called to my power. Tendrils of magic streamed softly above his blood, like wisps of fog dancing across a lake. Those streamers stretched toward me, eager to be used. Ready to be called, by me alone.

Ignoring them, I looked deeper, focusing on his blood that did not respond to me. It still looked the same, just shiny, wet blood. But that was with my power passively waiting to be used.

Intention was everything.

I concentrated on his blood and commanded my power. *Show Skye's blood to me. Let me see her touch on my alpha.*

The sticky surface of blood quivered, almost like it was being stirred by an invisible hand. Tiny globs pushed upward against the surface, making the puddle lumpy. Those bits did not belong in his blood—because they were *hers*.

Holding my finger out above his spilled blood, I willed those globs to come out. His blood was mine, and those bits were not. I wanted them out. Now.

The drops rose up out of his blood, hovering beneath my finger. It wasn't much at all—barely enough to fit into a thimble. He'd never fed from Keisha directly, so I would expect her blood to be diluted. How much more of her blood he carried... I couldn't say. This certainly wasn't all of it. Just what I'd spilled for the experiment.

Gina gasped softly. "Blessed be, I've never seen anything like that."

With my blood trickling down my thumb, I willed those dots to burst into flame. With a puff, sparks exploded in midair and the droplets burned away.

"And it only took a drop of you blood to do it." She stared at me, her eyes widening. "Goddess. I knew you were powerful but…" She shook her head. "That's Triune level shit, Shara. I mean it."

Chills dripped down my spine.

There was one empty seat remaining.

The thought of having to deal with Marne Ceresa and the unknown Dauphine on a regular basis because it was my fucking job nearly made me vomit all the delightful blood they'd fed me earlier. "No. I won't take that empty seat."

Even miles and miles away, I felt my grove stir. Trees rustled, restless and uneasy as if a tornado approached.

Deep inside me, a chime echoed through my mind, as if someone had gently tapped a gong. Wind swirled across desert sands, bringing the scent of night-blooming jasmine to me. Her words echoed in my head.

"*I, Isis, am all that hath been, that is, and shall be. What I will, will be.*"

22

SHARA

This was it. The final showdown. The kind of battle where only the winner walked away, and the other camp prepared for a funeral. Though I didn't know that I'd leave enough of Keisha Skye for her people to worry about burying. For all I knew, she'd find someone to bring her back from the dead.

Someone like me.

Riding in the limo toward House Skye's giant residential tower was nothing like my trip to meet Mayte Zaniyah. I'd been so nervous before meeting another queen. There was so much I hadn't understood. It was only weeks ago, but I felt like a lifetime had passed since I'd seen her smiling at me and realized she was just as nervous as I was.

Granted, she'd been hiding a pretty nasty geas from

me… But she'd been scared to meet me, too, and her entire family and nest had been on the line.

I looked around at my men, all dressed in gorgeous black suits and silk shirts. We were definitely going to a funeral. Gina had managed to find some golden tyet pins, or knots of Isis, in the legacy jewelry. There were twenty of them, which made me think either Mom's or Esetta's Blood had likely worn them. The gold looked incredible against their black jackets.

My white gown gleamed against their darkness. When I'd asked Alice for a white dress, I'd been afraid she wouldn't be able to find something un-wedding-like, but this sexy, gorgeous gown fit the bill. The full-length skirt was simply tulle, thin enough that my legs were visible through the delicate layers. Appliqué roses lined the hem and barely covered my groin. I'd never been so completely covered—and completely exposed at the same time. The bodice was composed of the same light tulle with appliqué roses strategically positioned to barely cover my dark areolae, but leaving most of my chest and back exposed in a deep vee.

Miracles of miracles, she'd even managed to place a few roses on my right hip to conceal a small pocket barely big enough for my pocketknife. With brutal fangs of my own now, I shouldn't need it, but I felt better knowing it was there.

It was time to get down to business and finish House Skye once and for all.

I focused on Xin. "Your former queen sent you as an

assassin to eliminate other queens."

It wasn't a question, but he nodded.

"So, you can circumvent a blood circle."

He didn't move a muscle, except one corner of his mouth quirked up in acknowledgement. His ghostly wolf bled into his eyes, making them shine in the murk of the car.

"Make a show of seeing me out of the car, get back inside with Guillaume and Mehen, and then make your way to me as you can. Let no one see you."

He inclined his head. "My pleasure, my queen."

Ezra was next. "I want you to be your normal belligerent, obstinate self."

"Who the fuck says I'm belligerent?"

"Exactly," Daire laughed.

"Don't lie, because House Isador doesn't lie. But if your former sibs suspect that things aren't all sunshine and bunnies in your nest, that's fine by me."

"I smell what you're cooking, my queen, and I like it. Is it alright with you if I break off from the main group? Wander around a bit? My old grizzly has a habit of smelling out things that aren't right."

"If that's your habit, then by all means."

I cupped Daire's cheek and rubbed my thumb across his lips. "I want you to be your normal amiable, lovable self, but be careful. Don't let anyone try to use you as bait."

"Or you'll wipe the floor with them?"

"Pretty much." I turned to my alpha. His eyes simmered with heat and he bulged. Everywhere. Even though he hadn't shifted. The gift I'd given him last night had pumped him up to ridiculous levels of strength. "My alpha can't get enough of me. I don't care what anyone says or does, I want you all over me every chance that you get. Even if one of those bastards tries to feed on you."

Daire snorted. "Why'd he get the hardest job?"

"Because I'm alpha, dickhead." He never looked away from my eyes. "Even inappropriate public affection?"

"By all means."

"This day gets better and better."

Next, I looked to Itztli, Tlacel, and Nevarre. "You'll be outsiders to this court. They won't know what to expect from you. Whatever you feel led to do in the moment is fine by me, but remember, I like my monsters bloody and sexy as hell."

Tlacel's eyes flared. "You have no specific direction for us?"

Itztli fingered the black blade on his hip. "We can do whatever we wish? Within reason?"

I nodded. "Whatever you wish, as long as it doesn't get me into trouble with the Triune later. If you pick a fight, wander off like Ezra, or make friends like Daire—whatever it is that you want to sell to Skye, do it, and do it well with my full permission. As long as you don't fuck or feed on another person outside my Blood. That's the only thing I ask you not to do."

Nevarre shifted slightly and I heard the rustle of feathers in my head. "As if we would ever even touch anyone but you, my queen."

Purring, Daire rubbed up against me. "Quoth the Raven, 'Nevermore.'"

Nevarre slung his long hair back over his shoulder in a careless, elegant motion that drew my gaze like a moth to a flame. "Now you've done it, cat. I challenge you. When we return to our queen's nest, I expect you to meet me on the green."

Naturally, I had to linger on his knees bared by the kilt. I'd never known a man to have sexy knees before.

Daire rumbled louder, trying to draw my attention back to him. "What the fuck does that mean?"

"You'll see." Nevarre smiled at me, his eyes sharp and eager. "Can we admit that you're a jealous queen?"

"Of course, because I am. Omission is fine. Letting someone make a stupid assumption without correction, fine. But don't outright lie."

"Understood, my queen," the twins said in unison.

"What are we supposed to do?" For once, my headless knight grumped like Leviathan. "Stuck out here in the fucking car."

"Be pissed. If anyone comes out to mess with you, tear shit up and make a scene."

"Goddess, let them come," Mehen growled. "I'm dying to show New York what a dragon looks like in the sky. Speaking of which, how do we get you out if things go badly? If she warded the building all the way to the top, I won't be able to get to you and fly you to safety."

"You don't," I whispered softly. I shivered under the intense, pissed scrutiny of my nine Blood. "I don't walk away from this. Either we win, and Skye dies, or she wins, and I die."

Rik squeezed me harder against him. "Then we all die. Understood? No one walks out of here if our queen doesn't make it."

Mehen flashed green eyes at Guillaume. "Do you think the headless knight can survive being eaten by Leviathan?"

"Do you think Leviathan can survive being gutted from the inside out?" Guillaume replied casually.

Mehen laughed softly, quiet puffs of breath very much like a dragon blowing plumes of smoke. "I guess we'll never know, because our queen is going to kick their asses."

Tears burned my eyes, but I smiled at each of them and stroked their bonds with pure magic. "The Great One has gifted me with the finest warriors of all time. How can we possibly lose?"

23

DAIRE

When we'd left Skye Tower a year ago, I'd sworn to never come back. Not for myself, but for Rik. I'd always known he'd be an alpha to be reckoned with, but with Shara's blood pumping through his veins, he was a fucking giant that made all of Keisha's previous males look like teddy bears.

I'd be lying if I said I wasn't fucking terrified to watch him step back into this hellhole. Let alone with our queen on his arm.

Oh, my fucking goddess, Shara looked incredible. She was the most powerful, motherfucking blow-your-mind queen I'd ever seen in my life, and I'd grown up with some powerful women around me. Ezra's formidable mother would make any male Aima twitchy, and our queen had kept her and her other sibs well in hand. Shara eclipsed them all. She'd give even Marne Ceresa a run for her money, and I'd swear off purring altogether if our goddesses didn't intend to put Shara on the Triune.

Assuming we survived this fight.

With any other queen, I'd laugh and joke about how quickly we'd be flying back to Eureka Springs, victorious and high on new blood our queen had claimed for House Isador, but Keisha Skye was not a queen to trifle with. She wasn't stable—which made her unpredictable. She couldn't be reasoned with. There was no alliance or compromise to be formed here.

It was kill or be killed, and though my head knew Shara could beat this queen with one hand tied behind her back, I couldn't help but worry.

Keisha had to know she was in trouble. Shara had broken Skye's geas on House Zaniyah that no other queen had been able to break for fifty years.

So what nasty surprises did Keisha have in store for us?

Two beefy men stood guard as doormen, human, both armed. They gave Itztli and Tlacel a hard look, did a double take when they saw Rik, and promptly lost track of Ezra, who slipped off down the alley.

"Name?" One of the men asked.

Carrying a large leather satchel, Gina stepped up beside us. "Shara Isador to see Keisha Skye."

Even though we were dressed like fucking royalty, they made us stand on the sidewalk while the other man made a big show of scanning a clipboard, flipping through several pages. "Ah. Here you are. Go up to the hundredth floor."

Shara inclined her head like the fucking queen she was. The twins pulled open both glass doors, and she swept inside like she fucking owned the joint. Which she would, when we were done here.

Her face didn't betray a single doubt or hesitation, even though she asked us in the bond, :*No blood circle yet?*:

:*The bottom floors are rented out and open to the public,*: Rik answered. :*The elevator will only take us to the fourth floor, and then we'll have to switch to a secured, warded elevator to get to the rest of the building.*:

We stepped into the elevator, and she aimed a frown of displeasure at the rude doormen's backs. Somebody would be looking for a new job tomorrow.

"Gina, make a mental note that we'll need to buy out whatever leases are in effect. When this building's mine, I'll bleed a circle on the sidewalk outside. Nobody gets in that I don't want here."

"Excellent idea, my queen."

We stepped off the elevator into a grand foyer complete with a huge chandelier, white marble, and lots of gold frames and vases. The public access areas were down a hallway to the right, with the second elevator directly across the foyer, where six women waited.

Women I recognized as Keisha's Blood, or, as she called them, her Furies. At least there were only six. She certainly hadn't sent her alpha, and couldn't be bothered to come welcome a visiting queen herself.

I took a deep, calming breath, and put on my most winning smile as I took the lead. "My queen, let me introduce you to Ashlee, Caryl, Melissa, Aliyah, Bethany, and Lissa Skye, six of Skye's Blood. Furies, this is my queen, Shara Isador."

Lissa smiled broadly. "Daire! We missed you. Welcome home."

It took all my training not to grimace. This place had never been my home, and after finding Shara… I would only equate Skye Tower with hell.

Each of them sidled up to one of us, and Lissa twined her arm with mine, leaning in to make sure she brushed her breasts against me. "No kiss?"

I pulled away slightly and gave a quick, apologetic glance at Shara. "No, I'm sorry. My queen doesn't like other women to touch me."

"Oh, she doesn't? Well that's too bad, isn't it, sugar. Let's get you upstairs. Her Majesty is excited to meet her new sib."

Shara arched a brow. "Excuse me? I'm not here to become a Skye sibling."

Lissa's eyes rounded and she laughed nervously. "I guess that's between you and my queen. We're here to escort you into the nest and upstairs to her throne room."

Shara nodded, stepping closer to Rik. He wrapped his arm around her waist and pulled her firmly up against him, while Ashlee, a tall slim woman with blue-black hair, took his other arm.

Shara's mouth flattened out in a hard, grim line. "Daire spoke truly. I don't like anyone else touching my Blood."

The woman laughed like it was a joke. "But we have to touch you to get through the nest."

"No, you don't. Not my three Blood who were formerly Skye. Hands off. Nevarre, Gina, with Rik and me. Itztli, Tlacel, with Daire."

Caryl, a petite red-head, asked "Where's Ezra? He's supposed to be here."

Shara shrugged. "He is, somewhere. He said he had some business to take care of."

The Furies looked at each other, and I felt the tickle in the back of my mind. They were using their bonds to talk.

Since Lissa had allowed me to feed once or twice…

She remembered it at the same moment I did and gave me a hard, toothy smile. "Let's go."

The twins came up on either side of me and with a hand on my shoulders, we three crossed into the warded nest at the same time. They immediately moved closer to the elevator, taking up a protective stance in case anyone popped out unexpectedly. I turned and watched as Rik led Gina, Nevarre, and Shara through the blood circle. She didn't shiver or make any indication that she felt the magic sliding over her skin. Once they were through, we pressed into the elevator.

Thirteen adults made for a cozy fit, which the Furies took full advantage of.

"Mmmm." Ashlee made a great show of leaning in closely to Rik and smelling him. He bared his teeth and rumbled a warning, but she ignored him. "Such a tasty alpha. But I remember when you were just a shy, awkward sib from an obscure house."

"Please back away from my alpha and kindly remove your hands from his person." Shara's flat, cold voice cut through me like a knife. Lissa shifted closer to me, whether for protection, or to try and draw Shara's attention away from her friend, I wasn't sure.

"He's one of ours," Ashlee insisted. "He passed through the circle. By Skye law, I could feed on him if I wanted. I'm Blood, and in Skye's Tower, anyone's game."

"I wouldn't do that if I were you."

Ashlee gave her a snotty look and then met the other Furies' gazes. "Her Majesty said to make a statement. I think taking a bit of Isador blood will show them who's house they're in. Don't you agree?"

The women all nodded.

Shara smiled, her eyes flaring. "Anyone who tries to feed on my Blood will die, and I won't have to lift a finger to accomplish it."

Ashlee narrowed her eyes, her jaw firming. "I think my queen will have something to say about that. Furies, feed."

Ignoring the suit coat he wore, she sank her fangs into Rik's biceps through the material. She was tall—but not tall enough to reach our alpha's throat. Lissa hesitated a moment, meeting my gaze. I shook my head, trying to warn her off. She'd been nice enough to me. Not all of Skye's people needed to die.

With a shrug, she leaned in to nuzzle my throat above

my collar. I clenched my jaws, fighting to control my reaction. I'd never had a problem feeding anyone before, but something about her made me want to flinch. Nevarre and Tlacel both moved back against Itztli, shielding him from the woman who'd paired up with him.

"Feed on me, if you'd like," Tlacel said. "But spare my brother. He cannot abide the touch of another."

"Oh?" Melissa drawled. "Your queen treats you so badly, then?"

Itztli jerked open the front of his shirt to reveal the long scar over his sternum. "Until you can take my heart out and put it back again, I'll pass."

She shrugged and sank fang into Tlacel. Bracing myself for Lissa's bite, I closed my eyes and concentrated on my breathing. Every cell in my body rejected her. Her touch, her scent, how sharp her fangs would be in my skin. If Shara had bitten me, I'd be melting and purring, crazy for her. But this...

This would be a violation.

Lissa bared her fangs, ready to bite me, but hesitated at a strange noise.

Ashlee spluttered, dribbling blood down her shirt. Eyes bulging, she backed a step away from Rik and slammed up against the elevator wall.

Lissa lifted her head. "Ash? What's wrong?"

She tore at her throat, bloodying herself. Gasping and spewing blood, the other Furies jerked back too.

Whirling on me, Lissa grabbed my arm. "What's wrong? What did she do to them?"

"Nothing," Shara said calmly. "I warned you. I don't take kindly to anyone touching my Blood, let alone feeding on them. I told you anyone who did would die."

By the time the elevator doors opened, five of the Furies were down on the floor, gurgling and choking as their throats swelled and blackened. Vega, Skye's female alpha, fisted her hands on her hips and glared at us all. "What the fuck happened here?"

Shara grimaced at the blood and black fluids on the floor, so Rik scooped her up in his arms and stepped over Ashlee's bloated body. "I warned them not to feed on my Blood, but they refused to listen. They paid the price. Look at my Blood if you don't believe me. They each bear fang marks."

Vega narrowed a hard look on Lissa. "Is that true? Or did the Isador bitch try something?"

Vicious sounds rumbled from our throats. Rik sounded like an earthquake. Itztli growled like a rabid dog. My fangs ached and my chest rattled on a warning hiss. Nevarre's eyes flashed, his head tipped like a raven ready to peck someone's eyes out. Even mild-mannered Tlacel was poised to strike, his hair flared up on the top of his head like a spiny ridge.

Lissa squeezed my arm, her nails digging into my skin. "It's true. She told us. We didn't listen."

Vega looked her up and down, her lip curled in disgust. "Yet I see you're still alive and kicking, Lissa. Are you taking up with another house over your own?"

"No, no," she babbled. "I started to bite you, didn't I,

Daire? I did. But Ashlee started choking. I was trying to help her."

She made another grunt and turned to glare at Shara. "What the fuck do I tell my queen?"

Clear of the elevator, Rik set her back down on her feet, but she leaned against him, the white skirt scandalously thin. I could easily make out the dark cleft of her buttocks. The long curve of her thighs. I could smell her heat and need, despite the magic trick she'd figured out to contain her blood. Rik tucked her up against his erection, folding his big body around her protectively.

"Tell her exactly what I said." Shara didn't even look at the other woman. With the scent of our blood in the air, her voice had gone husky with hunger. Something Rik wouldn't ever ignore. He lifted her up so she could get to his throat. "I asked them nicely. I warned them they would die. They ignored me."

She sank her fangs into Rik's throat. He groaned deeply, not trying to hide the fact that he was coming. His hips jerked, his big palms kneading her buttocks, pulling her harder against him. His eyes blazed with heat and he glared at the other alpha. He was so fucking big, pumped up, hormones blazing with the drive to protect our queen. Even while vulnerable in release, he was primed to kill in her defense.

Skye's badass alpha bitch couldn't fucking hold his gaze.

Vega's face reddened, her lips tight and jaw strained. She jerked her head at Lissa. "Get a clean-up crew up here. Not a word to anyone. Do you hear me?"

Lissa nodded and hit a button to close the elevator doors. Wide-eyed, she met my gaze and she didn't have to touch that old blood bond for me to read her mind.

Holy fucking shit.

Five minutes into Skye Tower, and we already had five bodies on the ground. It was going to be an epic trip.

SHARA

Standing outside massive double doors, I had flashbacks to the first time I'd been presented to House Zaniyah. That first night, our reception had been rather chilly from her people. They hadn't had any idea what kind of queen I would be. How much I would take from them. I hadn't had any reason to raze them to the ground, other than the geas Mayte hadn't warned me about on her nest.

These people...

Already, they'd fucking pissed me off.

I'd been fine, until I felt Daire's uneasiness and Itztli's panic as the two females moved in to take what wasn't offered to them willingly. How many times had someone been forced to give blood in this building? Penetrated by fangs they didn't want, forced to give up part of their own bodies and power to another?

They'd raped my men for their blood, used them against their will, and they'd paid for it with their lives. If I had my way, everybody in this entire building who'd ever taken anything from anyone against their will would meet the same fate.

:*You can absolutely do that,*: Rik whispered in the bond, his voice a soothing, deep rumble. :*But let's take care of Keisha first. Without her influence, I think you'll find that most of Skye will be more than agreeable to your rules.*:

:*I shouldn't have to make it a fucking rule that no one takes something from another against their will.*: Itztli took a hesitant step closer, his shoulders tight, hands fisted at his sides. I held out my hand and he immediately came to me, pressing up against Rik. For protection. Goddess, it broke my heart. :*I'm so sorry, Itztli. Go to the car. We'll be fine without you.*:

:*I would never leave you to theses vipers, my queen, but thank you. I'm not afraid of them, only terrified I might slip and unleash my darkest desires. I don't want to ruin your plans entirely when I start ripping hearts of their chests to feast.*:

Gina set the satchel on the floor and bent down to reverently lift out Isis's crown. The sight of the golden crown with arching horns holding the dark red sun disc centered me. I pushed my fury aside. I wouldn't give Keisha Skye the fucking satisfaction of rattling me in any way, shape, or form. I wouldn't be swayed from my purpose.

I was here to end her rule of torture and fear once and for all.

Gina set the crown on my head and helped adjust my hair so that tendrils curled down around my face.

:*The presentation room is one long, narrow hallway that runs the entire length of the building,*: Rik said. :*Her throne will be at the end against floor-to-ceiling glass windows. Her sibs will line the walkway, shoulder to shoulder and likely several people deep to get them all in.*:

:She'll want to impress you with her numbers,: Daire added. :So they'll be crammed in like sardines.:

:Will these sibs include other minor queens, or just weaker Aima?:

:Both. Minor queens that have been assimilated with their Blood and sibs from all over the country.:

I touched Mayte's bond and she flooded me with warmth. Her arms came around me and I felt the softness of rose petals against my lips. :Shara, be careful.:

:Always.: I concentrated on Xochitl's bond and sparkles filled my head like a glitter cannon had gone off. It made me laugh softly. :Have her unicorns shown up yet?:

:Not yet, but she insists she dreams of them every night.:

:Good. I hope they're on their way to her.:

I pulled back gently and focused on my Blood bonds. Xin glided unseen up a series of staircases. He'd be here shortly. Ezra felt further away, perhaps even underground. He moved slowly and carefully through dark, empty halls, his senses alert for the slightest whisper or sign of life.

Guillaume had his head tipped back against the leather seat in the car, pretending to sleep, his body completely relaxed. His scarred hands rested lightly on his thighs as he thought of each blade on his body like a mental exercise. Mehen had been driven out of the limo by his boredom and leaned back against the hood of the long car like a negligent lord surveying his kingdom.

Before I opened my eyes, I focused on the pocket of magic I'd used to hold the period blood inside my body. I cracked it open a little so the blood would start to trickle free.

Time for the demonstration of my life.

I opened my eyes and slipped my arm through Rik's. He wrapped his other hand over mine on his arm and slid closely enough to me that my skirts fell over his leg. "I'm ready."

Of course, it wasn't going to be that easy. Trying to get into my head and rattle my nerves, Keisha had evidently decided to make us wait. Forever. Long enough that my feet —trapped in ridiculous high heels—were starting to ache. Sweat trickled down Rik's face, his body so hot against me that my thigh and side were sweaty too. But neither of us moved a muscle. I didn't fidget or shift my weight or look at the woman guarding the door.

I refused to let any impatience tighten my face.

After what seemed like a lifetime, Vega turned and pushed the doors open.

Noise flooded my senses. The clamor of a thousand voices or more, also bored to tears and talking among themselves. The clink of glasses, the murmur of staff passing through the press of people offering trays of hors d'oeuvres.

Then, to make sure I fully understood how thoroughly Keisha Skye was trying to insult us, Vega didn't announce our names or provide an escort down the hallway.

Daire stepped forward, turned sharply like he was in a military formation, and shouted, "House Isador has arrived!"

The people closest to the doors whispered to the people

beside them, spreading news of our arrival through the press of people, even if they couldn't see us at the door. Slowly, the crowd quieted. Many of them knew Daire and recognized that a good show was about to start.

:*Would it be considered rude for each of you to shift?*: I asked through our bonds.

:*Extremely rude.*: Daire's bond chortled with glee. :*You heard our queen.*:

"Her Majesty's Blood, Nevarre Morrigan Isador."

Nevarre shifted into his glossy black raven, leaving his kilt and suit jacket puddled on the floor. He let out a raucous screech and flew down the hallway, dive bombing at people and tearing at hair and clothes to be as annoying as possible. I hoped to goddess that he crapped on somebody. Hopefully Keisha herself.

Daire scooped up the kilt and handed it to Gina for safekeeping.

"Her Majesty's Blood, Itztli Zaniyah Isador."

Itztli shifted to his gigantic black dog and bayed like a hell hound to start the Wild Hunt. Tongue lolling, he sat on his haunches, waiting for his brother. Tlacel picked up the obsidian blade and handed it to Gina with a flourish.

"Her Majesty's Blood, Tlacel Zaniyah Isador."

Tlacel leaped into the air, shifting so quickly into his Great Feathered Serpent that some of the people closest to us gasped with wonder. Bright green and teal feathers dotted with red, he cut through the air with a sinuous swipe of his tail that did look like a flying snake. His twin trotted beneath him. People oohed and awed as they passed when they caught a glimpse of such rare Blood.

"Her Majesty, Shara Isador, last daughter of the Great One, Isis, She who is all that has been and is and shall be, with her consiliarius, Gina Isador, and Her Majesty's alpha Blood, Alrik Hyrrokkin Isador. Not present are Her Majesty's Blood Guillaume de Payne Isador, Leviathan Gorgon Isador, Wu Tien Xin Isador, and Ezra Ursula Isador."

:Do you want me to shift?: Rik asked.

:No. I think we'll have more fun interacting this way, and I'd rather them not know what you are yet.:

Rik and I stepped up beside Daire, and Rik used his booming voice to announce, "Her Majesty's Blood, Daire Devanna Isador."

Daire shifted into his warcat and padded along with Gina behind us.

Head high, I stepped into the long room. I didn't look at anything or anyone, and I kept my pace slow and deliberate. I could feel blood smearing on my thighs as I walked. Spreading to the tulle skirt as it moved against my legs.

The first shock rippled through the crowd. Sharp inhales. Gasps. A woman, visibly bleeding from her period, in public, without a care. Entering a huge room crammed with ravenous vampires. Even more…

I was breeding, something that was so rare that their own queen had resorted to torture to try and recreate.

People started to inch closer to us, drawn by the smell of my blood and the promise of my power. Daire roared and snapped to keep them back. Itztli paused, bristling with a vicious growl rattling his deep chest. Tlacel and Nevarre swooped lower, sharp talons and beaks to add to the blood frenzy building in them.

Rik tightened his grip on me. :*This could get ugly.*:

:*I'm counting on it.*:

24

SHARA

If I ever needed a reminder that I wasn't human, I'd pull up this scene in my head again.

People in sequined gowns and elegant suits were shoving and pushing each other. To get closer to me. To taste my blood.

My period blood.

Which had dribbled on the white marble floor.

Daire pounced on each drop and licked it up, growling at anyone who thought to beat him to it. Energy rose in the room, a crackling promise of power that would tear through this skyscraper and blast it to rubble. Without turning my head, I asked Daire, :*Is Vega looking at us, or following us?*:

:*Yes. She's a few paces behind me. She tried to hold the crowd back at first, but now...*: He paused a moment to snarl and claw a woman in the face who'd dropped down to her hands and knees too close to my warcat for comfort. She fell back and writhed on the floor, like she was going to shift. :*She can't look away from you. A push, and she'll topple.*:

I wasn't sure how many of these sibs were queens or Blood that might have the ability to shift, but that would be one sure way to spread some seeds of chaos in the crowd, while also breaking Skye's hold on them.

A wolf scrambled free of the woman's shredded dress and looked at me. I stared back steadily. I didn't draw on my power. I didn't have to. My will was enough with the promise of my power flowing from me in waves of scent. *Submit. I am your queen. You will follow me.*

The wolf whined and dropped to the floor to inch toward me on her belly.

I shifted my focus to Vega. I didn't turn to look at her but let my intention ripple on the raw power licking through the room. She hadn't been able to hold Rik's gaze. She'd already lost to him. She belonged to me now. I wouldn't have to push very hard. And if I got Skye's alpha to submit to me without a fight, the rest of the Blood would be mine before a single drop of blood was exchanged.

Submit to your beast. I am your queen. You will follow me.

A mighty roar told me she'd shifted, and that roar had other people in the crowd shifting too.

:*They'll be more out of control as their beasts,*: Rik said grimly. :*I wish we could get Leviathan up here to roast some Skye cats and wolves for dinner.*:

:Brace yourselves,: I told them, closing my eyes. I tapped the blood dripping from my body and quivered at the instant rush of power tearing through me. I let the power flare out of me in a shockwave that sent the Skye watchers tumbling away from us. Many more shifted, and the roars, howls, and screams rose in to a deafening cacophony that made my lips curve.

Controlled chaos. Daughter of Monsters. I was born for this.

We started walking again. I let my power wash over the crowd, stirring up any hint of Aima blood that responded to me. A young, powerful queen sibling on my right, and her three Blood. They shifted and moved to follow Vega. An older queen with five Blood. Another.

No wonder Skye had ruled New York City for so many centuries. She must have pulled every queen in America to her.

:Except for Leonie Delafosse, Mayte Zaniyah, and you,: Rik said.

:Or they left.: Xin waited close to the throne for me as his ghostly wolf. *:Like my old queen. She refused to offer throat to Skye.:*

"What the fuck is going on?" A woman yelled somewhere ahead of us. "You know the rules in Skye Tower. No shifting!"

Oops. I smiled wider. People blocked the last few steps to the throne. Late afternoon sun streamed in through the floor-to-ceiling windows, making it hard to see. A large throne rose dark against the brilliant sunlight on a platform ahead, but I couldn't see if Keisha actually sat there or not. My eyes started to water and suspicion sprouted.

Maybe Keisha Skye had more to do with Ra than I'd thought. She was certainly taking advantage of his punishing light. The glittering chandelier overhead added to the brilliance spilling through the room. Rather than crystals, shards of copper, silver, and gold tinkled, stirred by the swirl of power rolling from me, spinning and reflecting the light.

:Nevarre, can your Shadow tone down the glare so I can see what she's up to?:

The raven flew straight toward the windows. *:On it, my queen.:*

I focused on the people blocking our way.

"Stand your ground," the woman said again in a booming voice. It had to be Keisha, but I couldn't tell for sure where her voice came from.

Tlacel swooped down over the shadowed dais. *:Look through my eyes, my queen.:*

I focused on his bond. I knew Rik could do something like this, where he looked through Daire's eyes.

:He's yours,: Rik's rumble rolled through our bond. *:His blood is yours. His heart is yours. Now make his eyes yours.:*

I reached through the bond toward Tlacel, sliding my mind closer to his. The path was narrow, since our bond was newer than mine with Rik. I hadn't shared nearly as much blood with the twins, but I was still able to slide inside him. I could feel his heart beating, the air rushing over his feathers as he dropped a wing and circled back lower over the dais. Through his eyes, I saw a large wooden throne, its back curved like an oval shield painted with Celtic runes. Spears made the frame and arms of the throne. His vision was so sharp I could see the delicate layers in the stone spear heads that had been painstakingly carved from flint over a thousand years ago.

But the throne was empty.

He cut a sharp circle back across the group of people blocking me from the throne. There. A woman stood in the back, her arms spread, her lips moving. A large golden crown gleamed against her dark curls.

:Up, away,: I told him and Nevarre. :To me, if you can. She's going to strike.:

They immediately wheeled away from the windows and dove toward me in a flurry of wings and feathers.

I pulled my power back toward us, wrapping us in layers of energy. I didn't want a visible shield. I didn't want to look afraid or defensive, because we weren't. But I'd be ready to absorb whatever she sent our way. She had the power of hurricanes and storms. She surely couldn't loose a hurricane inside the building without hurting her own people, but lightning... Yeah. She could try and blast us. That was what I'd do if I had storms as my power in close quarters.

Wriggling between my leg and Rik's, Daire licked a drop of blood from the top of my foot. When I didn't rebuke him, he nuzzled his head deeper beneath my skirt and swirled his tongue around my ankle and up my calf. Not to be left out, Itztli joined him on my left. I dropped my hand on his shoulders and pushed my fingers deep into his black fur.

Grounded. Braced. Ready.

I smelled ozone a moment before lightning arced from the glittering chandelier. Rik instinctively pulled me closer, wrapping his big body around me. Tlacel and Nevarre threw their wings over us like a shield of black and green-gold feathers.

Time seemed to slow. I had time to appreciate the smell of druid magic and ripe jungle rolling from my winged Blood. The stroke of Daire's rough sandpaper tongue on my knee. Itztli gripped my calf gently in his teeth, ready to pull me down to the floor if necessary. Nevarre's cold shadow enveloped the throne and slowly blanketed the dais, leaking toward us like a puddle of ink.

A million volts touched my power. Everything froze, like the world held its breath. Isis laughed softly in my head and I could almost see Her finger touch the tip of the lightning bolt. Her dark hair blowing in streams of power. Jasmine blooming around her feet.

Yes.

I pushed back. I willed the electricity to reverse. It sparked. Arced. And shot back toward its creator.

A boom rocked the building and time snapped back into full speed. People screamed. Smoke billowed up, reeking of burned flesh. The group of people blocking my path scattered, backing away from a pile of charred remains of several people, likely Blood, who'd taken the brunt of the recoil.

Keisha Skye stared back at me, slightly scorched and frazzled, but otherwise unharmed. Her ebony skin gleamed in the sunlight. Her face was gorgeous, sharp cheekbones and high forehead, her golden-brown eyes glittering as brightly as her crown. She wore a sequined gown that flashed like thousands of fireflies had descended upon her.

All that gold. The brightness and light, the twisting of her power and intention to darker urges. A hunger for pain and destruction. She had to be contaminated by Ra's influence.

She took me in, too, her mouth flattening into a hard, grim frown as she noted my shifted Blood. The way they crowded against me, the warcat and black dog both licking my legs and ankles. The blood.

I could see the moment she realized what it meant. Her eyes flared wide. The fresh glow of her skin washed away. Even the glittering brightness of her dress dimmed, though that was partially due to Nevarre's Shadow that slowly spread across the windows.

She lifted a hand to her head, as if she had a headache, or needed to adjust the crown. Her fingers trembled. Her lips paled, and she swallowed, hard, as if she was going to throw up.

Empathy welled up inside me. She'd lost a child. I couldn't begin to understand how devastating that must have been. How horrible. What lengths would I go to protect Xochitl? Even though she wasn't even from my own body? If Ra had taken her through the portal... If her hair had slipped through my fingers, and I'd watched her fall into the waiting arms of those horrible empty creatures...

I shivered, my heart aching. My eyes blurred with tears.

Keisha started to sob. At least, that's what I thought,

until I focused back on her face and saw the sneer twisting her lips. She laughed. She fucking laughed.

"Well, well, well. Your mother always did love to fuck the monsters. I guess I shouldn't be surprised that you're just like her."

25

SHARA

Keisha didn't say my mother's true name. She couldn't. No living Aima could say Esetta Isador.

But she knew that Selena wasn't my mother.

"Oh, yes." Still chuckling, Keisha stepped over the burned remains of some of her Blood without a second glance and sat gracefully on her throne. "My very good friend and Triune queen, Marne Ceresa, was only too kind to warn me that you were not quite what we first thought. I'm sure I would have recognized the truth as soon as I saw you, but I'm grateful she passed along that little tidbit. Now that we have crossed swords and tested each other's strength, let me lay the truth bare between us.

"*Your mother,*" she said each word like a curse, because

she couldn't say her name, "was my closest friend and ally at one time. Until she stabbed me in the back and crawled into the depths of hell to spawn you."

I took a deep breath but didn't dare blink or move. I didn't want to betray my surprise. Esetta and Keisha Skye had been friends. That...

That didn't compute.

I was only twenty-two. Keisha's daughter had died decades before that. She'd have been torturing people. When my mother knew her. When they'd been friends.

Keisha had laid the geas on Zaniyah's nest almost fifty years ago.

Had my mother known about that too? And done nothing?

Or, more likely, these were all the reasons my mother had taken the drastic step of wiping herself from Aima memory. So she could have me—and no one would know. In the vision I'd seen her hand me to her sister and say, *"let her fly."*

Let me fly free. Away from an Aima court, where I could be twisted and corrupted like her friend.

The clang of metal drew my attention to a dark corner to my right. Chains clattered. Something rose from the shadows. Something large, that shuffled toward me, dragging chains across the marble.

Rik started to slide in front of me, but I stopped him with a quick shake of my head. I needed to see what... who... this was. My power vibrated with sudden intensity, tightening around us. Drawing us together.

Pulling him to me quicker.

He staggered out of the shadows, a broad-shouldered giant of a man even taller than Rik, though he was stooped by the weight of massive chains looped around his body. A leather hood was buckled over his head. He couldn't see and could barely move, but he kept coming.

To me.

His head cocked, very bird-like, and he suddenly reminded me of a hooded, bound raptor.

"Isador?" He whispered, breathing so deeply I could hear it despite the hood that covered his entire face. "It is. My queen. You've come for me."

He fell on his knees before me, bent forward, and touched the leather hood to my feet.

"Aw, how sweet." Keisha's voice sharpened to a cutting edge despite her words. "He recognizes you."

I laid my fingers on his back and he straightened. "Who are you?"

He shuddered beneath my hand. "Llewellyn. Isador."

"Llewellyn *Skye*," Keisha said with a vicious smile. "You see, when your dear mother decided to abandon everything to sire you, she left her Blood behind. I took pity on them and called them to my side. Most of them chose to follow your mother in death, but Llewellyn hung on all these years. I guess that's why he was alpha."

Tears spilled down my cheeks. My mother's alpha? Chained and hooded and trapped in Keisha's control my entire life? I fumbled the buckles open, loosened the straps, and pulled the hood off his head.

I gasped, covering my mouth with horror. His eyes. She'd taken his eyes. Only pink, wrinkled pits remained. His skin was pale and scarred, though his dark curly beard and hair were well trimmed. Someone was taking care of him at least occasionally. But why the fuck would they put this hood on him if they'd already blinded him? What was the point?

:*To remind him of his place,*: Rik said. :*The same reason falconers use the hood and jesses. To control the raptor and break it to their hand.*:

Llewellyn tipped his head forward and breathed deeply. "I don't need eyes to know my queen's blood."

With power swirling around me, I focused on him. He glowed in the tapestry of my mind, the same as my Blood, only like flame rather than streams of lava. He still carried Isador blood. I could sense it winding through him. I heard weeping from a distance. Soft and mournful like a winter wind howling through the trees.

Esetta. For a moment, I could see her, a thin, wispy spirit of moonlight and shadow, laying her pale hands on Llewellyn's cheeks as she pressed a kiss to his forehead. *"I'm so sorry, Lew. So sorry. Forgive me."*

She looked at me, her black eyes suddenly blazing even as her form dissipated. *"Heal him, daughter. Give him back his sight as you give him back his heart."*

I pressed my wrist to his mouth and he sank fangs into me so quickly that Keisha couldn't stop us. She started to rise up from her throne, her eyes blazing with fury, but it was too late. He sucked me down like a man dying of thirst.

Actually, he probably hadn't fed in twenty years. Keisha had given him enough blood to bind his will to hers, and then locked him up.

Sinking into his bond, I couldn't hold back the tears. This man. Such honor. Even Guillaume would be impressed.

He had guarded my mother for centuries. He'd loved her more than life itself. When she couldn't have a child with him despite his alpha power, he'd sworn to do whatever she needed to fulfill her heart's desire. Like Rik had promised, he would even find a god so I could have a child.

Only Llewellyn had gone so far as to swear to allow his queen's greatest enemy to claim him as her own. So Isador would always have eyes and ears in House Skye, awaiting the day that the young Isador queen would come to put an end to the darkness and torture their queen committed.

He'd come to Keisha. Even knowing that she tortured alphas. Even knowing that she hated Isador. He'd put himself into her hands. Willingly. Gladly.

Simply because my mother had asked him.

So that one day, when I needed him, he'd be here and ready to come to my side.

Rage and hurt surged in me. I hated that this man had suffered for my sake. While I knew that Keisha had tortured men for decades, seeing how Llewellyn had suffered put it in more perspective. Worse, she hadn't used him to try and sire a child. He was still alive.

How many had she already killed?

She'd kept him alive—so she could torture him with all that he'd lost.

His sight. His queen. The daughter he hadn't been able to give her.

Volatile power crackled inside me. I filled him with strength. I focused on his eyes, drawing on Esetta's memory of him. Dark eyes, like hers. Sparkling with a thousand falling stars.

He strained against the chains, muscles bulging, pumped with my blood. I felt his flesh tearing, where chains dug deeply into his wrists and ankles over the years. I turned my rage on those chains and tore them away like they were spider webs.

His beast exploded free. Lion claws grated on the marble, but huge red-gold wings lifted him into the air. His beak opened, and his shriek made cracks splinter through the windows, though they didn't break completely.

Gryphon. No wonder Keisha had kept him chained and hooded.

He swept back down and snatched up someone in his claws, tearing her apart in midair and splattering the crowd below with blood and intestines. He hadn't given me his blood yet, but with my blood flowing in him, I knew exactly why he'd killed her.

She was the one who'd "cared" for him. She'd been his keeper. The one who'd taken his eyes.

He landed in front of us and settled in to tear at the body in his talons, tossing back chunks of flesh.

A slow, loud clap drew my attention back to Keisha. She lounged back on her throne like I hadn't just freed a man she'd kept imprisoned for more than twenty years.

"Now you owe me even more of that delicious Isador blood. Shall we get on with the proceedings, so you can pay the proper respect to your queen?"

I threw my head back and laughed. "You will never be *my* queen."

26

RIK

Looking at my former queen made every nerve in my body stand up at full alert. Every alpha instinct I possessed screamed at me to shift, grab Keisha by the throat, and beat her into a bloody pulp against her own throne until she was dead.

So my queen would be safe.

Because if anything happened to Shara, my fate would be much worse than Llewellyn Isador's had been.

Keisha looked at me, and it felt like she ripped all the skin off my body. "You've managed to turn my young sib into a fine alpha specimen. Tell you what. You give him to me, and you can keep the rest of my sibs free and clear. I'll settle the blood debt with the Triune. In fact, I'll throw in Vega. She can take over your alpha's spot." Her tone sharpened, her lip curling with disgust. "Evidently, she's already intoxicated on your power. She's of no further use to me."

In her lioness form, Vega slunk closer to me, though Tlacel bit a chunk out of her hide for getting too close. She might have submitted to Shara's power, but she sure as fuck wasn't Blood. She wasn't one of us.

I knew Shara loved me without question. But I couldn't help the fear worming through my mind that maybe she would take Keisha up on her offer. If it meant Shara would live, and we had no other alternative, I would do it. Without question.

:*No. Never. I'll kill us all before I allow you to fall into her hands.*:

"I don't know," Shara said aloud, her tone suggesting she might take Keisha up on her offer. "I've heard that alphas don't fare too well in your court."

"True. But none have been quite as hardy as Alrik looks to be. He's got giant blood in him. I think he'll hold up just fine."

"Why do you want him?"

"To have a child," Keisha replied quickly, but her words didn't ring true. For the first time, she seemed nervous. She reached up and twirled a tendril of hair around her finger and laughed, but it sounded forced and heavy. "What I've always wanted."

"But you already know how to have a child," Shara said. "You know how my mother had me."

Keisha shuddered delicately. "As if I would lie with a monster. Even to have a child."

"But you would become a far worse monster? That doesn't make sense."

Keisha jerked upright, and a sly smile spread across her face.

Not good. Not good at all.

"Where's Ezra Skye, by the way?" She said casually. "Did you not bring him?"

"He's here." Shara shrugged but allowed her lips to tighten with irritation. "He's always wandering off by himself."

Keisha nodded, a smile flickering on her lips. She stood and raised her voice to her people. "You're all dismissed. When we settle on a blood price, I'll call you back for a formal presentation."

She stepped down off the dais and came closer to Shara. A growl rumbled from my chest before I could stop it.

Unfortunately, Keisha seemed to like that sound a great deal. She ran her gaze over me and it was all I could do not to shudder with revulsion. "You'd best come with me, Shara. I have something to show you. It seems that your wandering Blood has gotten himself into a bit of trouble."

Dread churned in my stomach. I'd been so focused on Shara, that I hadn't paid any attention to Ezra's bond. I reached for him…

But felt nothing. Just a blank spot where her grumpy bear was supposed to be.

Shara's jaws clenched but she didn't say a word as we followed after Keisha. I felt her reaching for him, too, her rising worry for him. If he was in pain, we couldn't feel it.

Surely, he would have shouted or alerted us for help if he'd been captured.

"This is my consiliarius, Madeline Skye. She'll be my witness to the Triune that I'm satisfied with the terms of our arrangement."

"My consiliarius, Gina Isador." Shara hesitated a moment, and then asked, "you're not bringing any of your Blood? Aren't you afraid we'll try to kill you and walk out of here without a second glance?"

"Gina used to work for… *her*." Keisha's voice roughened, as if she was trying to say Shara's mother's name, but couldn't, which pissed her off. "I'm sure she's told you that the Triune will be most displeased if something happens to me before we can resolve this debt. Even if you're foolish enough to try and kill me in my own nest, surrounded by more than a thousand sibs, you won't be able to escape a Triune death sentence. Who knows. Marne has a twisted sense of humor. I wouldn't put it past her to command Guillaume de Payne to do the deed himself."

We walked down a hallway that I didn't recognize. I'd never been important enough in House Skye to warrant ever seeing the queen's personal areas. Daire and I had eventually shared an apartment on the fifth floor. One step up from the public leased areas. A true indication of how low in House Skye we were.

When we came to another elevator, this one a small service elevator that wouldn't hold more than a couple of us at a time, Shara balked. "Where are we going?"

"To the basement. You should leave your Blood here, or

at least make them shift back." Keisha stepped into the elevator and turned around to face us with a shrug. "Ezra is your Blood now. If you don't come with me, he'll die. It's as simple as that. If you don't care, you can wait here, and I'll be back shortly. But I assure you, I have something to show you that's most relevant to your interests."

:*I don't like it,*: I growled in our bond.

Shara sighed back, though outwardly, she didn't make a sound. :*I know. But what choice do we have? I have to find him.*:

She kissed each of her shifted Blood on their heads. "Wait for me here."

Daire wound around her, almost knocking her down on top of him in his furious determination to stay with her.

"No, Daire. I want you to stay here. I'll be back in a few minutes."

She untangled herself and took my hand. Gina and Madeline stepped onto the elevator, and then Shara and I joined them, though with my size, it was a tight fit. I hoped to goddess that Keisha had made the formal claim to the Triune. If she was lying about it…

Then we were headed straight into a trap and there wasn't a fucking thing I could do about it.

EZRA

I woke up with a start, unable to remember falling asleep. I had no memory of where I was. What I'd been doing. Who the fuck I even was.

I tasted blood. Not mine. There was a foulness in the

blood that made me scrub my tongue on my sleeve. Something rancid had crawled into my mouth and died. That was some fucking nasty shit.

What the fuck happened?

I sat up and rubbed my eyes, trying to see. It was pitch black and I couldn't see a fucking thing. My head throbbed like a giant icepick was drilling into my temple. It hurt badly enough that I reached up and felt for a wound, but there wasn't any blood. I held my head as I slowly turned around, trying to sense anything. A way out. A hint of light. A breath of wind.

Something glittered in the darkness. It wasn't bright, exactly, but it moved, and I could barely make out a shadow in the darkness.

"Hello?"

"Hello," something whispered back.

Something that wasn't human. Though I wasn't human, either. I couldn't remember what I was, exactly, but that sharp, metallic shriek wasn't a voice.

"Wanna play?"

I scooted backward, trying to move quietly, but the glinting darkness came closer.

"Play with me, bear."

Even while my brain was screaming to get the fuck out of here, something about the voice registered as truth. I was a bear. A grizzly bear, in fact. And my furry ass was getting the fuck out of here.

I surged to my feet and broke into a run, only to slam into an invisible wall. I fell with a shout, my wrist throbbing. My head tried to explode. I tasted blood again, but this time it was my own. Panting, I reached out and felt... nothing. But I couldn't push my hand through, either.

Some kind of blood circle. It had to be. Only instead of keeping things out...

It was keeping me in.

Sweat poured off me, ripe with the sink of fear. I was fucking trapped with something that wanted to fucking play, that had a voice like a knife sliding down sheet metal.

Voices echoed in the distance and memory crashed into me. I recognized that voice. Shara. My queen. I was hers. She would get me the fuck out of here.

"Shara!"

"Ezra? What's wrong? Where are you?"

"Get me the fuck out of here! There's something in here. Something that's not... right."

Lights flickered on, but they were blue in tone, rather than yellow. I saw my queen and alpha coming toward me, and fuck me sideways, I almost started to blubber like a baby. I didn't know why I was so fucking scared. Every hair on my body stood up quivering with alarm, and I was a fucking bear. I had a lot of fucking hair.

I did not want to turn around and see whatever thing had spoken to me. But it was like rubbernecking a fatal car accident.

I couldn't *not* turn around.

Then I wanted to laugh, because it was just a girl. A young girl, maybe ten or twelve years old. She had bright pink ribbons braided into her hair and wore a matching frilly dress. Her skin looked a bit… sickly. She looked almost green, though that was probably the blue light turning her skin a strange color. She had a stuffed toy in her lap, but I couldn't make out its shape.

"Mama!"

I glanced back toward Shara and my mouth fell open. Keisha Skye was with her.

We were fucked. So fucked. I couldn't even begin to describe the many ways we were fucked.

"Hello, babydoll," Keisha replied. "Are you being a good girl today?"

"Stop," I barked out. "There's some kind of blood circle here. It trapped me. I can't get out."

Shara jerked to a halt. She scanned the area, and I had the feeling that she was using her power to search out the trap, but I couldn't sense it. In fact, I couldn't feel her bond at all. I was alone in my head for the first time in forever. I couldn't feel Daire either.

Yep. Fucked. Royally.

27

SHARA

Since I didn't have Daire to lap up my blood, I'd used my magic to catch my period blood again. I couldn't do anything about the blood already on my thighs and dress. As long as I didn't drip any...

:I'll watch,: Rik assured me. :If a single drop falls from your body, I'll tell you so you can call it to you.:

I rubbed my arms, trying to get rid of the goosebumps that had absolutely nothing to do with the temperature of the room and everything to do with the scene unfolding.

My Blood, Ezra, was trapped inside a blood circle so insidiously hidden that I still couldn't feel it. The trap had almost gotten us too, and Keisha Skye would have fucking let us walk right into it without a word. I had a feeling that'd been her goal all along, despite bringing our consiliari down here with us.

Smiling, Keisha went toward the little girl. "Shara, let me introduce you to my daughter, Tanza."

I shot a quick look at Gina, who was so pale and visibly shaken that I took her hand and tucked her arm through mine. "Not possible," she whispered. "Tanza died in 1938."

"No, she didn't die," Keisha replied. "I told everyone she did and put a geas upon those who knew the truth."

"Or killed them," Madeline muttered.

While I was glad to know her consiliarius wasn't too thrilled with Keisha's actions, I couldn't count her as an ally, or even use my power to sway her like I'd done with Vega. Madeline was mostly human, like Gina, and immune to any shifter instincts that I could stir up.

"Her eyes," Gina whispered breathily.

I looked at Tanza's eyes and the goddess's warning shrilled through me. This wasn't a child, human or Aima or even a mix. Her eyes were completely black and faceted like an insect's.

My first thought was the spider goddess Itztli had told me about, but I didn't sense a spider behind the child's eyes. No, this was something colder, darker, and so far removed from anything I'd ever seen before that I didn't recognize it. And I'd been face-to-face with some weird shit, including goddesses that would have scared a human to death.

"Hungry, Mama." The child tossed her toy aside and wrapped her arms around Keisha's neck. "Feed me, Mama."

Ezra let out a sound that made me jump against Rik. "Holy fucking shit."

I followed his gaze. The toy the child had thrown was a head. A man's face looked up at me, his mouth twisted in a rictus of agony.

"Conall," Rik whispered. "Her last alpha."

"Shhh, dear heart," Keisha said. "You can have my blood to tie you over."

"No!" Tanza retorted and clawed at her mother's throat. "You know what I need."

Keisha stumbled back, clutching the torn bodice of her gown. "Soon," she gasped, moving closer to us. "You have a new male to play with. Feed on him."

Tanza stuck out her bottom lip and flounced away from Ezra. "He's not alpha. He won't last but a minute. I'm *hungry*. I need *more*." She looked at Rik and brightened. "Hungry. Give me that one."

I stepped in front of Rik, pushing against him, even though he didn't budge. "No. You can't have him."

"I was desperate to have an heir," Keisha said softly, staring at her daughter. "Desperate enough to believe *her* when she said we needed something more than our alphas to conceive. She'd done all this research from all the oldest cultures and insisted that we needed fresh Aima blood to rejuvenate our lines. Blood from the Mother, or as close as possible to Her. She went to her god of monsters. I went… elsewhere."

"You went to Ra," I said softly.

"Yes. He agreed that we needed to do something drastic

to conceive, but fucking the god of light wasn't enough, though he was only too eager to be used as long as I wished. He told me the only way I'd conceive was a life for a life."

Chills raced down my arms. That was exactly what Coatlicue had told me the cost of the red serpent would be. One of my loved ones would have to die for me to kill Ra. Evidently, he'd told Keisha something very similar.

"My alpha at the time was willing. Men are so stupid, Shara. Surely, you've come to realize that by now. Look at poor Llewellyn, waiting all these years for you to come save him. He refused to die because of a ridiculous promise he made to your mother. Silas was the same. He allowed me to kill him to give me my heart's desire. Tanza was born, and I was so happy. Very happy. But the cost of her existence did not end with Silas's death. As she neared puberty, she had no desire for blood. All she wanted was pain, and a great deal of it. She feeds on suffering, not blood, and her need is great."

My stomach churned. It all made a terrible kind of sense. "That's why you torture the alphas. Not to conceive another child, but to feed her."

"Yes. I don't usually let her have them to play with directly until the very end, because she kills too quickly. Slow torture is better for her. It keeps her happy, and I've learned how to make them last as long as possible. That's where you come in, Shara. I went back to Ra, furious that he hadn't told me that she'd need the constant pain of others to stay alive. She's stuck at this stage, desperate for pain, tormented by her own hunger. She can't develop any further, until you heal her."

"Me? What do I have to do with this?"

"Ra told me that your mother would make a similar bargain. A life for a life. You would be born with the key to unlocking Tanza's pain and end her suffering for all time. Your power would be great enough to heal her. But then she disappeared, and no one could even remember her existence. I knew she'd done it on purpose. She'd left with you to keep you safe from me. To keep you from healing my child who'd been born first. I searched for any sign of her for years, and though no one knew where you were, or what had happened to Selena after she left her nest, I noticed that no one mentioned inheriting the Isador legacy. It was still locked to Isador blood, rather than passing to the Triune. So, you had to be out there. Somewhere."

I closed my eyes, breathing too fast and shallow. "You sent them to find me. Rik. Daire. You wanted me to be found."

"Yes," she answered with a shrug. "They were my bait. The complaint to the Triune was my ploy to get you here in front of me, but I never wanted Blood for Blood, Shara. I want you."

SHARA

I couldn't think. I couldn't see a way out. My mind felt like a delicate, hand-blown vase that had been dropped from the hundredth floor to shatter into dust on the asphalt far below.

"The blood circle is hers," Keisha continued. "I can't get him out for you. Only you have that power. You can exchange yourself for him and heal her."

"No," Rik retorted, locking me against his side. "There's no way you're stepping one foot into that circle."

:*Can I break it?*:

I knew what the answer was. They'd told me the same thing when we'd gone to Zaniyah's nest. A blood circle could not be broken, unless it was broken from within.

From within.

:No.:

Despite his adamant answer, an idea started to tickle in the back of my mind. I felt again for Ezra's bond, drawing on my power until my heartbeat pounded in my skull. I could barely feel a thread where he should be. He was there, but extremely distant, as if someone had shot him on a rocket to Pluto. I tried to draw on our bond, but the tiny thread dissolved.

He didn't have enough of my blood for what I wanted to try.

Rik's bond weighed like a massive boulder in my mind. *:Tell me.:*

I didn't want to tell him, because I knew what his answer would be. We'd already talked about something like this, and I refused to risk his life.

Keisha was right in one regard. Men could be absolutely ridiculous in what they would do in the name of love and honor. I tried to think of any other way. I knew exactly how I wanted to finish Keisha. I'd already played it out in my head, how I would pull the Skye blood from my Blood and give it back to her. So easy. So clean. The Triune wouldn't be able to come after me, and my debt to her would be satisfied.

Then I'd fucking kill her.

But she'd never be satisfied unless I saved her daughter, who looked back at me with the glittering obsidian eyes of a demon.

Ra might be the god of light, but he'd managed to conjure something into Tanza that wasn't of this earth or any realm in our goddesses' dominion.

:*Shara. Tell me.*:

:*Our bond is stronger than mine with Ezra. I can't reach him through the blood circle.*:

:*But you could reach me.*:

I swallowed hard, my stomach fluttering with anxiety. :*I think so. The circle has to be broken from inside. If I can reach you through the circle, then I can break it.*:

:*We make the trade. I take his place. You get her to publicly acknowledge the debt is satisfied. Then you use our bond to break the circle and we kill them all.*:

My heart was trying to strangle me. He sounded so calm. So assured. So confident without a single doubt in my ability to save him. To save us all.

:*You'll have to sell it to her, or she'll suspect that you have something planned. Be furious. Be sad. But don't let on like we know a way to beat her.*:

Then he stepped forward and shoved me behind him. "Take me instead."

Keisha arched an eyebrow. "Oh? You're volunteering?"

"No, Rik!" I grabbed at his arm, tugging on him uselessly. My alpha could never be moved when he didn't want to be. "Please, don't do this!"

"I'm not letting my queen in that fucking circle until she does some research and figures out a way to break whatever curse Ra has put on your daughter. Let Ezra out, and I'll take his place. Tanza can feed on me while we figure out the best plan."

"No!" I was crying. I was fucking pissed. It wasn't an act.

But it certainly helped sell our plan. "Rik, I won't let you do this. There has to be another way."

"I'll do it," he retorted, ignoring me. "But you have to swear before our consiliari here and now as witnesses that you'll immediately declare that House Isador's debt has been paid in front of all your sibs. The rest of Shara's Blood are free to go. She loves me too much to leave me here, so you'll get what you want. But I want to be sure her house is secure and safe first."

Keisha looked at me and I felt her power on the air like a massive static electricity charge. I didn't try to hold back my sobs. The thought of Rik being hurt in any way fucking tore my heart out and shredded it to ribbons. How quickly would Tanza start to hurt him? How long would it take for us to get Keisha to live up to her promise, assuming she'd even accept Rik's deal?

I squeezed my eyes shut. *Goddess, Isis, please tell me this is the right thing to do. If anything happens to Rik...*

I gulped back another sob. I'd use the fucking red serpent. I would. I would do anything to save him. Even if someone else had to die. I couldn't live without Rik.

"Agreed," Keisha finally said. "I, Keisha Skye, Queen of Scathach, agree to publicly declare the blood debt with House Isador satisfied."

"Immediately." Rik's voice vibrated with intensity. "As soon as you go upstairs. You'll make the announcement."

"Yes. Now I want to hear Shara's oath that she'll return here to heal Tanza."

Each word tore from my throat. "I, Shara Isador, the

Great One's last daughter, will return to my alpha as soon as the blood debt is satisfied."

"Not good enough," Keisha retorted.

"I'll free Tanza from her suffering as soon as I figure out how."

Keisha nodded. "Yes. Agreed."

"Duly noted," Madeline said. "Gina, are you satisfied with the clarity of these terms?"

Gina was crying too, but she squared her shoulders despite the tears tracking down her cheeks. "I support my queen one hundred percent."

Keisha looked at her daughter. "Okay, babydoll, let's make a trade. You let the bear go, and you can play with this alpha."

Tanza clapped her hands and nodded. "My alpha. Hungry."

"Make him last," Keisha said. "We're going to work some magic and get you all better, okay?"

"Okay, Mama." Tanza reached toward Ezra. He flinched away, but she grabbed his arm and pushed him toward us. He stumbled and fell out of the circle on his knees. Panting, head down, he shuffled closer to me, crying as hard as I was. "Come play, alpha."

I clung to Rik's arm, but he shook me off gently. Without hesitation, he stepped into the blood circle with the demon.

Like the fucking prime alpha he was.

29

SHARA

I couldn't stop crying. Which I supposed helped sell the deal all the better to Keisha. Gina and Ezra both had their arms around me, supporting me as we rode up to the hundredth floor again.

The doors opened, and my Blood immediately breathed a sigh of relief when they saw me.

Until they realized Rik wasn't with us. Until they saw my tears.

Daire jumped up and draped his paws over my shoulders to lick my face frantically. :*Where is he? What happened? I can't feel him.*:

I buried my face in his fur and clung to him a moment. I wanted to say, *be glad you can't feel him.*

Because his pain had started as soon as we left the room.

At least I could still feel his bond, though it felt stretched and fragile. We'd shared so much blood that even Tanza's blood circle couldn't keep me fully out of my alpha. But that meant I knew exactly what she was doing to him.

He wasn't bleeding. Yet.

But she screeched so high and shrill that his eardrums had almost burst, and he'd fallen to the ground, clutching his skull.

The less Daire and the other Blood knew, the better we'd be able to conceal our plan. But it fucking broke my heart to let them believe that I'd actually be willing to trade Rik's life for mine. I shook my head, refusing to answer Daire even in the bond. He paced frantically around me, his tail lashing my legs, but he sensed a purpose in my actions. He trusted me to have a plan. To do something.

Even as we stood in front of Keisha's throne, waiting for her sibs to come filing back in.

Rik was bleeding now from his eyes, nose and ears, and Tanza hadn't even touched him yet. She lay on her back, staring up at the ceiling, giggling.

While my alpha twitched and bled and moaned with pain.

Panic welled inside me, but I beat it down. I wouldn't allow panic to affect my judgement or control. We had a plan. It would work. I just needed to get through this without falling apart.

Leviathan bellowed in my head. Night had fallen while we were down in the basement and I saw him fly past the cracked windows. Keisha had warded them with her magic, so even though the glass had cracked, he couldn't break them open, though he made a great show of trying. He landed on the roof and I felt him clawing at the stone and cement, trying to break through to reach me.

I clenched my jaws and clutched Gina's hand in mine, our knuckles white with strain. She didn't know the full plan either. Hopefully she knew me well enough to know that I'd never sell my alpha to save my own hide.

Finally, Keisha stood and raised her voice. "House Isador and House Skye have come to an agreement. The blood debt has been paid. Shara Isador is free to take all her Blood from Skye Tower when she leaves us. I formally withdraw my petition from the Triune."

"Duly noted," Madeline said, typing furiously on a small laptop. "I'm communicating your agreement to the Triune. It'll take a few minutes..."

I swayed, fighting down another wave of pain from Rik. I could only imagine how bad it really was. Even through the dimmed bond, the pain was nauseating.

Blinking away the tears, I focused on Keisha. She stood before her throne, smiling at everyone. Even me. She'd gotten what she wanted. She believed that once I healed Tanza that their lives could continue however she wished. All those alphas who'd died to keep her daughter alive were commodities. A sad casualty in her war to keep her daughter alive. If Tanza could live, she'd snuff out every single life in this room, if necessary, even though they'd sworn their blood to her for one reason only.

Her protection as the Queen of Skye.

Something flickered behind her.

Xin. He silently flowed closer to her, no longer in his wolf form, but still invisible.

My assassin Blood, who couldn't carry a blade on his wolf.

I met his gaze, his eyes flashing ghostly silver. Swallowing my tears, I let go of Gina's hand and stepped closer to Keisha.

She focused on me, a frown spreading on her face. A moment of doubt. Her eyes narrowed. She started to turn toward her consiliarius, but Madeline looked up with a bright smile. "Marne Ceresa replied. The Triune acknowledges and nullifies the blood debt."

I smiled at Keisha. Xin materialized and seized her, one arm around her waist, the other around her throat. She pulled on her power and lightning crackled and arced around her, but Xin refused to let her go. I lunged forward and sank my fangs into her throat.

I drank her down. Her power. Her blood. I claimed her in front of her people. She struggled a moment, wind tearing at me, whipping my hair and dress in a furious, desperate hurricane, but my assassin Blood had her locked tightly in his arms.

She tore at his skin, reaching back to claw at his face, but another Blood came to our assistance. The gryphon chomped down on her arm and held her pinned while she screamed.

Her mind opened to me and it was a horror story I didn't want to see.

I didn't care how much she loved her daughter.

All I could see were the countless broken, bloodied bodies of alphas who'd died to keep Tanza alive. The head rolling across the floor. The screams and wails of pain while she'd stood at the edge of the circle and watched her daughter feed on their pain. She'd known her daughter was possessed by something dark and demonic. That Ra had corrupted her from the beginning.

Yet she'd refused to end her daughter's torment.

Her power filled me. The deadly might of a hurricane. Million volts of lightning. The thousand lives that looked to her for support and protection. They fluttered into my consciousness like frantic moths circling the last gleaming lamppost in the middle of nowhere. They were mine, now.

Not that I gave a fuck about any of them.

The cold chill of the grave filled me. I remembered going to Isis's pyramid the first time, when she'd given me Her power. All Her powers, because I was Her last daughter. Keisha's mind flickered like a candle almost blown out. Its wick burned to nothing. I felt the choice. I could release her. Let her live. I could pull her back from the grave, like I'd done for Rik before.

But I chose death. I chose retribution.

The goddess's cold, hard smile confirmed Her acceptance of my choice.

30

SHARA

I raced down the darkened hallway to the room where Tanza held my alpha. He was still alive, but his body blazed like she'd tossed him in a pool of boiling acid. I could taste her blood in his mouth.

She'd forced her blood into him. Contaminated him. The same as Ezra.

I gripped Rik's weakened, stretched bond in my mind and prayed I wasn't too late.

Breathing hard, I stopped and made sure I found the edge of her blood circle. Now that I knew what to look for, I could feel the emptiness, the absence of warmth and life that marked the edge of her circle. If Ra was the god of light, which gave all things life, she was the opposite. The anti-life. The complete and utter blackness.

In some ways, we were very much the same. I had been conceived and born in absolute darkness. But the light of love still glowed within me.

She knew nothing but her hunger for pain.

He lay on the floor, his head in the child's lap. It could have been sweet and innocent, if he wasn't writhing with pain while she laughed, a sweet, high-pitched sound of pure enjoyment so evil that my stomach heaved. I almost vomited all of Keisha's blood on the floor.

He turned his head and met my gaze. Black blood dribbled from his lips, but he still managed to smile. :*Shara. You did it. My queen. So fucking proud.*:

His voice came from a million miles away, but I could still hear him.

Closing my eyes, I sank into our bond. I didn't dare force my will too fast and hard down the fragile bond tying us together, for fear it would dissolve into nothing. His pain washed over me. Stronger. I breathed through it, letting it flow through me. Tears trickled down my face. I shredded my lips, fighting the need to scream. He didn't scream, so I wouldn't, either.

I sank further into him. My rock, unshakeable. The low rumble of an earthquake. His extreme gentleness, utter loyalty, and selfless love. My alpha would lay down his life for mine in a heartbeat.

And I would pull him back from death's door to keep him with me.

For all his strength and alpha will, he surrendered to me.

He had from the first moment I'd met him. I remembered the gentle way he'd pressed his forehead to mine. His big hands so careful when he held me. A man of his size and strength could take anything he wanted from a woman, but he'd never do such a thing. My pleasure and enjoyment had been his number one priority from the first moment we met.

If that meant rolling over on his back and letting me have my wicked way with him, he'd be there for that, all night and all day, every day.

It was easy for him to let me in, all the way, without hesitation. He held nothing back. He opened up his heart, mind, and body to me. His soul brushed mine. I was inside him. I was him. I looked through his eyes and saw myself looking back.

Slowly, I rolled my head back to look up into Tanza's face. Her eyes glittered like black mirrors. Her blood seeped through my body like poison. A dark bond that I could trace back to its source. Her blood circle flowed around us like a black hole sucking up all the light of the universe.

Rik's eyelids fluttered. His body started to fail. But I didn't need his eyes to see any longer. I gathered my will and focused on Tanza's bond taking root inside him. I tapped my blood, both my period blood and the blood trickling down my chin. I focused it like a laser beam and pushed a searing hot flame through her bond.

I burned into Tanza. All my power, blasting into her with the heat of the earth's molten core. Her eyes flared, flicking with flames. My flames, burning inside her. She opened her mouth and screeched, a sound meant to deafen and maim. Rik jerked and spasmed on her lap, his body already punished with that sound while I'd finished Keisha. I felt the echo of pain and thrashing in my body, but it was distant, removed from Rik. I was inside Rik. I was in the circle with him. And he was dying.

I stoked the flames inside her, pushing harder. The blood circle wavered, straining beneath the force of power I pumped through him into her. So much power. Enough to blast the earth into dust. To tear the universe apart.

Or implode a black hole.

The blood circle popped, and the floor lurched beneath us. I slammed back into my body. On my hands and knees. Bleeding. I crawled toward Rik. Tanza lay on her back, thrashing and screaming as my flames boiled inside her. But she wouldn't fucking die.

My Blood raced ahead of me. Daire grabbed Rik's arm in his jaws and dragged him away from Tanza. Itztli and Tlacel grabbed her legs, pinning her lower body. Nevarre and Xin grabbed her arms.

She wailed louder and bloody marks tore open on my Blood. A slash across Xin's face. Deep, bleeding scratches on my black dog's flank. Invisible whips that tore at their flesh. But they kept her pinned, waiting for me to reach them.

I wasn't sure what to do. How did one kill a demon?

:*You kill the shell it inhabits and force it to vacate the body,*: Guillaume said in my mind. He raced toward me, knives in both hands. Leviathan had finally torn through the roof of the building and was blasting fire at anyone who thought to come after me.

My flames burned inside her, crisping her body, but she still lived. I wasn't sure what else I could do, short of sinking my fangs into her. But the last thing I wanted to do was risk giving the demon a hold in my mind and body too.

Then I remembered. My knife. I patted the tiny pocket Alice had sewn into the delicate skirt and found my old knife. I flicked it open and moved closer to Tanza's thrashing body.

"Help," she whimpered in her child's voice. "Help me. Save me. Please."

My mind quailed. I couldn't harm a child. Mom had died to save a child.

I thought of Xochitl lying hurt and scared like this and my stomach heaved at the thought of sinking my knife into her.

Sensing my hesitation, the demon chittered inside her, a high-pitched metallic laughter that tore at my flesh. Tanza's hand shifted into a black talon that lashed out at Xin and sliced deeply into his stomach, nearly disemboweling him. Doubled over with pain, he struggled to hold on to the claw, using his own body to shield me from the brutal weapon.

Gritting my teeth, I clutched the knife in both hands. The only way to save the child Tanza had been was to end the demon's dominion in her body. *Forgive me*, I thought at the universe in general, and slammed the blade into Tanza's heart.

Guillaume brushed past me and swiped his blades in a quick arc that sent her head rolling to the side.

Black blood leaked out of her. Not human. Not Aima.

I crawled over to Rik and pressed my wrist to his mouth. Eyes closed, he sank his fangs into me. Nevarre helped Xin up and brought him to me. I offered him my other wrist. I sank into them both, letting my power flow through their bodies. Xin was easy to heal, though his wound was ugly.

Rik didn't have as many visible injuries, but he was hurt internally, as if the demon had rubbed a cheese grater all over his organs and nerves, shredding them from head to toe. He fed long enough that I sagged against him, despite draining Keisha dry just moments before.

Guillaume stepped close and offered me his bleeding wrist. Nevarre pressed against my back, supporting me while I fed.

"Make sure you burn out the contamination from them both," Guillaume said. "If not, the demon may be able to track either of them down, even years later, and slowly infect them with its evil."

I cast my senses through Rik's body, searching for any hint of the blood he'd been forced to take from Tanza. Small drops had spread through his body like a black cancer. I took my time, making sure I touched each one with my power until all traces were wiped away. He sat up and wrapped his arms around me, though he didn't release my wrist yet. I nestled against his chest, breathed in his scent of smoking hot rock, and didn't mind the tears of relief that dampened his shirt.

When he finally lifted his mouth, I sighed with regret.

"Perhaps we could continue this once we return to your home, my queen."

I nodded, still feeling rather fuzzy, like my head would float away. Something wasn't right, though. I wasn't complete. I looked around my Blood and finally settled my gaze on Ezra.

He knelt at the edge of my Blood, head down with shame.

"Ezra." He flinched but lifted his head. I held my hand out to him, and he slowly crawled closer to bury his face against me. "Shhhh. We're all safe now."

"I'm so sorry, my queen. I fell right into their fucking trap."

I wrapped one arm around his shaggy head and held him to my chest. "This trap was set for me before my birth. If not you, then another one of us would have sprung it. It doesn't matter now. We won. It's over."

He lifted his head, his eyes haunted. "Is it? I still feel her inside me."

I looked over at the smoldering body. The fingers on her hand twitched.

Pressing my bleeding wrist to Ezra's mouth, I sank through his body, searching for those black cells of her blood. As with Rik, I took my time, making sure Ezra fed well, and that I didn't miss a single drop of contamination that he might carry.

Something rustled in the hallway. Rik dragged me up

into his lap. Daire crouched over our legs. Guillaume whirled with a foot-long bloody knife in his hand.

"It's me," Vega said hurriedly, stepping out into the blue-tinted light, hands up. "Just checking on you. The troops are getting restless. They don't know whether they should flee or swear to Isador."

I blew out a sigh. This was the part I'd dreaded from the beginning. The business of taking over a house as large as Skye was going to be tedious in the extreme. I held out my hands and Nevarre took one, Itztli the other, helping me stand. "Let's make sure this body is completely destroyed before we leave."

"Good idea." Guillaume used his boot to push the severed head closer to the body. "You may have to douse it with your blood and light it on fire that way, my queen."

I nodded, holding my hand out to him. He cradled my palm in his and carefully widened the bite in my wrist to allow my blood to drip in a steady stream. I coated the small body in blood, until my knees quivered, and I felt lightheaded again.

"Who... or what... is that?" Vega asked hesitantly.

I debated how much to tell her. Keisha was dead. The child she'd been so obsessed to save, also dead. Tanza had truly died a long time ago, because the demon who'd tortured alphas all these years had not been an innocent child.

Concentrating a moment, I lit my blood on fire. Flames roared higher, quickly consuming the body. Flesh cracked, blackened, and crumbled to ash.

Turning away, I said, "It was a demon. It twisted your former queen into torturing her alphas."

Vega nodded, and relief eased the harsh lines of her face. "She wasn't always like that. *We* weren't always like that."

I stared back at her until she dropped her gaze and stepped aside. "Let's hope the fuck not, because things will sure be different now. This is my fucking house, and nobody suffers in House Isador for another's whim."

31

SHARA

In the end, I had Keisha's throne removed from the dais and stashed in the basement. Mehen had gleefully blasted the ashes of Tanza's body to make absolutely sure we'd destroyed the demon's shell completely. Though I was going to have to spend a small fortune to fix the roof he'd also blasted through.

The gathered members of House Skye were quite depleted in number. Gina and Madeline had been working together to come up with a list of all the names of people who remained, their former house ties, and how they'd come to be a part of Skye. I had a feeling that Leviathan and Llewellyn had both snacked their way through the ranks. Many others had fled. I wouldn't begrudge any of them the chance for freedom after Keisha's reign.

Six-hundred-and-eight siblings stood before me. Looking at me. Waiting for me to make an announcement, or at least tell them what to do.

But first, I sat down between Rik's thighs and sighed as his arms came around me. Someone had found a comfortable chair big enough for us both to sit in. I was exhausted. Bloody. Another dress ruined beyond repair. My feet ached and fucking miserable cramps tore through my abdomen.

I wanted to curl up in a ball in the center of my bed with a cup of hot tea while Mehen read to me in French and my Blood pressed around me.

Instead, I sat looking out at a sea of strangers' faces wondering what the hell I'd gotten myself into.

Luckily, I had a most excellent consiliarius who gladly and skillfully took over everything to the smallest detail.

Gina raised her voice so everyone could hear. "House Isador now holds all Skye territories, including Skye Tower. If you were forced to swear an oath to House Skye, your new queen releases you from your oath. You're free to return to your families and home nests without fear of retribution later. If you're willing to swear to House Isador and stay on here, Shara Isador will take your oath of fealty now."

She paused a moment, letting people think about what they wanted to do. Several people did quietly head for the doors. I let them go. Gladly.

There were still way too many people staring at me, eager to swear their lives to me.

Gina smiled at me over her shoulder. "Our queen is

weary, so we'll make this quick. Rather than swearing an oath of fealty one by one, we're going to do this en mass. Some of you may also be chosen to become full sibs at a future date. For now, she'll accept your oath. Please repeat after me.

"My old queen, Keisha Skye, is dead. Her bond is null and void. I now swear my blood and my life to Shara Isador, last daughter of Isis, the Great One, She who was, and is, and all that will be."

Their voices thundered through the room. These people were fucking *glad* to have a new queen. They didn't hate me, even though they'd seen me kill Keisha not even an hour before. If they knew what I'd done in the basement...

:*They'd fucking kiss your feet and the ground you walk upon,*: Rik said in my head, tightening his arms around me. :*Long live the fucking queen. My queen. I love you.*

Daire rubbed against my legs and worked his tongue a bit higher above my knee, eagerly cleaning up the blood that had stained my skin. :*Long live Shara fucking Isador.*:

Shara's finale will be QUEEN TAKES CHECKMATE, tentatively set for an end of June release. Don't be too sad to say goodbye to Shara and the guys, because I already have plot wheels in motion for more stories in Their Vampire Queen's world, and I'm sure Shara will continue to drop ideas into my head as well. You may even see some Princess Takes Unicorns someday...

Be the first to read sneak peeks and discuss any questions you have about the series in Joely's Triune on Facebook. You can also receive notifications of upcoming releases and deals in Joely's newsletter.

If you're intrigued by the elements of Aztec mythology in this series, check out *The Bloodgate* series: Bloodgate (a free short story), The Bloodgate Guardian, and The Bloodgate Warrior.

ALSO BY JOELY SUE BURKHART

Their Vampire Queen, reverse harem vampire romance
Free in Kindle Unlimited
QUEEN TAKES KNIGHTS
QUEEN TAKES KING
QUEEN TAKES QUEEN
QUEEN TAKES ROOK
QUEEN TAKES CHECKMATE

QUEEN TAKES JAGUARS
Mayte's story available in Realms & Rebels boxed set
August 21, 2018

Blood & Shadows, erotic fantasy
Free in Kindle Unlimited
THE HORSE MASTER OF SHANHASSON

The Shanhasson Trilogy
A Complete Reverse Harem Epic Fantasy
THE ROSE OF SHANHASSON
THE ROAD TO SHANHASSON
RETURN TO SHANHASSON

Keldari Fire
SURVIVE MY FIRE
THE FIRE WITHIN

Mythomorphoses, Paranormal/SF Romance
Free in Kindle Unlimited
BEAUTIFUL DEATH

The Connaghers, contemporary erotic romance
Free in Kindle Unlimited
LETTERS TO AN ENGLISH PROFESSOR
DEAR SIR, I'M YOURS
HURT ME SO GOOD
YOURS TO TAKE
NEVER LET YOU DOWN
MINE TO BREAK
THE COMPLETE CONNAGHERS BOXED SET

Billionaires in Bondage, contemporary erotic romance
(re-releasing in 2017 from Entangled Publishing)
THE BILLIONAIRE SUBMISSIVE
THE BILLIONAIRE'S INK MISTRESS
THE BILLIONAIRE'S CHRISTMAS BARGAIN

Zombie Category Romance, paranormal romance
Free in Kindle Unlimited
THE ZOMBIE BILLIONAIRE'S VIRGIN WITCH
THE MUMMY'S CAPTIVE WITCH

The Wellspring Chronicles, erotic fantasy
Free in Kindle Unlimited
NIGHTGAZER

A Killer Need, Erotic Romantic Suspense
ONE CUT DEEPER
TWO CUTS DARKER
THREE CUTS DEADER

A Jane Austen Space Opera, SF/Steampunk erotic romance
LADY WYRE'S REGRET, free read prequel
LADY DOCTOR WYRE
HER GRACE'S STABLE
LORD REGRET'S PRICE

Historical Fantasy Erotica
GOLDEN

The Maya Bloodgates, paranormal romance
BLOODGATE, free read prequel
THE BLOODGATE GUARDIAN
THE BLOODGATE WARRIOR

RECOMMENDED READS FROM THE AUTHOR

Stolen: Saving Setora
Dark Dystopian Reverse Harem MC Romance
By
Raven Dark and Petra J. Knox

It all began when the road warriors found me outside Hell's Burning, lost and dehydrated. When the bikers took me into The Compound, I thought I was saved.

Especially when, as a Violet—a rare genetic anomaly prized above all—I'm taken in and raised by one of the wealthiest men in the world. Educated and groomed by the best teachers money could buy, I mistakenly thought he had a great future planned for me, one in which I'd be cared for and cherished.

I was wrong.

For centuries, women have been sold as slaves. In my 18th year, my benefactor reveals a truth that shatters my world. I'm to be put on display before the wealthiest of society at one of the biggest auctions this world has ever seen…as a slave.

But that night at the auction, something goes wrong. I am stolen by members of the infamous Dark Legion, a road warrior crew feared the world over. Torn from the only world I have ever known, now I have not one master, but four.

I shouldn't want these dangerous, deadly men with their leather cuts and their growling bikes, but the deeper my captors draw me into their dark and twisted world, the more I crave what they do to me. They stole me from a powerful man who'll stop at nothing to get me back. If I don't find a way to escape soon, my new masters might just steal my heart.

*****Stolen is Book One of the Saving Setora series, a dark, dystopian Reverse Harem romance with biker tones. There is no cheating, and the final book ends with an HEA for Setora and her four men. This full length novel contains triggering elements and four twisted heroes who know how to own a woman right.

Made in the USA
Monee, IL
07 December 2021